The Talont... es:

A Second Chance

**Written By
Ronald Steven Lessiter
and
Casey Thomas Lehman**

COPYRIGHT NOTICE!

This book, series and its characters are both © <u>Ronald Steven Lessiter & Casey Thomas Lehman 2015</u>

ISBN 10: 1518868665

ISBN 13: 9781518868665

———

Copyright will be planned to register upon date of publication

I have strict fanfiction/fanart guidelines going from most to least severe in offense in this order:

1. **<u>ABSOLUTELY NO NON-CANON PAIRINGS – ESPECIALLY SLASH!!!</u>**
2. **<u>NO FETISH IMAGERY/STORIES!!!</u>**
3. **<u>NO ADULT IMAGES/STORIES WITHOUT PERMISSION FROM THE CREATORS FIRST!</u>**
4. **No AUs**
5. **No gender-swapping**
6. No using the dragon characters in fanfiction in *any* way, shape or form
7. Ultimar's use *must* follow cannon
8. Cross-overs are *only* allowed with Ultimar/Mian due to the nature of their canon.

Special Thanks/Dedication

Shalone Howard, A.K.A. ShaloneSK@DeviantArt

The talented artist who created the original pictures of TalonFyre, Angel, Flare and Hikari. Thank you so much for getting me into fanfiction, as this series would not have been possible without the original inspiration of a certain draconic world. God bless you for your help, Shalone. Even if it was indirect, you've allowed this to come to fruition.

Abby Williams

The young woman who created the inner art for the book. Thank you, and I hope the drawings you've done add a lot of credit to your portfolio!

Clare Keating, A.K.A echodusk@DeviantArt

The amazing creator of the "Demon on the Battlefield" comic. She has inspired me to make original stories with her works and has also reawakened and furthered my love for dragons. She is also a novelist at this time. I look forward to reading her books as well. I have also commissioned a comic to be made of War of the Third Demon, the prequel to my book. This will be published sometime after the second book in the Chronicles.

Panthera Arven, A.K.A ARVEN92@DeviantArt

Another creator who inspired me to make original content and also the artist for this book's cover/ending picture. She has a comic by the name of "Chakra: Battle of Titans", which is very interesting, especially if the reader prefers talking animals as heroes instead of samurai or psychic warriors.

DragonLordMarkJ@DeviantArt A.K.A Montecristo709@fanfiction.net

Although I'm without an official name, his stories took away my fear of using religious references in my books.

My friend Karen, A.K.A Karebear-4ever@Deviantart

For the inspiration to keep moving with the story and her kind remarks.

Gary Gygax and David Lance Arneson, creators of Dungeons and Dragons®

This game had massive impact on War of the Third Demon's multitude of species and other aspects of the world The TalonFyre Chronicles is set in.

E. L. James, Creator of Fifty Shades of Gray, for showing a fanfic can be made into a real book and complete universe of its own.

Table of Contents

Table of Contents

Prologue and History as told by TalonFyre 8
Chapter 1 11
Chapter 2 16
Chapter 3 19
Chapter 4 22
Chapter 5 24
Chapter 6 26
Chapter 7 30
Chapter 8 33
Chapter 9 36
Chapter 10 39
Chapter 11 42
Chapter 12 45
Chapter 13 48
Chapter 14 51
Chapter 15 54
Chapter 16 57
Chapter 17 60
Chapter 18 63
Chapter 19 67
Chapter 20 70
Chapter 21 74
Chapter 22 77
Chapter 23 80
Chapter 24 83
Chapter 25 85
Chapter 26 88
Chapter 27 91

Chapter 28...94
Chapter 29...98
Chapter 30...102
Chapter 31...106
Chapter 32...109
Chapter 33...113
Chapter 34...116
Chapter 35...119
Chapter 36...121
Chapter 37...123
Chapter 38...126
Chapter 39...129
Chapter 40...131
Chapter 41...133
Chapter 42...135
Chapter 43...138
Chapter 44...140
Chapter 45...142
Chapter 46...144
Chapter 47...146
Chapter 48...148
Chapter 49...151
Chapter 50...153
Chapter 51...159
Chapter 52...162
Chapter 53...164
Chapter 54...166
Chapter 55...168
Chapter 56...170
Chapter 57...172
Chapter 58...174
Chapter 59...177
Chapter 60...179

Chapter 61..183

Prologue and History as told by TalonFyre

THERE was a war a few years back. Pretty horrible stuff. A demon dragon, who went by the name Rayburn, came from a faraway land and declared war or enslavement on every dragon alive, and *death* to all non-dragons.

Only thing that can stop a demon dragon is a balance dragon, born fifteen years before a demon dragon comes to call. The balance dragons have a power called "soul breath" – rips an evil being's soul from its body and burns them both to nothing. Name was Electus. Means chosen or something, I dunno.

The guy led the Wings of Angelus – a bunch of dragons that fight for peace against the Demon Flame Army. The guy also had a tail-held obsidian sword the Council gave 'Im called the "Dark Reaper".

Rayburn had a daughter called Nocturnal - half demon dragon, half red dragon. She did a lot of his crap – never complained once.

When the gal went up against Electus halfway through the war she got her ass handed to her. Heard he planned to put her head to the "Reaper" as soon as he took her down, but then he got a look at her eyes – said they had pure sadness in 'em. Guess he didn't have the guts to finish the job. I woulda. Still, turned out to be a good thing. The gal turned into the right hand of Electus, a General with all the tactics the Wings of Angelus could use. Even ended up being his *mate* near the end of the war. Mate… word makes me cringe.

Rayburn had control of golems, black-blooded demon animals, lizard men, undead and a whole bunch of other creepy things. His worst weapon was the Thanatos Golem. Thanatos means death, or so I heard - used it to attack the city of Resistance's main hold where the Seven-Dragon Council lived - Darastrix Charis. The damn place had fifty-foot thick steel walls that were enchanted to make magic and physical attacks bounce off of 'em. The problem was that this thing had the power to rip through then absorb barrier enchantments like they were made by an amateur. Rayburn thought ahead for that.

The Seven Dragon Council was made up of dragons that represented virtue or something. The thing didn't reach 'em though – ended up breaking down halfway through the fight with Nocturnal's branch of the wings. Dunno why, probably ran outta gas… heh.

Anyway, the Angelus ended up cornering the bastard in his castle. Electus was **pissed** when he heard Rayburn kidnapped his mate and threatened to have his way with her if they didn't give up. Bad idea on his end.

Electus went borderline crazy after the guy said it and led a full-scale assault on the guy's castle. They lost a lot of good warriors that day, but Rayburn was toast. The asshole didn't have a chance to do anything to Nocturnal. Worst of all, she was the guy's ***daughter*** for crying out loud! Who the hell does that shit!?

Enough about the war, on to me. I was just a kid when I became a mercenary. Well, I don't have enough scales to count all the jobs I've done, some good, some bad, some just plain wrong. One was so bad I just took off when they weren't looking (wanted me to smash an unborn dragon in its nest! I'm not that desperate!)

My main employer was Scrape, an old S.O.B. who would kill you so much as look at you. Heh, he got one of his very best top mercs to come at me my first day. Rip they called him. Well, all I said was, "Rip you're gonna' need a new arm when I'm done with you." Of course, he was at least twice my size and ten times as rough looking.

He tells me, "You have ten seconds to tell me why I shouldn't skin you alive, creep. This is my territory!" Funny - he only waited nine. Then he says, "Time's up, time to die."

I stop him and say, "I'll give you one chance to cut through me and my armor. You lose; you lose a forepaw, maybe a few other things."

He laughs making the whole place roar with laughter. "Alright," he says.

Well, his attack was pretty much brute force with a hidden surprise, a hidden sword under his arm. Dirty S.O.B. The minute that blade hits my armor it shatters. He just looks like he's seen a ghost. In fact, the entire place does.

"Well, guess what that means?" I ask him.

He stands there speechless. Well, one hit of my blade not only takes both his right horns clean off spreading blood on me and the others watching, it takes his forepaw too. "Didn't I say so?" I yell.

I just stand there watching him writhe in pain, I didn't enjoy it - he just needed to be shown his place. "I'll get the medics to fix you up so you'll live, but not happily. Mind the lopsided stares too, you'll creep the kids out," I tell him.

Scrape just hands me the employer's deed for the guy, says he's no use now and he wants me to take his place.......funny. I point my blade straight at his neck and I swear he stopped breathing, "Please....no," he begs.

"Hey, I'm not evil," I say as I pull it away.

When I went to work for Rayburn he noticed my claws, but never asked me why I had flames running through them. I only did one or two jobs for him, and after he found out who I was, I barely made it out - almost lost an eye and got a claw knocked clean off which he kept. Meh, it grew back, admittedly crooked but still works.

All I remember was him saying, "You're just like your parents, but even more foolish. I will enjoy snuffing your existence clean."

Well, he got damn near close, but not close enough. If you're wondering why he had all those scars and the gash over his eye – well, that was me. Didn't say I wasn't strong, did he?

Heard Rip is looking for me, probably still mad. That's gratitude for you. If Rip finds me knocked out cold, both of us go down....

As for my home world - well more like home world in hell anyway. It's mostly desolate landscape with merc camps dotted everywhere. Occasionally there's a camp with Rayburn's troops that escaped the war. Gotta' find my way back, but sitting here thinking to myself isn't going to help anything!

Chapter 1

Awakening

IT was late, and the white dragon was at his wit's end concerning what to do about his dilemma, which was over a year old. His mostly white, slightly yellow tinted, scales were covered in dirt. His light blue, somewhat plated, underbelly had a slight stain of grass. His pointed, yet slightly tilted-back; bright yellow horns had bits of leaves on them. His golden wing membranes were slightly irritated.

He walked through the dark forest on his golden claws, deep in thought with his emerald-green eyes half-closed. The noises of the late night didn't bother him; it was something he was used to by now. The eyes that stared at him through the forest were nothing but creatures that dwelt in it, after all. He had gone deeper than he had imagined and the underbrush was thicker. However, he needed to find what he was looking for…or someone. Exactly who it was that he sought? This he did not know.

"What'll I do about her?" the white dragon said worriedly, head in the clouds, unsure of what his vision meant.

He stopped in an instant when he saw a ghostly dragon before him. It had blade-like spines down his back, and a tail shaped like a scythe, almost like a draconic grim reaper.

"Well *this* is awkward – anyway, mind helping me wake up?" the specter asked nonchalantly.

The white dragon looked puzzled.

"Sorry I meant to ask for a name, my mistake," the specter continued in a slightly apologetic, yet still nonchalant voice.

This turn of speech put the white dragon at ease. "My name is Flare. I'm a light dragon," the white dragon replied. He then cocked his head and asked the question he assumed he needed to, "How do I wake you?"

"Heh, two opposite ends of the color spectrum," the ghost laughed. He then paused. "Ok, I'm acting too smart. I need help getting up," the specter reiterated in a gruff sigh. With that, he handed Flare a glowing claw with a sliver of bone on the end.

This puzzled Flare even further. "What is this?" Flare asked, scratching his head.

"One of my claws I tore off - has my life's blood in it," the specter explained. Flare knew at this point that he had found the dragon that his vision had informed him of.

A portal opened up behind the specter. "Where does this lead?" the light dragon asked, slightly curious about what he'd have to face.

The specter looked at him intently, "To another world where I'm laying out cold - and hurry my back itches."

The portal led to a desolate crater, almost burned to charcoal. It was evident there was a massive explosion that caused the large indent in the ground. Flare stepped through, ending up next to the specter's body.

"Ah, here we are," the ghost sighed in relief.

The light dragon walked up to the slumbering dragon. Flare attempted to attach the claw.

"First off, my blood is filled with hot lava so don't get..." the specter stopped when he saw the light dragon's incorrect method. "It doesn't work that way," the specter said in a slightly annoyed tone as he looked at Flare, who had pulled back the claw and looked at him, confused.

"You never explained," the light dragon replied calmly. It was true, the ghost never told Flare how to revive him.

"My body has a shield up and in the presence of my claw it goes down enough to get to my heart. You bite the end off and stab me right in the heart, mind the spray," the specter told Flare, taking a warning tone at the last three words. He disappeared into his body after saying this.

"Very well - as a light dragon it's in my nature to take risks in order to protect others," Flare said seriously, stabbing the claw into the former specter's heart. After this he jumped back as the blood sprayed out.

"Ahhh, there we go," the dragon sighed happily as he stood up, proceeding to immediately scratch his back afterwards. "Ohhh man, way better- thanks," the dragon went on as he pulled the claw out. The hole patched up with lava, hardening to normal within seconds.

This was something the likes of which Flare had never seen – a dragon with blood of lava. "Like I explained earlier, light dragons tend to help others," the light dragon reminded the dragon he aided, who was still scratching his itch. This wasn't exactly true and Flare knew it. His vision still puzzled him however.

"Ok, there – sorry," the dragon mumbled in a slightly apologetic yet still uncaring tone, ceasing to scratch his spinal area.

Flare paused, "I sense you have a troubled past..." he half-lied to the dragon. It was true, he could sense a dragon with turmoil in their heart, but there was another reason for him to say this.

"Yeah, well most people in my part of town don't *ask* about the past," the dragon said in a gruff voice. "Forget it, I need to get back," the dragon said, quickly changing the subject.

Flare could sense this dragon was keeping something from him, but replied with a defeated, "Very well," nonetheless.

After a few minutes of walking through the desolate landscape, the dragon tripped over a rock, resulting in an embarrassing face-plant. "OW!! Dammit!" the dragon grunted in an annoyed tone then picked himself up, slightly disoriented.

Flare gathered light in his forepaws and put it on the dragon's face. "Healing Light," Flare murmured softly, calling upon his element.

The dragon just sneezed in reaction and gave a gruff response once more, "Yeah, not happening."

Opening a portal, the dragon turned to Flare. "Doesn't work for me, they tried - had to work it out myself," the dragon explained as he walked through the newly-created glowing wall, still in a daze. "Come on," he said in a half-ordering tone as he made a gesture that gave the same impression.

Flare was puzzled, "Hmm... That's strange... You're not a normal dragon, are you?" he asked ponderingly as he stepped through the portal, following the mystery dragon.

This only got him an eye roll and a sarcastic "No, what made you think that?" from him.

All this time, Flare hadn't asked a question that he should have a long time ago, "What's your name?"

The mystery dragon replied, "TalonFyre," as he began to reach the other side of the portal.

On the other side of the portal was a dust land, void of all life but armored dragons, lizard men, and a few other creatures that clearly belonged in such a place.

"Ah, the crater, home sweet hell hole - Merc City," TalonFyre sighed in a glad tone, walking over to a towering stone wall.

Flare looked seriously at TalonFyre, "I only do mercenary work if the target is unjust," he said worriedly.

TalonFyre scoffed angrily, "Yeah, they wanted me to smash an unborn dragon. I *killed* the guy who asked me - no one stopped me - guy was a waste of flesh."

The light dragon flinched, disgusted by the idea of such a job. "Serves the bastard right," he growled in a hateful fashion. Flare was easy-going, but not apathetic by any means.

TalonFyre turned to him and looked him directly in the eye. "Only time I've ever eaten dragon flesh. Never did again, it was pure hatred - horrible crap too," he said cruelly.

Flare looked at him warily and replied with, "Dragons aren't very tasty," while a bit unnerved.

"Mphh..." TalonFyre smacked onto a hidden doorway and rubbed his snout grumbling. "Damn door," he growled as a torch emerged. TalonFyre took his paw off his snout, "I'll get the door stand back," he called to Flare, backing up.

A massive blast of black fire shot from the mercenary's mouth, opening the door. "There, finally home," TalonFyre sighed, walking into the bunker. "And yes, dark flames - before you ask. Sort of a gift and a curse," he went on, finding a smaller torch. He then lit the end of his claw and set ablaze the torch, revealing a massive cavern. TalonFyre looked around.

This black fire made Flare question TalonFyre's heritage, was it truly evil? If it were such, he would have sensed it when it was first demonstrated. The fact that his vision told him to help the mercenary added onto his theory about this. It wouldn't have been good for an evil dragon to help him out with his current situation.

A splattering sound was heard after the two stepped inside the cavern. "Ah, great!" TalonFyre yelled in an annoyed tone once more, stamping a creature with brown and white stripes upon a long bumblebee-like body. It had six legs, wasp wings, a scorpion-like head and tail with three stingers as well as wide, bulging red eye. "Vespatites... I hate these things," he grunted angrily.

Set into the side of the cavern was a smaller, yet still fairly large room, which TalonFyre proceeded to enter. "Follow if you want," the mercenary said with an uncaring tone followed by a shrug. Flare followed him through the doorway out of curiosity.

TalonFyre blasted a pit that was seemingly dormant, lava began to flow. "Ah, this is the good part," he said with a smile.

"The generator, I presume?" Flare asked curiously.

To his surprise, TalonFyre got into the lava, submerging his body. "Nope, loosens me up. That's why I was half drunk," TalonFyre answered, as he began to glow a shade of bright red, matching the lava. "Ohhhhhhh - nothing like it."

"What power..." Flare whispered, astonished at the spectacle.

"I'm my *own* power source," TalonFyre stated proudly as his claws, eyes, underbelly and wings began to resonate with the same glow as his body. He stepped out and shook off, splattering his new ally's tail by mistake.

"Ah, **geeez!!**" Flare yelped in alarm, his scales burning off.

"Oh, sorry," TalonFyre apologized embarrassedly.

The lava dripped off, leaving a third-degree burn on Flare's tail. This wound was no problem for him, however. He gathered light into the burn, mending his wound without need for medical supplies. "I've had much worse to heal from, it's fine," Flare replied calmly, wincing.

As he began to stretch in a doglike manner, the mercenary's neck made a disgusting crack and his spine followed suit. "Ah man - way better," he sighed in a relieved manner. He then proceeded to unlatch a seemingly invisible hook, a layer of armor dropped off with a massive thud afterwards.

"Yup, matches everything and absorbs heat. How do you think I stayed alive in there?" TalonFyre asked rhetorically.

Flare shrugged, "Your life essence was rather faint, so it makes sense."

At that moment TalonFyre's stomach started to rumble. As such, he ran off toward the other rooms. "Just remembered - I haven't eaten in *so* long..." he moaned, as he approached a massive stone door. He then opened it, revealing rows of frozen meat. TalonFyre looked around for a few seconds for a choice piece and grabbed one with some decent bone in it. "Good, don't have to cook it separate or at all," he remarked with a smile as he bit into the meat, half crunching the bone. He then held it in his mouth and roasted it with his flame, swallowing part of it and proceeding to eat the rest in the same manner. The last piece was about to be devoured when TalonFyre began to choke, concerning Flare. "Hang on," the mercenary gargled, drooling lava, "There."

TalonFyre turned to Flare. "You sure you don't want any?" he asked politely. He had to repay Flare in some way after all.

Flare shook his head, "Like I said, I'm good. I don't need to eat much," he replied uncaringly, 'Unlike *someone* I know', he thought to himself.

The door was slammed shut upon Flare's response. "Fair enough," the mercenary said with a shrug. He then walked over to a heap of scrap metal. "Where did I leave it...?" he whispered.

This concerned Flare, "Leave what?" he asked.

TalonFyre was too busy digging through the scraps to notice the light dragon's question, however.

Chapter 2

The Letter

 TALONFYRE dug through the metal until he found a gray 15-foot sword with a three foot wide blade, almost like that of cobblestone. Its hilt and grip were created from volcanic rock and crudely made. "Ah!" the mercenary exclaimed as he gave the sword a few waves, getting the feel of it once more.
 "A Golem-Flesh sword…" Flare gasped.
 "Yup - off of one killed by 'soul breath', making it much better," TalonFyre added smugly as he turned back to Flare.
 "So you use any weapons?" TalonFyre asked Flare in a slightly curious yet uncaring manner.
 At this Flare straightened out his tail in preparation while TalonFyre went on talking, "I don't use this unless it's another golem or some big idiot who needs a reality check," his tone still smug.
 Flare's tail started to glow a shade of white. "Photon Blade!" he yelled as a 9-foot, needle-shaped plasma sword sprouted from the tip of his tail out of nowhere.
 "Nothing I haven't seen," the mercenary remarked with an unimpressed demeanor, "Any claw-like weapons?"
 Wanting to show the mercenary something new, Flare put his forepaws in the air and to the side, almost making it look like he was trying to scare someone. After this, two needle-like blades appeared upon his forepaws. "Light blades, the same as on my tail."
 This was indeed new to TalonFyre. "Oh - well that's one thing I'm not familiar with," he replied, slightly impressed.
 Flare continued with his explanation of his powers, "I can also create maces and spears. It took a lot of practice to be able to focus light energy into photon weapons."
 TalonFyre's claw began to glow with a reddish-black hue. He then approached Flare, poking the area around his heart. After this was done, his powers shut off. "Never seen this then?" the mercenary asked with a grin.
 Flare backed up, surprised, "Pressure points?" he asked wondering.
 TalonFyre smirked. "Hotpoint - senses the source of the powers and shuts it down."
 This turn of events worried Flare, "Temporarily or for good? I kind of *need* those," he asked, his concern showing in his voice.
 TalonFyre continued his explanation, "It shows the heat signature of the powers and lets me deactivate it simply by touching it," he went on as his tail turned into a black blade with a red glow.
 "Uhm - nice trick, so…" Flare started.

TalonFyre touched Flare's heart area again, "Here - too flashy for me," he said nonchalantly, transferring them back.

Flare was relieved, but also impressed. "So, it's like power theft?" Flare asked.

TalonFyre shrugged, "Not permanent, just gives me a much more powerful version for a short time - almost mimicry. But it has its disadvantages." His expression darkened, "Leave it too long and I start losing my own. Sort of changes to a permanent version replacing mine - which is why I never use it unless I have nothing left to lose," the mercenary finished with another shrug.

This caused Flare to ponder for a moment. "If you found a power that was great enough, would you trade it?" he asked.

The mercenary walked into a pitch black room and responded with an uncaring, "Nah- I'm fine as is," as he entered.

Upon his arrival in the dark room, TalonFyre placed a lit claw upon the wall, lighting the room just enough to see. The room was filled and plastered with scrolls and maps upon shelves, boxes, and even the wall. "Ah, my archives," the mercenary sighed.

Flare was astounded, "I didn't take you for a scholar..." he whispered to his new friend.

TalonFyre walked up to a drawer, pulling it open. "One thing I found when I was young was a letter from my father. It said 'do not open unless revived'. Since you did that I'm able to open it and here we are," he explained, reaching into the drawer gently.

Flare walked up to TalonFyre. "May I.... see it?" Flare asked politely.

"Oh sure..." the mercenary answered, pulling out a clearly aged piece of parchment, igniting it with his breath. The letter appeared in front of them as an illuminated message.

Dear son, if you're reading this then you are ready now so here it is. The reason your mother and you never met...

During laying of your egg she began having heart issues; right after you were laid she died.

She gave you your dark fire and glowing blood and you are the last of your kind. She would be proud.

In TalonFyre's eyes, tears of lava began welling up. "It's not your fault," Flare told the clearly distraught TalonFyre in a very kind yet assertive tone.

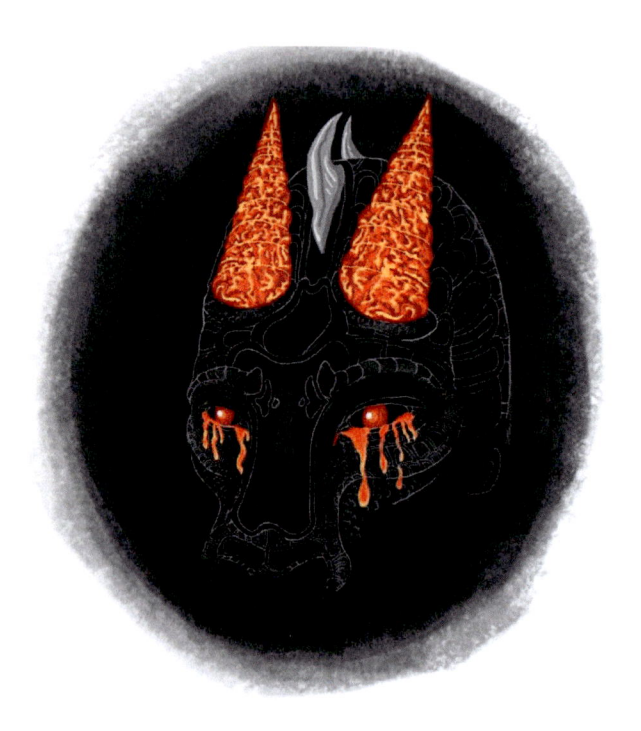

The mercenary was silent for a moment, and then stormed off, breaking through a wall in tears. "I KNEW IT *WAS* MY FAULT!!" he yelled in a mixture of anger and sorrow. He ran into his room, locking a large door behind him. Flare put his paw on the door, sobbing fully audible behind it.

"I knew I was a waste of space....." the mercenary cried, shedding tears behind the door. A few minutes later, the door unlocked. "**ARRRHHHH!!**" he screamed in misery.

Flare could see his eyes narrow darkly after this. He was worried - and he was right to be.

Chapter 3

The Pinnacle of Depression

THE mercenary began opening his chest after his heart. "I'll end it all now..." he said with a sinister smile.

Flare saw this and punched him in the face, which got him nowhere, as TalonFyre merely bit into his paw, causing blood to flow. "I'm done with this life. I'm just a nobody," TalonFyre sighed.

At this point Flare knew he had to say it. **"DO YOU REALLY THINK YOUR MOTHER WOULD WANT THIS YOU MORON!!!?"** he yelled at the top of his lungs.

TalonFyre stopped his claw just shy of his heart leaving a gash in it. "No...." he said softly, lying down sobbing.

Flare gently put his bleeding paw on TalonFyre's, "She died giving you life - do you *really* think she would want you to *waste* it?" he asked in a soft and fatherly voice, although it was a rhetorical question.

Eyes full of tears, TalonFyre looked up at Flare. The light dragon's expression showed pure pity. "Look at me - a merc as tough as me crying like a hatchling. And how would I know if I never even **met** her?" TalonFyre wailed, slashing his face. He then put his head back down after saying this and started crying again. He was covered in blood. "It's all just a mess I made. All of it," the mercenary sighed miserably, starting to place holes in his heart.

Blood flowed from TalonFyre's body, and Flare saw this. "Well looks like I'm...not so tough after all," the mercenary coughed, spitting blood. "Yeah, funny how I thought I was helping with those damn jobs. All to get rich - to get some notoriety and fame..." he continued, his eyes closing slightly.

The situation looked grim at this point. Flare knew he had to do something to help, and fast. "This takes a lot of power to do, but..." Flare began, creating bandages of light.

"I'll see her again now..." the mercenary sighed in a mixture of sadness and false joy.

Flare attempted to dress the wound, but a snap of the jaws from TalonFyre destroyed them. "No, I'm going home. I'm sick of this crap life - have no purpose," he said miserably.

"Your purpose is clear - to help Electus through his quest to unite this world in peace after the war," Flare said capriciously, struggling to find the right words to get TalonFyre to live.

The pleas merely caused TalonFyre to stand, but blood gushed out of his chest. "No....I was just a **pawn**," the mercenary scoffed. Flare didn't know how to help him at this point.

"Well, it's over now," TalonFyre sighed, barely audible as he began to lean over, his eyes closing again as he sadly whispered the words, "I'm....coming."

By this point, Flare had had just about enough. "You're **pathetic**.... You're really going to *give up* like this?" he said cruelly.

TalonFyre merely smiled. "Better than be killed by some damn idiot mercs - and no, not me," TalonFyre growled, attempting to get up.

At this an idea struck Flare. It was the entire reason he set out on this quest. "You could always come with me," Flare suggested hopefully.

TalonFyre wobbled. "Although I do feel kind of....." the mercenary started in a disoriented fashion, only to be interrupted by Flare.

"I have a home where you could find peace. Also, I have a-" he began, only to see that the mercenary had nearly blacked out in a pool of lava-like blood. His heart was still beating, but was slowing down - and fast

"Uhh.... well......that's that. I'll be at peace soon enough," TalonFyre sighed in a falsely happy tone.

Flare knew of only one thing that he could do. "The ultimate power of the light - donating a part of one's own life force to another...." he started.

TalonFyre stopped him short. "It's fine - no sense wasting it on me," TalonFyre sighed. After his words, the dying mercenary teleported himself outside.

"That light dragon's got too much to live for - has a lot to do yet - too much to waste on a stupid merc like me," the dying dragon chuckled somberly.

"I didn't even get to tell him my life force *regenerates*..." Flare sighed, his voice disheartened.

"Yeah well, it's not worth it anyway... yes I can hear you," the mercenary growled.

Flare was too lost in thought to hear and merely continued talking to himself, "It's a gift, and a curse - just like TalonFyre's power."

The door opened slightly. Flare then realized the mercenary could hear him speaking. "We're alike in that way," Flare said softly.

TalonFyre opened the door entirely after this. "Unless you didn't notice…" the mercenary partially said. There in his bloody hands, was his still-beating heart. "Wow all this just for me - what a mistake," he whispered with a look of pure sadness.

Taking his claw, TalonFyre began to stab the beating piece of glowing rock as blood gushed out. "Ugggghhhhh….!" he moaned in agony. At this point his heart was stopping completely.

"Well - at least *someone* will have remembered my past. So long Flare," TalonFyre said with a sad smile on his face.

"**DAMMIT**!!!" Flare screamed in a mixture of fear and anger.

Even though TalonFyre was trying to kill himself, his paw stopped short of the last puncture. "Something's holding me back…" he said with a furrowed brow. A single look at what was causing the situation, and TalonFyre's expression turned from a look of frustrated sorrow to pure shame. There, standing before them, was the specter of TalonFyre's father. His angered glowing red eyes seemed to pierce TalonFyre's very soul. His horns were shaped like a tilted ant's jaw with a slight curve at the end, moving in unison as his head came down to meet his son's. It was impossible to see his coloring, but he seemed to have embroiled markings on his back and paws.

"***YOU FOOL***!" the specter boomed in anger, cleaving TalonFyre in the jaw.

"Oh man, now I'm in deep crap," TalonFyre whimpered in fear.

The specter turned to Flare. "You, light dragon - help this fool of a son!" he ordered Flare. Flare quickly grabbed an orb of light out of his head. "And quick, he's bleeding out!" the specter continued. Obliging him, Flare placed the orb upon the heart of the mercenary's lava-filled heart. "Yes, that will do," the specter sighed, relieved.

The orb of light glowed as Flare began the incantation, "Ini wer vers di mitne, si majak tobor ekess wer ir persvek rigluin."

TalonFyre gave a disapproving growl - which earned him another smack from his father. "No - nngh!" he yelled.

"Tobor ekess wer ir ios coi - erekess svabolen vi cirau sepa tepohaic majaktor di astaha ekess shala," Flare continued.

"Nnnghh!" the mercenary yelled disapprovingly once more.

"Origato wer mamiss arise vur qe naktada wer ro togofor - **Tiichir di Tobor**!!" Flare cried out, finishing the incantation.

With this, TalonFyre got up, fully restored. "Fine, I'll stay a bit longer then - didn't say I have to like it," he scoffed.

After he said this, another form appeared. TalonFyre was shocked. Standing before him was his mother - the one who died giving him life. Although slightly transparent, her shimmering black scales matched his own. Her angry yet sorrow-filled eyes were a deep blue, almost like sea next to thick enchanted steel walls of Darastrix Charis on the purest and clearest day.

"I have something to tell you. I was sent... by *these two*..." Flare said with a sigh. "And-" Flare started, but the mercenary paid no heed to him. Instead he struggled to rise, heading toward his mother - who promptly slashed his face.

"First, *that's* for trying to *KILL YOURSELF!*" she yelled at the top of her spectral lungs. After this, she embraced him as they both shed their tears. "And this is for never seeing you," she continued, sobbing. Flare watched this and shed tears as well. He knew it was time to tell him.

A/N: The words to Flare's incantation are,
By the power of light, I give life to the one in need.
Life to the one without it - through which a kind soul has given of themselves to allow.
Let the body arise and be kept from the eternal plane - Blessing of Life!

Chapter 4

The Past

THIS was what the vision told Flare to do – "Help a dragon in need. In return, you will receive comfort from your troubles. However, it will not come through without effort. Otherwise it will be for naught." That was what TalonFyre's mother had said to him in the vision. This meant Flare would need to make TalonFyre feel like he was no longer alone in the world, and to do that, he needed to make sure he knew about what had happened to cause Flare to search for him.

"I have something to tell you TalonFyre – about my past," Flare sighed, looking at the two.

"What... about... it?" he asked, still crying in his mother's embrace.

"When I was young, I decided to venture into a forbidden cavern," Flare started, looking up with an unreadable expression.

Blood began to seep out of TalonFyre's heart again through a hole that had reopened. Upon seeing this, his mother shot the light dragon a glare.

"It was said to contain an artifact of immense power, but carrying a curse," Flare continued, giving TalonFyre more of his energy and fully healing him. At this point, his parents disappeared.

"This artifact... gave me eternal life..." Flare went on.

"What....*wait*! **DAMMIT**!" TalonFyre cried angrily out as the two vanished.

Ignoring him, Flare drooped his head, disheartened at the last words that he was about to say, "But as you know, eternal life is exactly that - a blessing and a curse."

The mercenary stood up, back to normal and fully healed, "Thanks. I kind of well, lost it all," he said sadly.

Flare looked down and shed a tear as he began his next story, "I can see spirits as well. I was banished from my village, became a vagabond... a wanderer."

TalonFyre walked up to him and gave a sad smile, "Heh, not a merc then. Well, not a job for most – hell, or me. I only took it to get stronger."

TalonFyre looked at the spot where his mother was and shut his eyes while Flare continued his tale, "Eventually I found a place where I could live in peace and have a family. But then - Rayburn came. He slaughtered the entire village, every male, female and child. My mate, Angel... she got eternal life from me, but not immortality. She was his first target. He killed her in a way too horrific to describe, burning her with demonic fire - then he tore her apart. We never found her head." He clenched his right forepaw with an angry look on his face.

During this time, TalonFyre was in thought about what his mother had whispered in his ear. He decided to tell Flare now that he had finished his tale, "She told me she wasn't planning on living at all... *She* was the Thanatos Golem's heart. She made herself have a heart attack to prevent it from killing the seven-dragon council in Darastrix Charis," TalonFyre sighed, shedding a tear.

"That's something she didn't tell me," Flare said, eyes widening in surprise.

This made TalonFyre grin. "Yeah, a hug from your long dead mother says a lot without a word," the mercenary replied, picking up a necklace. "My mother's..." he grasped it, tearing up yet again. "I cry too much... not very tough is it....?" he sobbed.

Flare put his paw on TalonFyre's shoulder. "My friend, you have a place... but it's not as a mercenary. Your place is helping rebuild the world," he said, a little unsure of his own words.

"Yeah, well - Electus finished my job. He did it for me," TalonFyre shrugged.

"Your power... you can use it for more practical means than *killing*," Flare went on with a grin.

"Yeah - I guess so," the mercenary replied uncertainly.

"Did you think of helping to rebuild Darastrix Charis after Rayburn's last ditch effort to kill the council?" Flare asked in a hesitant voice.

TalonFyre rolled his eyes. "Well, I did find a souvenir," he said sarcastically, walking into an armory. TalonFyre then pulled a lever lowering a crane containing an ice ballista from Darastrix Charis.

Flare was tired of kidding himself. He got up his courage and began to tell his new friend what had truly weighed on his mind, "And also... there was *one* survivor of my family's slaughter, besides me."

TalonFyre wasn't paying attention however. "Don't ask - my merc "buddies" made me. How do you think my father **died**?" he asked with a growl.

In his anger, Flare's eyes narrowed at the question and he jumped to a conclusion, "I'm sure the same way my mate and son died – Rayburn," he clenched his paw as he said the name.

This thought was dismissed as TalonFyre shook his head and began to tell the real story. "Those wastes of life grabbed him while I was asleep and took him hostage," his expression showed the same amount of anger as Flare, who loosened his paw slightly as TalonFyre said this, his expression turning less angry. "Yeah, they said steal the ballista so they're not as well defended from the Thanatos Golem and my father lives. I did it and they *still* killed him!" the mercenary screamed angrily.

Flare began to put the pieces of the puzzle together about the crater of ash, but he needed to ask a question to be sure, "Are they still alive?" he was already sure of the answer, but he needed to know for certain.

The truth was obtained when TalonFyre confirmed Flare's suspicions, "The fiery blast I made after that was a mile wide - nothing survived. I barely did. Even managed to turn my father to ash. I saw him leaving - said I was doing well so far but wasn't finished....he was," TalonFyre sounded sad as he said this.

It became apparent to Flare that it was hard for TalonFyre to talk about this, so he decided finally to say what was on his mind the whole time. The problem was whether the mercenary would even accept. It was now or never.

A/N: Darastrix Charis means "Dragon Hope" in Draconic. It was named this due to the hope that it would never fall, which it nearly did in the War of the Third Demon, as the fight against Rayburn would come to be known.

Chapter 5

A Favor for a Favor

"I have an idea. Do you know how I said there was a survivor... of my family...?" Flare asked, still a bit uncertain of the response he'd get.

TalonFyre was listening, but said what he wanted to say at the end of his story, "Even thought of going right to Mr. "High and Mighty" Rayburn and ripping him a new **asshole**."

Turning to Flare with false hope, replying with, "Yeah - let me guess - me right?"

Flare shook his head no, "It was my daughter... Hikari," he sighed with a sad look on his face.

TalonFyre merely gave a semi-interested, "Oh."

Flare looked down. "Her name means light," he explained with another sigh as he thought to himself, 'You need to help her before it loses all meaning.'

The mercenary, however, had trouble paying attention. "Sorry, I'm still a little dazed," he said, shaking his head. TalonFyre came out of his stupor, "Anyway, you were saying?"

After this Flare continued, "My daughter was the *only* survivor of my family. Her name is Hikari, it means light. The death of her mother filled her with grief. Now she won't even talk to me. She says I failed them," he sighed once more, a depressed expression on his face as he shed a tear.

A Vespatite's insect-like screech was heard from the corner of the room. "Oh my **God,** I am *so sick*...!" the mercenary smashed it with his foot as he growled. He then turned to Flare, "Well, anyway - I can try talking to her..." His helpful expression quickly tuned to a hurt one. "No - she'll get scared and run off like all the kids," he retracted sadly.

At this, Flare looked him straight in the eyes. "Hikari needs someone who's lost a lot to talk to her," he said seriously.

"Oh," TalonFyre said as he grasped the situation.

This response caused Flare to smile hopefully, "And, she's almost your age."

TalonFyre became disturbed at his comment. "Ah - **no**! Before you **EVEN** *suggest that* - I literally *can't* mate. It's well - impossible..." he said with a disgusted look on his face, cringing at the thought.

"No, nothing like that," Flare replied with a chuckle, rolling his eyes.

"Oh - ohhh ok," the mercenary grinned embarrassedly as he said this. Flare merely chuckled again.

"Yeah, you'd be surprised how many of the ladies ask me. I just growl and walk off," the mercenary's brow furrowed as he said this. He then clenched his paw. "Never again will I even attempt," he mumbled angrily.

Flare understood this; however, that's not what he needed to be done. "She needs someone to talk to - that's all," he reiterated softly.

TalonFyre nodded. "I can do that. Well, where is she? At your place?" he asked Flare.

This was a question Flare was glad to answer with, "Yes, she is…*thankfully*," whispering the last part.

Making a quick trip back to his archives, TalonFyre returned with a map marking the caves of every dragon in the vicinity that Flare lived in. "Here you are," he pointed to the area of Flare's home as he said this, "The Phosphorus Groves… Yup, I've scouted there before," the mercenary continued, picking up a gem.

"Let's go now," Flare suggested hastily.

TalonFyre then slammed the door and the bunker sunk. "Fine - ok, this portal here," he said as he threw the gem to the ground, revealing a pearl-white portal in the shape of a 60-foot cylinder. He approached it only to realize that it was unpowered.

"Huh!? It won't work! Damn merchant's a **liar**!" TalonFyre yelled angrily. "Well, he's gone now - tried to snatch my sword. Yeah, didn't turn out well," he then paused, "Huh, it matches you - odd. I've been through it before no problem."

A touch of Flare's paw opened the portal, revealing an image of Flare's homeland. TalonFyre was surprised at this, "Well…that's handy. You're like a generator with legs," the mercenary chuckled, stepping up to the portal. "You're leading right?" he asked hopefully.

Flare stepped through the portal and answered, "Yes, for more than one reason."

Chapter 6

Hikari

THE portal led to a very thin forested area. The trees however, were covered in a strange blue, glowing moss. The foliage had a tint to it as well. The grass was also covered in a strange white glow. This was the reason it was given the name 'Phosphorus Grove'. It was a beautiful place, especially at night.

 They stepped out of the portal, and as soon as that happened, the mercenary let out a sneeze. This turn of events resulted in the ignition of a tree. "Uh, oops – air's different here," TalonFyre gulped embarrassedly.

Flare whipped his tail around the tree and put the fire out by smothering it. He then healed his wound with his light powers.

The mercenary looked around and huffed, "So, where to now? That map is *not* accurate." Flare was about to say something when a blast of light shot into TalonFyre's face, "What the- GAH, damn sun!" TalonFyre growled in an annoyed voice as he began to stagger around, dazed and blinded.

"Oh dear..." Flare sighed worriedly.

"Huh?" TalonFyre grunted as he looked up, his eyes watering and his vision still greatly blurred.

Flare rolled his eyes again. "That wasn't the sun," he started, keeping his worried tone.

"Oh great - *another* disaster," TalonFyre interrupted in a half-sarcastic, half-concerned tone.

Flare put his paw to his face and corrected him, "No, that was Hikari's light breath."

TalonFyre became depressed at this fact. "So... she doesn't like me," he sighed.

"No, she thought that was me," Flare once again corrected the mercenary, who obviously wasn't listening as well as he should have been.

"Your point? Not many people like me..." the mercenary continued. He then realized what Flare told him and responded simply with, "Oh."

Slowly but surely, Flare walked up to the cave. "Hikari, there's someone here that I would like you to talk to," he half-yelled, half-whined.

TalonFyre then tossed a rock in the general direction of the blast. "Blinding me...." the mercenary growled as he began to turn his head with a mixture of anger and odd disappointment. As TalonFyre was walking away, he heard a thud.

The dragoness walked out angrily and looked at the two. "Um- oops," the mercenary whispered quietly. "Great, another injury - at least it isn't *me*," he grumbled, barely audible.

 After this, he started to see more clearly. A slender, beautiful pearl-white dragoness with a sleek pink underbelly, blue sclera, pink irises, and blue wing membranes with a purple tint was standing at the entrance to the cavern. TalonFyre then noticed she had a blood spot on her head. "Uh oh... **great** - *not* a good start," he sighed in an embarrassed tone, concern showing in his face.

Flare knew he had to do something to make sure his daughter didn't start off on the wrong foot with TalonFyre, so he did the only thing he could think of and yelled out, "Sorry, I was trying to get your attention!" Flare placed his mouth near the mercenary's earlobe after this. "Just pretend like it was me who threw it," he whispered.

"Oh, good," the mercenary whispered back. Pointing his claw at Flare, TalonFyre nervously yelled, "He did it," at the top of his fiery lungs.

"Sorry about that," Flare yelled apologetically.

"Yeah, she's not gonna' be happy *YOU* threw it," the mercenary continued with the same nervous tone.

Unconvinced, the dragoness turned her head. "Who is this?" she asked, annoyance and spite evident in her voice.

The mercenary decided to sock Flare in the foreleg to add to the ruse. "Ow…" Flare moaned, rubbing the spot where he was struck with light. TalonFyre pointed at Flare again.

A small, sly grin appeared on Hikari's face, and then faded. The mercenary noticed this and gave an embarrassed laugh. "You're a terrible liar…" she scoffed.

"Hey, mercs don't lie much or they get killed," TalonFyre shrugged. A Vespatite bit his tail after he said this. "**OW, YOU LITTLE…!**" he grunted angrily.

Although TalonFyre would have killed the creature, Hikari sprang at it and slashed its head off with nothing but a three-foot photon blade on her tail.

TalonFyre ran after it and laughed, "Yeah, it's still going," as he ran up to it. Unfortunately in his haste he collided with a tree, his head becoming wedged in its trunk. "Mphh… Oh, great…" His attempt to take it out merely uprooted it. Although she thought it was a bit funny, Hikari pulled TalonFyre out.

"Thanks," TalonFyre sighed in relief, rubbing his head with one of his forepaws. In the other paw, he had the Vespatite by the leg. He paused for a moment and decided to leave it be. "Aw, forget it," he mumbled uncaringly, throwing it into a rock.

The Vespatite skittered away headless. Its retreat would have been successful, but Hikari had other plans. Forming a photon claw, she sprang after it, ripping its legs off. TalonFyre was shocked, "Naw, just…" Hikari didn't listen as she mauled it to a bloody pulp. "Whatever, I don't care for them," the mercenary shrugged, hiding his impressment.

"Why haven't the dragons figured out how to make *pesticides*? It's beyond me. Even found a few fried in the bottom of my lava pool." Hikari giggled at the idea of this. "Clogged the thing up and it blew up on me. At least it felt nice. Sure as hell woke me up," he continued.

This story intrigued Hikari. "You can withstand lava?" she asked curiously.

"Blood is filled with it," TalonFyre answered in a slightly proud voice as he pulled back a layer of flesh and bled lava. "Doesn't hurt," he shrugged nonchalantly.

Hikari was even more curious now. "You're not your everyday dragon, are you?" she continued with her questioning.

"Nope, I'm sure as hell not," the lava-blooded dragon answered in the same nonchalant tone. He thought for a second what to say next. He then got an idea. "Actually won a bet once on that. Guy was absolutely sure I was a regular fire element. He had a huge cart of gold. I let him keep it," he said, finishing his story.

There was something Hikari noticed about the mercenary. "Your eyes are also… they look sad," she whispered in a slightly concerned voice, her face keeping her curious expression.

TalonFyre was confused as to how Hikari could have known about his sorrowful past, or even his current situation of the emotions he was withholding. "She can read people's eyes," Flare explained softly.

Attempting to change the subject, TalonFyre added, "Yeah, not to mention glowing. Scary as hell to the Vesps in the dark - gives them strokes." Hikari laughed upon thinking of it. TalonFyre continued happily, "If I'm bored I'll knock the lights down and hide… then scare them to death and watch them run into each other. Oh **man,** it's fun! One even attacked another and they all *killed* each other out of *fear*!"

Picturing this in her head, Hikari burst out into a fit of laughter with TalonFyre joining her soon after. After it died down a bit, Hikari exclaimed, "That's *so* **cool**!"

Surprised by her reaction to his stories, TalonFyre decided to continue. "Yeah, well that's back home and I'm sure they're actually *in* the damn bunker again…as usual. I can never find out where they get in. I've sealed **everything**," he moaned disgruntledly.

The outcome of the meeting was better than Flare could have hoped for. It was at this point that he decided to explain about his daughter's attitude, "I have to mention she's kind of… abnormally into violence. For a dragoness I mean."

Upon hearing this, TalonFyre pulled out his sword from his armor, stopping it within a hair's length of her face. He got an unexpected reaction - she smirked. This made him confused – he was happy. Why was he so happy?

TalonFyre pulled the sword away from the dragoness and put it away. "I never use it unless it's either a golem, or a dumbass merc employer who *doesn't know what's good for business*," he said, the last words having a sly tone to them, "It helps pay the 'bills'." This caused Hikari to chuckle a bit.

"Come to think of it…" the mercenary pulled out a smaller version and handed it to her. "It's light-infused instead of black fire," he explained.

Hikari became ecstatic at this and only managed a happy, "Thank you!" before composing herself. She felt strange. What was this feeling she had? Her stomach felt slightly odd. It wasn't that strong, but she still had an unfamiliar feeling in it.

Flare had an idea how he could make the situation even better. "Oh, tell her what happened when you were asked to *kill* that unborn dragon," he said smugly.

TalonFyre smiled at this. "I ate the guy who asked me to do it. Damn if that's how I taste then I'd just throw up - like eating old burnt rocks covered in rancid meat," he said, gagging.

"That's awesome..!" Hikari cried with a look of vengeful joy. This surprised TalonFyre even more – it was almost as if she was enjoying the story more than he was.

TalonFyre continued happily once more, "He deserved it. Not nice at all. Oh man, he had *lots* of the others actually do it. He was Rayburn's second-in-command. Everyone was scared to stand up to him."

Hikari interrupted with a sly remark, "I can guess why he tasted bad - shit tastes really nasty."

This earned her a good laugh from TalonFyre before he went on, "Five times my size - just a *huge* ****ing moron. I ate his damn face first - while he was alive. The others just ran. I think I finished half of him before I started puking," he said, ending his story.

"That's pretty hardcore," Hikari laughed mischievously.

TalonFyre looked at her seriously. "*No one* like that deserves life - just killing dragons while they're defenseless... Sick," he growled.

Hikari's expression hardened. "You have no idea how much I agree. I would have ripped his head off, put it on a spike and sold it off to the highest bidder," she hissed, clenching her front paw.

TalonFyre started again, "Even came across his mate who *obviously* gave me this." He uncovered a gash across his eye. "She was pissed but had an unborn dragon in its egg. Hypocrites. I left her alone after she swiped me. I just told her how her husband tasted, and said she has bad taste in men. She just started sobbing. Me? I laughed," the mercenary shrugged. Hikari giggled cruelly at this. "Even left behind a horn of his. I didn't care - she deserved to have him killed - but *not* the hatchling. No... I'm no murderer without a reason - I only kill those who deserve it," the mercenary finished again with an assertive voice.

"As long as the innocent will be harmed, the evil cannot be either." Hikari said softly, the fact hinted that she couldn't bear to see a hatchling grow up without a mother or father.

"Anyway, Flare, what's new?" TalonFyre asked in a somewhat uncaring tone as he turned to his new friend, although he wasn't exactly certain as to the meaning of his question.

"You got her in a better mood, I can tell you that!" Flare answered with a laugh.

TalonFyre scratched his neck. "Damn, what is making me itch? Oh, the air - damn scales are going hard. ...Hang on." The mercenary walked over to a dried pond and bulked his arm twice as muscular. He punched the ground, going down an entire layer of earth. He then jumped into the hole and rode the lava back up. "Ahhh..." he moaned happily.

"Now that is one hundred percent bad-assery," Hikari laughed.

"You picked a good place, I'll give you that. Lava is actually more earthy - better for me," TalonFyre said with a smile, relaxing in the lava. "Yeah, I'll just..." he yawned, falling asleep mid-sentence, snoring a few seconds in. Hikari giggled again at this. TalonFyre flicked lava at her and gave a tired, "Trying to nap here," as a response. This would have made many a dragoness angry, but not this one.

"Yep, a total badass," Hikari said with a smile. The mercenary's snout stuck into the lava making bubbles as he snored.

A/N: Vespatites have the odd cockroach-like ability to live without a head, albeit for a week or so. They also have two circulatory systems: one sends blood to the brain, but most of it stays in their body.

Chapter 7

Mothers

ROUGHLY an hour later, the sleeping mercenary got up, glowing as normal. "Yeah, it doesn't take me long," he shrugged, once again uncaring.

Hikari felt strange. She wanted to stay close to him for a reason she didn't understand. "Mister TalonFyre... Will you stay here with us?" she asked him, eyes full of hope.

"Great, now there's a lava pool out here burning the..." the mercenary stopped mid-sentence and answered, "Yeah, sure nothing going on at home. But I'll sleep out here. I snore – bad," although he wasn't entirely sure why he agreed so fast.

"I know," Flare laughed.

TalonFyre felt a sneeze coming and was about to say this but it was too late to stop it. The exhalation sprayed lava onto Hikari's forepaw, burning it. "Uh, oh, bombs away - aw **crap**!" he yelled unnerved. The mercenary took flight, certain that he had blown his chance to stay.

"Ow! Ah, well..." Hikari healed her wound with her light powers only to notice TalonFyre had taken off. "Wait!" she called out, taking off after him.

As he flew, TalonFyre had a strange feeling. Why did he feel guilty? Why did he feel like he was leaving something behind? Most importantly of all, why did he want to go back?

The scenery passed him until he came to an open cave. The cave was empty all but for the skull of a dead dragon. TalonFyre walked up to it, unaware that Hikari had followed him. "Hey, you look scared stiff!" he laughed.

Upon seeing the skull, Hikari's face changed to a look of pure despair. "That's.... my mom's..." Hikari gasped, her voice showing hurt.

TalonFyre's heart sank as he heard this. He backed away, crushed. "Yeah, too many dead moms in a day thank you," he gulped in despair, tearing up once again.

Hikari gave a sad sigh, "It's okay... you didn't know. Wait - what?" She was puzzled, but didn't have time to ask about it - TalonFyre had taken off again, flying back to Flare.

The scenery passed by TalonFyre once more, but his eyes were too tear-filled for it to be visible. Hikari was following close behind him, full of questions and guilt.

When he arrived back at the cave, the mercenary charged towards Flare with tear-filled eyes, Hikari landing behind him. "What's wrong?" Flare asked in a concerned voice.

TalonFyre put his head in his forepaws, "I'm *so* **sick** of it!" he wailed. Flare was about to ask when TalonFyre continued in a broken voice, "*All* the dead mothers! No one has *any* alive anymore!"

Hikari looked at him sadly, "Talon..." she whispered in a sorrowful and sympathetic tone.

He turned away. "Just forget it," and upon saying this, he disappeared.

"I think you should tell her about it," Flare started to say, but didn't have time to relay the message. The mercenary had already gone, crying in solitude in a valley a half of a mile away.

"Why did he run - I'm going after him!" the dragoness exclaimed with a worried face. She took off, following the smell of lava. She already felt attached to the dragon for some reason. Why did she want him to stay? When he threw his blade in front of her face, her heart was racing, but she wasn't scared. She didn't have time to think about such things right now, she needed to find him.

Meanwhile, TalonFyre had found another cave and began to check for corpses or remains. "Looks clear finally," he sighed, relieved. He then lay down and drifted off into a sad sleep.

The scent of lava led Hikari to the cave. She entered to find the mercenary. She looked at him with sorrowful eyes. He sensed her presence and replied with a growl. However, Hikari approached him, unafraid of his anger. "Talon... why did you run?" she whispered sorrowfully.

TalonFyre was silent for a moment, then handed her his necklace.

"What is..." she began.

"All I have left of her now....." the mercenary said sadly.

Hikari began to cry into TalonFyre's forelegs. "I'm... so... sorry!" she wailed, tears flowing from her eyes.

TalonFyre put his wing over the dragoness to comfort her. "Not your fault - she was the heart of the Thanatos Golem. She caused her own death to stop Rayburn's attack on Darastrix Charis - she saved me."

This caused Hikari to calm down slightly. "She saved us all, including Electus and the council. She was a true hero," Hikari whispered, her eyes still filled with tears.

TalonFyre nodded, "Yeah... brought me into this world without my dad.... Gave me my claws, lava infused blood, my scales, everything," he continued, feeling a bit better. "Guess my dad kept it all secret to save me," he finished with a sigh and fell silent.

"I don't care *what* you are. No matter what, I want you to stay," Hikari said with a comforting smile, drying her tears with her wing.

TalonFyre nodded once more. "Fine by me - I've got nothing else going on," he shrugged. Hikari smiled in pure joy when he gave this answer.

At this moment, TalonFyre had sensed his bunker's door bombs detonate. "Dumbasses - they *never* learn," he chuckled.

"Something funny?" Hikari asked, confused.

The mercenary grinned. "Just my door bombs setting off. Yeah, I'm tied to that place sort of," he explained with a smile. Hikari laughed. "Actually..." he mumbled something incoherent.

After the odd words were spoken, an explosion was heard. "There, now it's gone," the mercenary said. "Aw, hell - archives are gone too," he muttered. He thought about it for a second and shrugged, "Meh, nothing I don't already know."

What TalonFyre had done shocked Hikari to the core, "You destroyed it all ... for me?" she asked softly.

"Meh, I was sick of the Vespatite infestation in that place - but yeah...," he turned, "So now what? I'm homeless, as usual," he went on with a sense of hope he was unaware of.

"We *go* home," Hikari replied with a smile.

TalonFyre was confused. Why did he destroy his own home? Hikari was kind, that was certain - but not someone he should blow up his house for! Yet why did he say that he *did* do it for her? And why did he feel glad when she said those words? What was wrong with him? All these questions circled about in his mind as he took his wing off of her, and he had no answer to any of them.

Hikari on the other hand, knew what she felt. She loved him. She actually *loved* him. This was a new feeling for her. She never actually loved a dragon until she met TalonFyre, and she hadn't known him for more than a few hours. Why did she feel so attracted to him? Was it because he had a tragic past? Was it because of his hardcore attitude and soft heart? The only thing she did know is that she had fallen for him, head over paws. Maybe it was a crush – infatuation and nothing more. How many male dragons had she met at her old village? Two? Maybe three at most? She hadn't seen a male besides her father in at least a year. That would make it likely that it could very well be a crush. Still, what if it wasn't? What if she truly desired to have him as a mate? She was not aware of any sexual interest in him whatsoever at this point. So the idea of hormones being the driving force behind her attachment was out of the question. That could only mean one thing – she really did have a romantic interest in him. The one thing that filled her with fear however, was her 'problem'. No dragon would want her, not even this one. But TalonFyre was the dragon she needed, she was sure of it – wasn't he? Whatever the case, she knew it would be better to tell him about her secret sooner rather than later in their relationship.

Chapter 8

Hunting

TALONFYRE got up, the entirety of his spine making a crack, "Ahhh - better."

'Maybe Hikari has found someone she can actually be with. I can tell she's fallen for him.' Flare thought, standing outside with a large smile upon his face.

"I can *tell* you're there - it's called sense of smell. That and I can see you in the damn dark," TalonFyre yelled to the light dragon with a grin.

Flare continued smiling, "I have no problems with you staying with us - *for good*," he said proudly.

"Well, that's **great**!" the mercenary chimed.

"By the way - around your room there's a crack in the wall. It's a Vespatite nest," TalonFyre informed them. They were somewhat disturbed by this - at least Flare was. "Yeah, I picked it up in the lava. They're actually eating something... sounds like they're eating a *lot* of food. Wow, one of 'em just puked on the food - and now they're eating the puke," he gagged at the last sentence.

"We don't have any..." Hikari began, puzzled.

"Yeah, I beg to differ," TalonFyre replied sarcastically, looking to one side. He took off following the scent of Vespatite vomit, Hikari and Flare behind him. Soon, they arrived at Hikari and Flare's cave. The scent led them to the crevice. It was a small, diagonal crack a few feet in diameter. "Easy smell to find," the mercenary said with a smirk.

Flare carved an entrance with his photon tail blade and knocked down the wall, revealing 13 Vespatites.

Hikari made a sly grin and pulled out the dagger. "What do you say I test this bad boy out?" the dragoness asked rhetorically with a menacing smile.

"Go ahead," the mercenary answer, smiling in return.

This was all the inspiration Hikari needed. TalonFyre sat down, eager to see what the dragoness would do. Hikari charged her light breath to daze them. Talon covered his eyes this time, "Not getting me twice."

The dragoness fired a barrage of light bullets directly into their eyes, blinding the Vespatites and disallowing them from attacking her.

"And don't fire one at me - I know you're thinking it," TalonFyre went on in a semi-serious tone.

Hikari paid no heed to the mercenary's comments, slashing them all, stabbing their necks, and ripping their heads off.

"Heh - *nice*," TalonFyre laughed.

Hikari then proceeded to rip off their legs and cut them up as if they were sushi.

"You know, you can use your tail to hold it, it works even better. Mine's too big for that," TalonFyre commented. "Just don't stab yourself," he added, slightly concerned.

She gripped the weapon in her tail, charging it with photo and creating slight spikes in it. She then sliced the Vespatites to ribbons, uncaring that they were already near death.

"There - see? ...I'm too damn big for it," he mumbled.

Hikari put the dagger away. "That felt *good*," she sighed, once again sounding menacing.

TalonFyre was pleased. "Yup, first time always does – uh, the sword I mean," he grinned embarrassedly after saying this. Hikari, however, laughed happily.

Just then, TalonFyre's stomach growled. "I just ate back at .... Oh wait... crap, blew all that meat up!" he moaned loudly.

"Gold, I don't need really," he continued in an uncaring voice. He threw another gem on the ground, the lava pit from his bunker appearing through the portal. "Ah, here we are," he said, then turned to the Flare, "A little help?" he requested. Flare obliged happily.

TalonFyre lifted one end of the pit, Flare the other. "Put it over the hole I made," he instructed the light dragon. Flare did as he was asked, starting to move the pit. As they were doing this, the portal fizzled out, crumbling to dust. "Ah, just ignore it - it was a fixer upper," the mercenary shrugged.

The two dragged the pit onto the lava, fitting it snugly. "Well, that's one thing fixed," the mercenary said happily.

"Our home is your home," Hikari told the dragon with a kind and hopeful voice.

"Oh, I was just bringing it here anyway. Lava here makes me a little tipsy," TalonFyre replied with a smile.

Hikari was glad he was staying, but was concerned about one thing, something that always drove a male dragon away. She decided to say what was on her mind anyway. "Talon, there's something I need to tell you," she whispered, unsure of what his reaction would be.

"Yeah?" he said.

Hikari began to close her eyes as she sighed, "I'm infertile," her voice filled with fear.

"Yeah, same issue. Drop the subject, I'm starving," the mercenary scoffed. Hikari was disappointed, but at the same time extremely happy, when she heard this. TalonFyre went off after a deer, paying no attention to Hikari's smile.

"Let's go kill us some game!" Hikari yelled in joy, running after him.

TalonFyre had caught his deer and was ripping the deer apart as if he were a beast. "Damn that's good," he mumbled, mouth full of deer.

'Wait... hunting? This is my chance to impress TalonFyre!' Hikari thought as she spotted a bear. It was reaching for food in a nearby bush, and would make a good meal. She jumped on top of the creature, biting the neck and promptly ripping its head off afterwards. "Nothing like a challenging kill!" Hikari bit into the bear after saying this and started to devour it.

Raw bear was enjoyable, but there was a way to make the meal more pleasing, and for some reason, TalonFyre wanted Hikari to enjoy her feast as much as possible. He walked over to the dragoness, "Hang on - stand back a sec." The dragoness took a few steps back from the carcass. After this the mercenary immersed it in black fire, roasting it to perfection. "There - now eat," he said with a small grin, returning to his own meal. After the meat was gone, TalonFyre began devouring the bones, picking his teeth with the antlers.

"This is *great*!" Hikari exclaimed, still devouring the bruin.

Unable to hold it, TalonFyre let out a belch, "BUUUURRRP- Oh sorry." He thought she'd be disgusted, but instead, Hikari let out a larger belch after hearing him.

"Beat you," she said smugly.

This caused TalonFyre to laugh joyously, leading him to choke on a bone.

"Talon! Careful!" Hikari yelled worriedly. The bone melted in the lava lining of his throat. Hikari saw this and was relieved.

After both of them had finished their meal, they headed back to the cave, "Now what?" the mercenary asked uncertainly.

Hikari only answered, "We live in peace."

Peace was something that was long unknown to the mercenary, and he was uncertain if he could cope with it.

"I *do* have some scrolls that you might not have read," Hikari added hastily.

"Yeah, all mine are gone, not to mention boring," TalonFyre shrugged.

"Also, there are a lot of ruins around here that need exploring," Flare stated, joining the conversation.

TalonFyre shrugged again, "Better than merc camp. In fact, everyone I meet I note in my mind and if they're pure evil…. I can set this off." A messy explosion was heard after he said this, causing Hikari to laugh. "*That* would be the **bombs**. All the evil in the dustbowl is dead. Didn't say I had to let it *stay* that way. Doesn't fix the damn dust," he shrugged.

"You really are something," Hikari said, once again smiling.

TalonFyre wasn't sure what to make of Hikari. Her figure was so feminine, yet her attitude was more tomboyish than any female he'd met. She was certainly unique, and someone he'd like to know better. She was also infertile, just like him. She would never go into heat, and never have a child. He had one question, however – why did he feel sorry for her instead of happy for himself? An infertile dragoness was a dream come true for him! Why did he feel pity for her? Why did he feel like he wanted her to have a child of her own? He decided to ignore these questions and focus on the here and now. After all, he had no desire to mate, let alone have a child.

Chapter 9

Arsenal

FLARE looked to TalonFyre, "I didn't mention this before but... we're in the field of archeology."

The mercenary remembered what Flare said earlier, "Yeah, didn't you mention eternal life or something?"

Hikari nodded. "Yeah, that's the thing - I got it from my dad, but only part of it," she replied uncertainly.

"Ah - I got the same issue - sort of....last of my kind," the mercenary looked a bit sad at the last words.

The whole idea of longevity made Hikari curious. "How long do you live?" she asked ponderingly.

TalonFyre thought for a moment. "Don't know - never knew. I've outlived everyone in the merc camp by well, centuries. Well, no, decades," he shrugged at his answer.

Flare spoke in a glad tone, "Something tells me we're going to spend a lot of years exploring together."

The mercenary's nose twitched, "This air is getting to me." He sneezed after this, spraying lava, which Hikari dodged. TalonFyre coughed, "Think I swallowed a fly... protein I guess."

A few drops of water hit the mercenary's nose. It had started to rain. "Oh, *great!*" TalonFyre moaned worriedly as his body began to steam. "Yeah, I'd better get inside," he grumbled.

Hikari was concerned when she saw this. "Are you going to be okay?" she asked the mercenary in a concerned voice, placing her wing over him.

He felt a little uncomfortable with this, but ignored it. "Oh yeah, as long as I get inside. The pit will be fine. It has a sort of spell on it - reflects rain," he replied in a slightly nervous yet grateful voice.

"Water doesn't go well with you does it?" Flare asked rhetorically, tilting his head.

"No," the mercenary answered a bit annoyed.

"Lava *isn't* that good with water," Hikari stated, still looking concerned.

"Nope and I'm full of it," TalonFyre added in a smart yet nervous tone.

The rain started to become swifter and heavier, causing more steam to rise off of TalonFyre. "So now what, are we staying outside?" he asked worriedly, already sure of the answer.

Hikari's concern increased. "We're going in," she replied assertively.

Flare nodded, "You bet."

The mercenary followed them inside, Hikari's wing still over him. When he got inside he cracked his neck, which turned out to be deafening. "Ow, that actually hurt - not much," he shrugged, leaning upon a smooth wall.

It was then that TalonFyre noticed something about the wall he was next to. "Hang on," he rapped on it – it was hollow. "Uh, guys - do you *know* there's a cave complex back here?" he asked in an oddly curious voice, looking back at them. They shook their heads no, confused.

Without hesitation, he rammed the wall headfirst, revealing a cavern the size of his bunker. Flare and Hikari walked up to the crevice, surprised this had been there without their knowledge.

"Well - and OWW!" he groaned in pain. He then realized it had happened a second time. "Uh, my head is stuck again – great," he mumbled, once again annoyed. Hikari pulled him out once more. He then rubbed his head. "Thanks... I need to stop doing that," he sighed embarrassedly.

"I was going to say that," Hikari said with a grin.

The three walked inside, finding the cave walls were as smooth as TalonFyre's scales. "Well, I can tell it's just empty, and I don't sense any residual energies - just a random space," the mercenary said looking around, "Talk about home decorating."

"Do you want to make a lava pit here?" Hikari asked kindly.

TalonFyre shook his head no. "I have mine outside, it's fine," he replied, declining in an uncaring voice.

Flare had an idea. "How about we use this to store the artifacts we find?" he suggested happily.

"And my weapons," TalonFyre added with a grin, pulling out a shard of gem.

The mere mention of the word 'weapons' made Hikari excited. "That would be nice," she remarked happily, her face matching TalonFyre's. Flare simply shook his head and stood back.

The mercenary drew a circle in the floor and a portal opened, revealing all of his armaments. "Wasn't going to blow these up!" the mercenary exclaimed with a smirk, "I'm not that stupid."

Hikari admired the weapons in joy, "Kickass gear here," she said with a sly smile.

"Yeah - oh careful," TalonFyre warned.

Hikari backed away. Unfortunately she had walked upon a piece of equipment. Claw shaped shoes then latched onto her feet.

"Great – well, you're getting new claws. Try not to move," TalonFyre instructed her.

The dragoness stood still as the device stabbed her directly in the tips of her paws. "OW!" she yelped as the mold dropped off, making a casting of her claws from a mix of golem skin.

"There...yeah I knew I should've thrown that away," TalonFyre shrugged in a nonchalant voice, masking the fact that he was slightly concerned for her.

"What happened?" Hikari asked, admiring the piece of weaponry attached to her paws.

"It clones your DNA and matches it with the metal. Makes it ten times sharper and infuses it with your element," the mercenary explained.

Returning to the pile of weaponry, TalonFyre grabbed a chunk of golem. He proceeded to sniff it, gagging at the smell. "No more left in it," he remarked, tossing it backwards. Unfortunately, Flare was in the way of its trajectory and was struck on his nose by the blackish-gray piece of rock. "Oops - you ok?" the mercenary asked, a bit concerned.

Flare rubbed his nose and healed himself. "Yeah, I'm fine now," he replied without anger.

"Yeah, fancy trick - anyway get it out, it stinks," the mercenary requested in his usual uncaring voice.

Hikari grasped it in her tail and walked towards the exit of the cave.

"I thought I threw these out," TalonFyre whispered, pulling out some strange, wingtip-shaped pieces of metal. He examined them for a moment and threw them behind his back, which landed by Hikari as she arrived back inside.

"What a bunch of *junk*..." TalonFyre mumbled.

Hikari picked the blades up, "What are these?"

The mercenary turned to her, "Stabilizes your flying and allows you to use your wings like a sword," he explained, digging through the pile once again. "There's another right...here - catch Flare!" he tossed them over to the light dragon, who caught them on his wings.

TalonFyre continued through the pile until he found his own, then it hit him, "Oh right, I nearly cut a wing with these damn things. The one time I try to enhance my wings I nearly rip one." With that, he bit them in half and blasted them with fire, melting them.

Unnerved by the idea of getting his wings torn, Flare quickly unequipped the armaments. TalonFyre saw him do this, and realized the light dragon was afraid of the blades. "It was my fault. Mine were second hand. I copied them and fixed the mistakes. They're safe," the mercenary informed him. However, Flare was still a bit unsure, and left them on the ground.

After a few more minutes of digging, TalonFyre found what he was looking for. "Ahh, *here* it is!" he pulled out a small table, armor dropping to the floor. "Invisible armor - well seemingly, matches your scales and color. Just put your foot on the plate in the center. It'll scan you and make a set of armor to match your style of fighting and level of protection," he explained, happy with the knowledge that Hikari would find it amazing.

Hikari was indeed amazed at this, but before she could try, Flare interrupted, "It's getting late... we should head to bed before our next outing in the ruins."

The mercenary heard him say this and realized how late it truly was and yawned. "Yeah, I'll..." he began only to be cut short by his own exhaustion as he fell over in slumber.

The dragoness looked at him. "Dad is it okay if Talon sleeps next to me?" she asked pleadingly.

Flare nodded and said in a parental voice, "As long as it's okay with him."

Hikari looked at TalonFyre once more, a hopeful expression on her face. TalonFyre saw her face and uncertainly gave her the answer she wanted, "Yeah, it's fine. Just don't try to wake me up." He handed her earplugs after this, which she put into her earlobes.

He moved over a bit. After this, Hikari draped her wing over him. "Goodnight Tally," she whispered contently.

"Night Hikari," he mumbled sleepily, not realizing what she just called him. He fell asleep once more with a slight smile, but still snoring.

TalonFyre didn't know what it was about this dragoness that made him so comfortable. Was it gratitude, kindness, friendship, or something else? Why did he allow her to sleep next to him? Why did he trust her? These questions were driving TalonFyre insane, albeit subconsciously. Whatever the reasoning was, he wanted to do something for her, and he knew exactly what it was.

Chapter 10

True Nature, part 1

TALONFYRE snuck away in the darkness of the night, headed for the cave which housed the skull again - this time with purpose. When he reached his destination, he approached the remains of Hikari's mother. "Well she told me only once and not for my own use - this should help," he whispered in a kind voice.

He grabbed his mother's necklace and began to revive the skulls owner, casting a shroud around him so no soul would see the deed. Bones emerged from the skull, the bones became muscle, and the muscle became flesh. The dragoness then opened her eyes.

A few hours later, he came back to Flare and Hikari's cave. "Guys come out here, it's very important!" he yelled happily.

They both walked out sleepily. Their drowsiness vanished the moment they saw who was next to TalonFyre. There, standing next to him, was a pure white dragoness with a yellow, sectioned underbelly and light blue wing membranes. Her eyes were a deep blue color. Her upper horns were near the shape of Hikari's – spiraled like a unicorn. Hers, however, had a goat-like shape, while Hikari's were much longer and conical. Also, she had no horns near the bottom of her jawline. It was her mother – Flare's mate.

"I believe you know each other," TalonFyre said, beaming.

Hikari's jaw dropped. "...Mom..?" she gasped in amazement and near-disbelief.

The mercenary's smile grew wider, "Yup - must be she was worried about you - even tried to scratch me - anyway..."

He was about to say more, but Hikari and Flare both ran up and embraced her. "How... is this possible?" Flare whispered, tears of joy in his eyes.

It was at this moment that TalonFyre's mother's necklace burst into flames, turning to ash upon hitting the ground. "My mother - her pure soul was in this necklace. She said only someone who truly died innocently deserved it," the mercenary explained, albeit softly.

Hikari was shocked beyond belief at what he had done. "I....! You...Talon... Thank you so much!" she cried gratefully.

"Yeah, well if I tried using it I'd just waste it. Besides, she *told* me to help you guys," he shrugged, not wanting to show what he was truly feeling. His claws faded to jet black. "Yeah, that's the end of that. No more glowing claws. I mean sure, I still have lava infused blood but they were a nice showpiece," he remarked.

Flare walked up to TalonFyre and took a soft and grateful tone, "You brought Angel back to us. Thank you."

The mercenary merely looked at him kindly. "Can't stand to see good people suffer - I'll take the suffering around here," he replied, walking inside to his weapons.

While the family enjoyed its reunion, TalonFyre was rummaging through his belongings. "Ok, now where....Ah!" he exclaimed, pulling out a bag of still-glowing claws. "Ok, now this will smart," he complimented himself. "Nnnnggh!" he snapped a claw straight off with a growl of pain, and placed the glowing one where the end broke. It started glowing again. "Yeah...that's better – God, I'm still a bit dazed," TalonFyre sighed, his head spinning a bit.

By this time, Angel had walked in and approached him. She put her paw on his front shoulder. "You're not a monster like you thought, TalonFyre, nor are you a waste of space. You're a virtuous dragon who took the wrong path," she said in a loving and kind voice.

"Well, anything to help someone who died unjustly - died for no reason by the hands of evil, I mean," he shrugged, once again hiding his emotions.

Angel, however, knew the truth. "I'm half psychic dragon. I can tell someone's true self," she smiled at the last two words.

"Yeah, well, search away then. I'm not hiding anything," TalonFyre lied nervously.

Angel, however, already knew he was. Placing her paw on his chest, Angel began her reading of TalonFyre's heart. "You're a lot softer than people realize. Also, you have a kind heart that was hardened after years of mercenary work. You are no monster; you're a loving dragon that took the wrong path in life," she said with a motherly smile.

"Well - nice work," the mercenary shrugged, both impressed and embarrassed.

Once again, TalonFyre began digging through more of his arsenal. "I know I left it.....aw forget it," he moaned.

Angel looked at him with a kind smile and said what she thought he wanted to hear, "You have my full permission to be with my daughter."

The mercenary was silent for a moment. "Uhhh...." he stuttered.

Angel continued, "I know about the fact that you both cannot have children," she sighed, still keeping her kind voice.

"Oh good," TalonFyre's fears were alleviated at hearing this. He pulled out an inert black quartz orb. "There – eye from the Thanatos Golem - damn thing lets me sense lesser ones. Not getting anything," he shrugged uncaringly.

The mercenary was distracted; however, Angel wanted to make him understand what he meant to her daughter. She took a slightly parental tone, "Have you forgotten my daughter is the same? She never thought that she'd find a dragon who would accept her."

TalonFyre started to get the message after hearing this, "Well, that's good. I know I'm just used to being the same. I just let the subject go unnoticed." With that, he smashed the black piece of quartz. "Not gonna' need that anymore - don't want memories of that day..."

"Anyway, you guys should be catching up right? I'll be in here messing around, making the usual junk," TalonFyre shrugged, turning back to his equipment.

Angel smiled at him. "You're going to be doing that with us," she answered, still somewhat keeping her parental tone.

"Well, I don't want to intrude any more than I have," he started nervously, but was interrupted by Angel.

"Have you already forgotten you're part of our family now?" she continued, sounding even more parental.

"Yeah, my mistake," TalonFyre replied sheepishly, grabbing Hikari's armor from the night before. "Well, this turned out nicely," he stated proudly. He followed the dragoness outside to where Hikari waited.

TalonFyre was conflicted after Angel said what she did. Was he really family to them? Even more so, did he *want* to be? He wasn't sure. Did he actually *love* Hikari? No - it couldn't be. He never loved a dragoness, and he never would. He was sure of it...but would it really be that bad to fall in love? He was sure it would be. He was completely certain this dragoness was the same as the others. Maybe she was even as bad as 'her'. Or was she? Maybe she wouldn't be like the others. She had made no sexual advances on him whatsoever. He was in a war with his own emotions and memories at this point, and no side could get a foothold. He decided to wait and see where this whole thing led before he made any rash decisions.

Chapter 11

True Nature, part 2

THEY walked out of the cavern back to the main area where Hikari and Flare waited. "Hikari, here!" TalonFyre called out, tossing her the armor, which she promptly grabbed. "I worked on it while you slept," he said with a grin.

The dragoness quickly strapped on the piece of equipment and gave a joyful, "This is badass!" instead of thanking the mercenary. He strangely appreciated this more.

"I see your tomboyish attitude hasn't changed Hikari," Angel sighed in a disheartened tone.

TalonFyre smiled happily, "Yeah I..." he stopped, losing his train of thought as he realized his own armor was missing. "Oh, guess mine is gone somewhere. Meh, I don't need that stuff - too heavy.... cooks me like a damn potato," he shrugged.

A few seconds later TalonFyre spotted the armor on the floor. He thought for a moment, eventually deciding he had no need for it. He handed it to Angel and the color changed to pure white. "There, new owner," he said, then he turned to Flare, "You want any? I made it all overnight." Flare nodded to the mercenary in acceptance.

"Oh my...this is surprisingly snug," Angel stated in a slightly amazed voice.

"Yeah, fits to match your shape and size," TalonFyre explained, tossing Flare a set as well. "Go nuts. I actually made them while I slept," TalonFyre stated proudly.

"If we're going to be exploring ruins, we need all the protection we can get," Flare remarked seriously, putting the piece of equipment on.

Once again TalonFyre cracked his neck making a disgusting sound. "Ok, that's *definitely* better," he moaned happily, stepping outside. "Well, we going exploring or catching up first?" he asked, ready to go.

The family had been broken apart for so long they needed to spend some time together, along with TalonFyre. Hikari did adore him after all. Her parents both knew this. "Let's catch up first," Flare replied in a slightly parental yet kind voice.

Upon hearing this, TalonFyre laid down in the lava pit. "Yeah, I'll multi-task," he sighed uncaringly.

The mercenary's nose twitched – he knew what was coming, and Hikari and Angel were right next to him! He didn't want to cover them in lava! He turned his head, sneezing *away* from them this time. This caused Hikari to chuckle a bit, at which TalonFyre gave a fake frown. This however caused her to laugh even more.

Angel approached him and softly asked, "You're in more peace now than you have been in a long time, are you not?" reading his expression.

TalonFyre smiled at this. "I have to say you're pretty sharp – yeah," he sighed happily, closing his eyes.

Overjoyed at this, Hikari went into a daze, 'I hope he stays forever. He's the only dragon I ever want to be with. I'll never go into heat or have a child, but maybe just to become one with him we could...' she was taken out of her trance by a snapping of her father's claws. He had noticed she was looking at the mercenary longingly and wanted to keep her from scaring him off.

A few minutes went by as the family conversed and eventually TalonFyre opened his eyes again. Thankfully Hikari was no longer looking at him as she was earlier. It wasn't a lustful look per say, but it may have been enough to drive him away permanently.

"For being only half psychic dragon her powers are very potent," Flare explained, seeing that TalonFyre was once again aware.

The mercenary was no longer paying attention, however, and was rummaging through his armor's satchels. This confused the family, but there was a method to his madness.

TalonFyre brought out a small tree the size of a grass blade, tossing it to Hikari, "Plant that anywhere barren and it's green the next day - the whole land. Learned it from an old-as-the-earth mountain dragon," he remarked with a smile. The pun earned a small giggle from Hikari.

Upon hearing this, an idea formed in Angel's head, and she quickly suggested what was on her mind, "Let's use this where you father died. He deserves it."

This was something that was in the back of TalonFyre's mind, but he never had the strength of heart to do it. Somehow, seeing the three of them gave him the drive he needed –most of it being from Hikari. Why did this dragoness make him feel so strong – so powerful? When he looked at her he felt as if he could take on the world – everything seemed possible. It was as if he felt like nothing could stand in his way. He cursed his mind - What was it? What was happening to him!? Why was he feeling like he was so invincible!? Most of all, why was this one dragoness causing these feelings? It confounded him how a single being could give him so much drive; let alone the fact that it was a female. Whatever the case, he knew he was able to do what he desired to do long ago – to mark the grave of one who cared for him.

The mercenary emerged from the pool and shook off, once more raining lava upon the ground and a plethora of other areas. "And I do it *again.* Lovely," he sighed, checking to see that the family wasn't hurt.

"It's okay Tally," Hikari replied in a forgiving tone.

The mere mention of that name caused TalonFyre to cringe. "*Please,* just Talon is close enough," he gagged disgustedly. The very idea that the tomboyish dragoness could come up with such a name for him baffled the mercenary.

"Okay, sorry," she apologized, an ashamed and embarrassed look on her face.

Paying no heed and throwing yet another gem down, TalonFyre created a new, faintly white portal - unpowered. "Flare, you mind..?" TalonFyre started, once again taking an uncaring tone.

Hikari walked up and touched it, opening the gateway. "Oh - well, I guess this works," the mercenary shrugged. He headed through, and the family followed suit.

The portal led into the half-mile wide crater which Flare had seen before, at which time TalonFyre ended up face-planting onto the ground. "Watch your step," he advised, spitting rocks out. This, of course, earned him a giggle from Hikari as she and her family swooped down.

"Yup, this crater is all me. Get me mad enough, I can do this stuff," TalonFyre laughed as he walked to the center of the detonation zone, Hikari behind him. "Well…" his gaze wandered to the charred armor, "I learned armorsmithing from the best. Yeah…" he whispered, starting to cry slightly.

Hikari hugged him upon seeing this to comfort him. This time he hugged back – he had to. For some reason, this dragoness made him feel at ease.

After TalonFyre composed himself, he placed the small twig-like piece of greenery in the center of the blast zone – the exact place where his father had perished. "And right now we should take off," he warned. The family took to the sky, and the mercenary took off hovering over the crater.

The crater started to turn green as a blast of cool air hit them. "And here we go…." TalonFyre said happily as grass appeared across the horizon. The next thing that happened made TalonFyre desire to leave - the center turned into a pond. "Ugh, water - only thing that can make me weak," he cringed, "Let's get going…. it'll finish off."

With that, he went through the portal, and the family followed. "Heck, there's gonna' be trees, rivers, the whole thing - too nice to watch," he added as he exited the portal and the family followed. After they had gotten out, the portal then turned to dust.

"Your father would be proud," Hikari said in a sweet and comforting voice, nuzzling TalonFyre.

He smiled at the thought of this, "Yeah… so anyway, catching up - everyone knows me I'm sure. That and I'm sick of explaining it." He placed himself in his lava pit after saying this and yawned. A few seconds later, he was asleep, snoring once more.

"He sure does sleep a lot, huh?" Angel whispered quietly.

"I was awake all night," TalonFyre mumbled, rolling over in his sleep.

"Yeah, he made that armor for us," Hikari added gratefully.

TalonFyre continued snoring and his snout fell into lava, creating bubbles. Hikari snickered at this. They were about to re-initiate their conversation when TalonFyre snored again, spraying lava upon the ground. "…sorry…" he murmured, rolling over once more.

"It's fine - no one was hurt," Flare replied in an uncaring tone.

Although TalonFyre was sleepy, he was awake enough to put his snout out of the lava to snore so that he didn't spray the molten rock on his new friends and… whatever Hikari was to him.

Chapter 12

Bonding

AS he remembered what Angel had said, TalonFyre felt the need to wake up. "Oh, right – sorry," he apologized.

"What is it Talon?" Hikari asked, wondering why he decided not to sleep.

"Catching up, I forgot – well, you guys are. I'm just spectating - and cooking," the mercenary answered, his voice taking a joking tone for the last two words. He started to glow once more, got out, deciding against shaking off this time. He then sat down beside Hikari. Why her, he had no idea.

Beginning the conversation Angel asked, "So, what have you been doing while I was gone?" but TalonFyre had spotted a Vespatite.

Angel would have just ignored it normally and continued on, but after seeing the looks on TalonFyre and Hikari's faces, she couldn't resist helping further their relationship. This mercenary was the only dragon her daughter had ever loved – she had to help them, or rather him, realize the fact that they should be together. To do this, the first thing she had to do was appeal to their personality – to show the similarities between them.

Suspending it in front of them telekinetically and rolling her eyes, Angel waited for the mercenary to take whatever action he desired. Wasting no time TalonFyre pried its scorpion-like jaws open, placing a small fireball inside, and finally tossing it into the air.

"**Boom-time**!" Hikari yelled happily as it exploded. TalonFyre sneezed from the ash and green goo.

When TalonFyre looked up, he spotted five more Vespatites hunched together, their fear paralyzing them. He put his face to theirs with an evil grin.

"BOO!" was the only thing that emerged from TalonFyre's mouth. This was all it took for them to scatter, trampling each other with their bee-like legs and emitting spider-like screeches as their vast amount of fear took hold of their entire psyche. The display caused Hikari to burst out laughing.

TalonFyre laughed as well, "I swear they should make a *game* out of this," the mercenary said as he walked over to his former place next to Hikari. "Who says they're not fun," he added.

Flare looked at his mate. "In case you were wondering Angel, Hikari has been training nonstop to get stronger ever since you died," he said with a small, sad smile.

Angel was curious as to the time that had passed and asked, "How long was it?"

He was about to answer but TalonFyre called out, "Hey- Hikari!" With this, he tossed a dummy Vespatite in the air. Hikari bit its neck and slashed it to bits with a photon claw.

The surprise came when meat rained down from the 'slain' Vespatite. "It's actually filled with meat, so you can eat it. Stuffing wasn't very tasty," TalonFyre snickered at the last sentence. Hikari devoured it like a slob, jumping from one piece to another.

"Dear!" Angel yelled, about to scold Hikari, only to be intercepted by TalonFyre.

"Well she worked on that, too," he stated with a grin.

Hikari then let out a resounding belch, causing TalonFyre to laugh. "Hey, guys like gals who eat," he laughed.

Angel shook her head back and forth and sighed, "You two... are perfect for each other."

This phrase gave TalonFyre a shock he was unaware of as he capriciously agreed, "I guess so."

He was about to retract his statement when an odor wafted to his nose, causing it to crinkle. "Yuck - I thought I was bad," the mercenary gagged as he smelled the air exhaled by his new potential 'lover'.

The mercenary got up after this, taking off after a deer. "Just remembered I'm hungry," he yelled back. He caught it within moments, roasting it alive as it screeched. He decided to mimic Hikari, ripping it apart, eating it like a beast, devouring the skeleton and all. Once again he got a bone stuck in his throat, but again the lava-drool took care of it. "Ok, now I can think straight," TalonFyre sighed, sitting upon the ground covered in blood.

Flare finally answered Angel's question, "It was about one and a half years since Rayburn killed you. Hikari has been training nonstop since then."

TalonFyre decided to make their day by informing them of his defeat. "Heh, Electus kicked his ass good - only time I saw *fear* in his cold, unfeeling eyes," he laughed, licking the blood off.

Hikari's eyes narrowed. "Serves him right - I wish I could have seen that bastard's face," she growled cruelly.

TalonFyre grinned at this. "Well...." he said as he pulled out an orb, "Heh, I sent it in when they were busy fighting."

Hikari's face turned to a sinister smile. TalonFyre saw this and gave it to her. "Here, I've seen it too many times," he said with a smile.

Hikari gave a vengeful "Thank you!" with the same sinister grin.

The orb's illusionary capabilities projected the battle at Rayburn's castle where he had fought Electus.

Rayburn was a monstrosity. His four eyes were sunken and glowing red. His jagged, sword-like scales were black as night and his six horns like that of a goat. He had six legs with long, sharp claws. His saggy underbelly was a dark red. His six thin wings were a pale, sickly greenish shade and nearly bone. His tail-tip was like that of an old-style pitchfork, but blood-red.

Nocturnal was chained to the wall, her blood-red scales and two bull-like black horns chipping off from her struggle to get free. Her onyx-colored underbelly was cut at the top. Her dark black, pitchfork like tail-tip was also dulled. Her sharp, long claws were filed to a point where they were stumps.

Electus however was in top form. His muscular and trained body was both black and white, separated in a linear wave. His left foreleg was black, complimenting the white part of the wave. His right foreleg was white, complimenting the black part respectively. His back legs were the opposite. He also had a black and white underbelly with plates that transitioned from white to black for each segment. His head had an odd symbol upon it that matched his body coloring. His eyes were golden.

After teleporting behind Rayburn, Electus clawed a soft spot at the back of his neck and severed his spinal cord, taking away his ability to move. The black and white dragon let loose a large blast of golden energy as the demon looked on in horror. The blast collided with his head as his body began to glow gold as well. After this, his soul came out of his vaporizing body and erupted in flame. After that, the demon dragon was no more.

"Even if he didn't get his soul burnt to a crisp, I would have kicked his ass," TalonFyre said with a smirk as he pulled out his sword, which was now twenty-five feet long.

Hikari laughed at this.

"Even worked on the golem part - sharper now," he said, then he put it away, "Oh, reminds me – nah, I'll wait till later."

Vast amounts of weaponry flashed in the dragoness's mind. Hikari couldn't wait until later. She couldn't contain herself until then. "Heh, a new toy for me?" she asked smugly.

"Maybe..." TalonFyre winked.

TalonFyre was confused again. Why in the world did he agree so quickly with Angel's statement? Had he really ended up falling in love with this tomboyish dragoness in such a short time? No, love was out of the question. Why would he keep giving her gifts and doing things for her if he didn't though? That was it! He liked her more than anyone he'd ever met! He didn't love her! Or did he? He never had been in love, so how was he supposed to know what it felt like? Whatever it was, it felt good, and he wanted to stay with the family – for a long time.

Chapter 13

New Powers

SOMETHING was bothering Flare about Hikari's training for a long time, but he never got a chance to question her about it. Now was a better time than ever.

"I never got to ask you this Hikari. Why didn't you ever work on your psychic powers?"

Hikari's head drooped at her father's question. "I figured with only a quarter blood in me they won't be good enough," she sighed.

TalonFyre nudged her, "Better than no blood."

This caught the dragoness's attention. "You're saying I should try?" she asked a bit hopefully.

TalonFyre nodded. "Well, yeah - it's better to try and *use* them instead of letting them waste away," he replied in a somewhat kind tone.

At this, a twig was tossed to the dragoness by her father. Hikari gazed at the twig and concentrated. It first began to rock back and forth, eventually standing upright, and finally snapping.

"See?" TalonFyre smiled as he said this.

"I... I did it," Hikari gasped in surprise.

Angel's mouth dropped. "You... you got it right on the first try. *I* couldn't even do that," she whispered.

The mercenary then had an idea to make her even more inclined to train with her powers and gave a happy, "I'm going to go get you something," as he walked inside.

Entering the cavern, TalonFyre searched through his scattered belongings until he found what he was searching for.

"Ah..." he pulled out a pure white shard, grasped it in his tail and walked back out.

The family saw the shard and wondered what the mercenary's intention could be – Hikari especially, since he had handed it to her.

"What's this?" she asked curiously.

"Don't break it. It's pure psychic energy - balances it out. Dug it up one day when I was building that damn bunker," TalonFyre answered with a joyous grin.

"How do I use it?" Hikari asked with a curious yet excited expression.

TalonFyre was surprised she hadn't heard of dragons eating gems to get stronger, but decided not to wait upon asking if she had no knowledge of it. "Well... you eat it - it'll melt. Don't know why everything I have is edible," he shrugged.

Hikari placed the gem in her mouth.

"By the way - it tastes like rotten Vespatite, so just put up with it," the mercenary added.

After a few seconds Hikari's eyes widened in disgust, but she continued to hold the gem in her mouth. "*That* would be the *center* – yup, it's **nasty**. Makes you feel like everything is significant, kind of like a drug - so it's gonna' get **weird**," he continued.

This word confused Flare, as he had never heard it before. "What's a drug?" he asked, a little concerned.

"Oh, strength enhancers, magic boosts, some are just plain for relaxing. Even saw one old guy take a past-date one of those. He was spinning around in circles. Actually passed out cold but woke up feeling really giggly. I never take that crap but it helps when it's the right type," the mercenary finished the explanation.

TalonFyre looked at Hikari's face and asked, "Feeling a bit zoned yet there?" as her eyes widened even more. "Yup, it's hitting her. She'll be fine. Might even have fun," he laughed.

A minute later, he decided to see if the gem had taken effect. "Hikari, you feeling it?" he asked. He didn't need an answer, because as soon as he had asked, her eyes changed shade to a glowing blue.

"Yup, there it is - now the best part," he grinned at what he was going to say next, "It's called carbonation. The thing is loaded with it, meaning...." he continued covering his ears and nose as Hikari let out a giant, resounding belch. "Meaning all ladylike things go out the window," he laughed and gagged at the same time.

Hikari's body began to shine with a blue light. "And now the glowing starts - meaning the powers are being doubled," TalonFyre explained. The shine intensified after this, and the dragoness's aura grew exponentially. "Holy crap, that's **some** power! I feel that right *here*!" the mercenary exclaimed.

Flare was a bit scared. "Shouldn't you have given it to her *after* her powers matured?" he asked.

TalonFyre shook his head and replied, "No, it's safe."

The glow increased in strength, causing the cave to shake slightly. "Uh-Oh! Great, I didn't think...!" the mercenary began.

Flare looked at him. "What is it!?" he yelled angrily.

TalonFyre looked back at him and answered, "Well, one word – unstable."

This caused Angel to panic, giving an angry, "**WHAT!?**" causing the mercenary's own worry and guilt to heighten.

TalonFyre knew he had to do something, and fast. "Hang on, hang on!" he gasped tensely as he approached the dragoness and pointed his glowing claw at her chest.

"This should..." he whispered fearfully as he pressed his claw against her chest. The glowing died down and then halted. "...and stable. Yeah, I feel it now, they're perfect. She should be fine," he sighed, his fear alleviated.

"The more you train with them, the stronger they get, and you should feel pretty dizzy," the mercenary informed Hikari, looking her in the face.

The dragoness then started to wobble. "Get ready to catch her!" he called out to the dragoness's parents.

Angel propped herself against her daughter as she fell to her side, exhausted.

"Yeah, she just needs a nap - anyone else?" TalonFyre offered with a laugh. The two shook their heads no. TalonFyre walked off after this.

It was strange – TalonFyre had never been that worried about anything in his life! Why did have such concern over her? He should be more worried about himself, because that's what mercenaries do! Why – why did he care about that dragoness so much? Why did he feel she was so much more important than him? He didn't love her – he didn't! How could he bring himself to love a female after what happened!? But if he didn't love her, why did he care about her so much? Why did he feel so scared? The fear that gripped him when Hikari became unstable... it was overwhelming! If it weren't for his mercenary training he might have been paralyzed due to it! It was odd to say the least. Whatever the case, he decided to help the three with their archaeology.

Chapter 14

The First Adventure, part 1

A/N: If text shows up in ()'s or parentheses, it means they're using telepathy

HEADING to the family's archives, TalonFyre prepared to mark down his parents' hoards. He knew his old maps like the back of his volcanic paw, and decided to make use of that knowledge to help out with the couple's hobby. Pulling out a map that showed treasure caves buried in the land, he put down a new mark.

"Well, he wants to explore so…" he then handed the map to Angel without finishing.

She was astounded. "This looks promising," she remarked.

"Here, take it, I'll watch Hikari," TalonFyre instructed, tearing a claw off of his paw. He then gave his signature glowing talon to Angel. "Here's the key. It was my dad's treasure cave."

Knowing his father's mercenary history, Angel decided to ask the normal question, "Is it booby trapped?"

TalonFyre shrugged and answered with, "As long as you don't step on the marked traps - pitfalls mainly. Some spells, but nothing harmful. Good luck."

TalonFyre then thought of Hikari. "Where is she now anyway…?" he asked the dragoness's mother ponderingly.

"She's in the cave resting. She's still a bit tired from the whole affair with the gem," Angel replied, her tone a bit concerned.

The mercenary was a bit worried at this, so he decided to see her. He entered Hikari's room and lay beside her. Angel had followed however; as she had something she wanted to suggest to the mercenary, "You deserve to explore it… with her."

TalonFyre however had no desire to leave. "Not how she is right now, she's too dazed. You guys go. I have my mother's yet. That will be for later," he replied, grinning at the idea.

Angel walked off after his answer, Flare following. "Also, try to duck when you go in!" he called after them.

He closed his eyes after this, draping his wing over the dragoness and falling asleep next to her. Strangely, his snoring problem hadn't occurred.

Nearly two hours later in a rocky clearing littered with grass, Flare and Angel were looking around the general area where the spot was marked on their map. Sadly their search led to no avail.

"(Hey, you find it yet? Yes, I have some telepathy - not much)" the mercenary both asked and stated using his psychic powers. They shook their heads.

At this point, TalonFyre decided to help with the search. "(Hang on…)" a projection of him appeared beside the two mates as he said this. "(Remember this Flare?)" he asked smugly. The light dragon merely rolled his eyes.

"Astral projection…. I suppose you're part psychic dragon too," Angel stated in a gasp.

TalonFyre gave an unsure, "(Very minimal, but I guess so)" as he gazed at the map.

He then proceeded to check the scenery. "(Ok, should be around.... Ah, there we are!)" With this, he pointed to an engraving on a rock with the same crest as his father's armor. Taking to the skies with the two mates behind, he headed for the piece of terrain that bore his father's crest.

The three landed beside the marked rock. "(I think Flare knows the procedure)" TalonFyre said with a grin.

Flare walked up to the marked piece of stone. "This is it, huh?" he rhetorically asked, placing the claw into the marking.

The mercenary sighed, "(Same one that revives me. Just drip the blood on the mark - you have to bite the end off. Watch it though, it'll melt teeth,)" explaining once again.

Flare repeated the earlier procedure and quickly moved his mouth away.

"(Ok, now just drip the blood over the mark,)" TalonFyre instructed. Flare did as he was told, and the door revealed itself and opened.

"(**DUCK!**)" TalonFyre warned as cannon fire was heard. There was no need to do this however, as the shots stopped short before they hit them – this was due to being blocked by telekinesis.

"Angel, do you really have to show off like that?" Flare moaned in a voice of false anger. TalonFyre laughed at this.

"(Hang on.)" The mercenary disappeared for a moment to check on the slumbering dragoness next to him, "(Looks fine.)"

Angel smiled warmly upon hearing him say those two words. "You really care about her don't you?" she asked the mercenary sweetly, already knowing full well the answer.

"(Yeah…)" he sighed, reappearing once more.

After sidestepping a few traps, they arrived at the treasure room. "(Ok, time to see what he left me, I mean us,)" TalonFyre said, walking in and laughing at the last three words.

When he saw the hoard, he was amazed. "(Holy mother of-!)" he gasped, astonished at the sight. Before them was a room twice as full as his own hoard and full of jewels and gold. "(I think money won't be an issue,)" he remarked, his jaw open wide.

"Yeah, *some* of it we might not even *need*," Flare said, mouth agape as well.

TalonFyre composed himself after a few seconds, as he didn't truly desire money anymore. "(Take whatever,)" he shrugged.

"Make that a *lot* of it," Angel added to her mates comment, making a giant light tray.

"(Fine – anyway, I'm off to see how she's doing. Good luck and happy looting. Also, some stuff in there is encrusted with jewels so…)" TalonFyre disappeared without finishing.

"We know what to look out for," Flare replied, shrugging.

Angel was smiling again, happy that her daughter had found someone who accepted her infertility and tomboyish attitude.

TalonFyre knew he cared about Hikari, but love was another matter. But if he didn't love her, why did he feel happy instead of uncomfortable lying next to her like he was at this very instant? Why did he feel so happy giving things to her? Most of all, why was he actually enjoying every moment he spent with her? He kept asking himself all these questions over and over; unable to come up with a single answer besides ones he did want.

Chapter 15

The First Adventure, part 2

GETTING back into his body, his wing still over Hikari, TalonFyre lay back down with a smile on his face. 'Why am I always tired for crying out loud?' he thought to himself. He sighed and made the decision to see how Flare and Angel were doing now that they discovered the treasure room.

"(How's it going over there?)" TalonFyre asked.

Flare replied with, "We got a pretty good load," as he brought the treasure out.

"(Great, now lock the door - normal lock. No one's gettin' in.)" Flare heard this and locked the door behind him.

"(Thanks – anyway, bring it all back so we can see,)" TalonFyre finished happily.

Angel knew what they were going to do with the money and replied, "Okay, but we're not going to keep it at all. Darastrix Charis needs all the help it can get," once again using a parental tone.

"(Hey, if we had to, we could give it *all* to Darastrix Charis, it's my dad's anyway,)" the mercenary shrugged.

There was something TalonFyre had forgotten about, "(Aw, shit - left the ballista in the bunker.)" With this, he opened a portal in the other room, dropping it and shaking the cave. "Ah, there it is! Good thing I left a portal open near it! " he exclaimed, looking at the ice-enchanted piece of war machinery.

"You're going to return it, aren't you?" Angel asked the mercenary in a caring tone.

TalonFyre nodded. "(Well, not broken. Firing mechanism is shot, the whole thing is bent. So, yeah...)" he sighed in a disheartened manner, realizing he had a lot of work ahead of him.

"(Another sleepless night fixing it, right?)" Flare asked, concerned.

TalonFyre replied with a sigh, "(I guess so. I don't need sleep really - only gives me a tiny bit of energy.)"

A few minutes passed and flapping was audible from outside the cave. "(Well, have fun guys,)" the mercenary said with grin, ready to see the spoils.

"(Is Hikari up?)" Angel asked hopefully.

TalonFyre wanted her to see her parents return and gave a concerned, "(I don't know,)" as a reply. He felt movement on his side after he had said this - it was Hikari.

"Ah, perfect timing sleepy," he whispered, taking his wing off of her. "You probably feel like you've been smacked by a golem," he chuckled.

She looked at him and smiled. Her voice was soft at the time, but she had to ask it, "You were here the whole time I was out?" already knowing what he would say.

Just as she thought he gave a soft, "Yeah..." as an answer.

This made the dragoness so happy. She was at a loss for words and could only manage, "You're the *greatest* Talon..." in a sigh.

This made TalonFyre uncomfortable, or maybe it was another feeling. Whatever it was, he had to change the subject. "Yeah, well, don't try anything power-wise for a bit. It can hurt - mainly headaches," he warned, pointing to her head.

"Okay, I won't," she replied in an understanding tone.

TalonFyre began another story, "Yeah, one guy tried a flame booster and actually tried his powers too soon and cooked himself **alive** - guy was an idiot," cruelly saying the last words.

Hikari didn't need psychic powers to tell he was actually informing her of this to prevent her from hurting herself, or to know that he was worried about it.

By this time, Flare and Angel were almost back. Hikari walked out with TalonFyre to meet them. The two looked for Flare and Angel. "Heh, must be a heavy load," he joked. After a few minutes, Flare and Angel appeared over the horizon with a 30 square foot box of gold and treasure.

"Heh, not that much. Go nuts - take whatever," the mercenary shrugged, once again in an uncaring tone.

Angel shook her head. "There's no artifacts here, and we mainly live off the land. This is for Darastrix Charis," she informed him.

If the treasure was all for charity, TalonFyre had one thing that would make the deliverance much easier, "Oh - hang on..." he created a portal to the treasure hoard with another gem. As he said this he motioned for them to follow. "Could've made that earlier," he reminded himself as the three trailed behind him.

Confused about why he didn't merely create a portal instead of staying inside the cave, the mercenary was about to ponder his reasoning. However his train of thought was interrupted by Hikari. "You just wanted to stay with me, right?" she asked smugly.

TalonFyre was taken aback by her bluntness and replied, "Your words not mine, but maybe," not certain if it was true or not.

TalonFyre looked around for a few moments, attempting to find what he needed. "Ok, let's see.... Ah!" he exclaimed, pulling an odd lever. The mechanism caused every bit of treasure to be lifted into a metal crate - gold, jewels, and all. Knowing he was possibly a wanted dragon he wrote a letter saying "from anonymous" and threw it on top of the pile. He then pulled the lever again and it disappeared.

"Yeah, I don't need them chasing me around," TalonFyre remarked with a worried face.

"You're right. Peace is best enjoyed with people you know," Hikari said with a smile.

TalonFyre began to step back through the portal to the family's cave. "Anyway, we going home or what? Oh, and your powers should be ready now." Hikari looked happy that TalonFyre had said this.

"Try them out Hikari," Angel suggested, nudging her.

Hikari was more than ready, but needed something as a test subject. She looked around in an attempt to find a suitable target.

"Try that," TalonFyre instructed, pointing to a boulder in the far left of the cave. Hikari focused on the boulder as it levitated above the ground and exploded. "Hikari keep practicing, I need to talk with Flare and Angel," the mercenary said with an unhappy sigh.

"Okay!" she replied happily.

What TalonFyre was about to do made him upset for some reason. Why, he didn't know. He wanted to see Hikari happy, and he knew of only one way that he could do it. He just hoped the three wouldn't take it the wrong way, especially her. He knew he couldn't satisfy her after what he did. He was dense, but he knew Hikari had a deep emotional attachment to him. He couldn't keep lying to her. It was impossible to keep a secret forever, and he knew this. She could never be his, and he could never be hers. Even though she desired for him to take her with all her heart, he knew it could never be. He had to end this and make her let go before it became any harder on her. He had to stop her advances on him before they began. Mating was impossible for him, let alone something he desired. If it became a fact for Hikari that it was impossible for her virginity to end at his hand – if it was impossible for him to break the literal wall that bonds two mates for life… she'd have to let go.

Chapter 16

The Cure

THE three walked to the back room, the door sealing. "I think we need to talk," TalonFyre sighed in a sad tone, pulling out a small, bright orb.

The sadness in the mercenary's eyes told Angel all she needed to know, "It… it's about Hikari's infertility, isn't it?" she whispered, her pain showing in her voice.

The mercenary nodded, "Yes - I have a solution. This orb contains the purest form I can create."

This was something that the two mates knew Hikari would never accept. Flare shook his head no, "She *won't* want a child with someone else."

The mercenary looked down sadly at the comment. He knew he couldn't hide it forever, and now was the time to tell them. "Only once in my life. No I…. I did a job once. She was the most pure evil dragoness ever born. Basically she tried to force me over," the mercenary growled.

The words shocked Flare. He had no idea TalonFyre's hatred of mating came from the fact that he was nearly raped. Angel, however, had a look of pure sadness on her face. She could only imagine what it could have been like for a dragon to have that happen – much less from a female!

"No, wasn't having that. So I took that part of my life out," TalonFyre continued, a tear forming in his eye. "I, well, stopped my ability to mate. I wasn't having it. After that - no. It's irreversible. But she has a chance - I don't. But her powers aren't balanced enough yet," he sighed, finishing his tale.

Flare shook his head again and reiterated, "She won't want that…" while tears formed in his eyes. It was clear that he cared very much for his daughter's happiness.

TalonFyre's expression darkened. "No… she'll have to take that choice. Either she absorbs it or my heart shuts down. Call it a curse," he informed them with a gruff voice.

Angel's head drooped. "She'll do it then," she replied in a somber and nearly broken tone.

"Yeah, I have a lot of those do-this-or-I-die things," the mercenary shrugged. "Well you keep it Angel. It has no trace of me anywhere inside it. She won't know." With this, TalonFyre placed the orb in the grip of her tail.

Curious, Flare decided to ask, "How did you destroy your ability to mate?"

TalonFyre looked away. "Yeah….not saying. Let's just say it involved a lot of *blood* and *ripping.*" He followed the statement by showing them a scar upon his underbelly stretching the entirety of his lower half.

This scar actually gave Angel hope. "You said it's irreversible, but I have a feeling it's not. If we had an artifact that could regenerate body parts..." she started, but was cut off by TalonFyre.

"Yeah... No. I'm not - not all that again!" he yelled angrily, disappearing. "(You let her know the stakes. I'm not staying around when it all starts back up. Just don't follow me. I'll be nearby.)"

Flare looked at Angel. "We need to give this to Hikari, but she won't mate with anyone else," he sighed, his tone becoming barely audible and becoming cracked at the last few words.

The mercenary spoke again through telepathy. "(Yeah, about that – if it comes in contact with me when she absorbs it, it kills me. So that's a definite no.)"

Flare was confused by this. "What do you mean if it..." he started to ask, only to be cut off with an almost demonic-sounding "**NO!!!!**" from TalonFyre.

Angel sighed, "Let's go give it to her."

After the door had opened the mercenary snuck through a portal to his home as he covered his trail. "(Yeah, like I said, *DON'T FOLLOW*!)" He screamed as he headed into the remnants of his bunker. He then blocked the portal he had created. "(Give her my best - I'll be watching.)"

The whole ordeal would break Hikari's heart – Flare and Angel knew this. However, they also knew it would shatter her heart if TalonFyre died.

"What's this?" the dragoness asked, confused.

"(Part of my soul, but not. It's purified of all of my traits)" TalonFyre said with a monotone.

"It's a cure to your infertility. Before you say no, Talon will die if you don't take it," Flare explained, closing his eyes and letting tears escape.

Hikari was hurt beyond words upon hearing this.

"(Yeah, and if you do take it - I'm the one watching who you bring home, too. Three phases I guess,)" he said in a gruff voice, trying to mask his sadness.

The orb floated to Hikari, disappearing into her heart. "(Yeah, I figured you'd hesitate.)" TalonFyre emerged from the shadows behind them unnoticed, grinning.

"Talon?" Hikari sobbed.

"Well, she has a chance now - one I don't want. It's either that or you will be denied the joy of having your own," he said, once again using a gruff tone to mask his sadness.

"I don't want anyone else!" Hikari wailed, leaning onto TalonFyre.

He backed up and showed her the scar. "It's done," he sighed, starting to lose his nerve.

Hikari had started to cry at this point. "Then I won't have a child..." she said with a serious expression.

After this, TalonFyre disappeared once more. "(Urges will be urges. You have to...)" he whispered. He had to leave before his own sadness made it harder for her to accept.

Attempting to console his daughter, Flare put his paw on her head, "I know you don't want to have a child with anyone but him, but..." he was interrupted by a slash on his face by Hikari.

"**NO!! NEVER!!!**" she screamed in hysteria.

TalonFyre appeared again in front of the dragoness, putting his forepaw on hers. "Hey, trust me - you don't want what I had for a life. Orphaned... left alone. You can take care of all that and care for your child, I can't. Better you than me. Besides everyone that knows me knows it."

He then handed her a glowing claw on a necklace. "Keep that....." he said softy. After this, he vanished and cut off his telekinesis. 'She's better off figuring this out herself with family. Never said I was, but never said I wasn't,' he thought to himself.

Seeing Hikari in such a state crushed TalonFyre. He should have known giving her the ability to bear a child was a mistake! He cursed his own stupidity at what he did and wanted to make it up to her. The problem was that he couldn't mate. He ripped his entire reproductive system out. Also, after his experience with 'her', mating disgusted him. Besides, what kind of father would he be?

Even with all these reasons, his heart ached after what he did. It ached for Hikari, her parents, and for some other reason. Was it because he actually *loved* her!? No, love is when you gave freely of yourself with kindness as an intention and expected nothing in return – and he did. It's when you care for someone more than yourself – he did. It was when you want to see someone happy even if it hurts you – and he just did. He loved her.

He didn't want to admit it, but he loved her. Worst of all, since dragons mate for life he just sealed his own fate! He just made it so that she'd never be his! He was so stupid! He could have been happy with Hikari without mating, but he just HAD to screw it up! He was more miserable now than when he thought that his laying killed his mother. He was even thinking of killing himself again. He'd never find another dragoness that was like her. He'd never find another Hikari. This was it, he was done with love. Nothing but divine intervention could help him now.

After TalonFyre left, Hikari was distraught beyond words. She looked at her tail, constantly wanting to create a blade and pierce her heart with it. She didn't want another mate. She wouldn't let herself have anyone but TalonFyre. If she was going to die without having him as a mate, she was going to die before she mated with anyone else.

Flare saw her gazing at her tail, his heart sinking. He knew what her thoughts were. If it came down to it, he'd make her unable to. He'd break the bones in her tail and her forelegs. He wouldn't fix them until she came to her senses.

Last there was Angel, who was in tears along with Hikari. She saw how her daughter was. She saw her despair. She felt her sorrow. If Hikari killed herself she'd be devastated! When Hikari slashed Flare it crushed her. He was her father! He was only trying to help comfort her and she nearly cut his eye open! The kind heart that she was, she could never tell Hikari what she did wrong. She couldn't let her hurt more. All she could do was try to stop her daughter from doing something they would all regret – TalonFyre included.

Chapter 17

Where You Would Have Gone

TALONFYRE was brooding, slumbering in the lava under the earth's crust. 'No, it's never going to happen or change. I won't let it – no - not on my watch...' he was lost in thought, which was broken as a wormhole opened up right next to his lava pit.

A six-foot seven, muscular man with crimson, white, and gold armor, odd prismatic eye-coloring and flowing pure gold hair down to his knees walked through the wormhole.

Alongside him was a humanoid creature with a snakelike, elongated head, pure blue eyes with pale blue reptilian pupils, pink scales, fairly large breasts and a snake's lower half. At the height her underbelly came up to, she was at most four-foot two – smaller than him by far. Her arms were rather thin, and her hands were more like humanoid claws with long nails. The latter also wore a large, semi-tight white top with mesh netting below it that covered her entire upper body from her thin neck down, cutting off at her shoulders and upper belly, which was far longer and thinner than the part that her shirt covered. Oddly, she wore a medium-sized golden belt around her upper underbelly for some reason. TalonFyre watched from his pit giggling, albeit hidden at the same time.

"I hate seeing scenarios like this," the man sighed in a disheartened tone.

The mercenary appeared behind him, hidden by a shroud. "Well......fancy armor," he growled menacingly.

"I know you're there, TalonFyre. I can sense life forces," the man shrugged, his voice showing slight sternness.

Out of options for the violation of his home, the mercenary walked out of the shroud, his entire body twice its normal size. He was also glowing bright red, as if reflecting his pain and anger. "I'm not going through with any of it!" he boomed in a demonic voice.

This display may have deterred many, but due to his will and sheer power, the stranger was unfazed by any of it. He grasped the mercenary's muzzle, screaming his resolve, "I won't let you throw away your one chance at happiness!!!" his voice devoid of all fear.

"No... I'm not letting you change a *thing*!" the mercenary cried out, blasting him with black fire - which bounced right off the man's skin.

This turn of events caused TalonFyre to be silent for a moment, then charge at the man hooking his neck with his jaw, pinning him. The mercenary then charged up a powerful and massive blast of dark energy. "No.... NEVER!!" he screamed, eyes pure red.

"You *do* know I **let** you do that, right?" the stranger asked with a cruel smirk.

TalonFyre paid no heed, considering it to be a bluff, "This is the "me" I keep hidden under the lava..... my true darkness..... I'm not pure... never was," TalonFyre growled. An ear splitting roar was released from the mercenary, about to fire this dark blast.

In a seemingly bold move the man grabbed the blast from TalonFyre's paw, throwing it away effortlessly. "Well....nicely done..." the mercenary sneered. He then grabbed his blade, now glowing black. His tone became cruel as he spoke again, "I "upgraded it" to kill anything I wish."

The man had had enough of the farce by now. He knew it was time to show him he was serious, and just how outmatched he was. "Do you want to see *true* darkness? **HERE!**" he snapped, putting his hand on the mercenary's forehead and sending him into a trance. The mercenary fell over, dazed.

Before TalonFyre, a fortress shrouded in darkness was shown. Abominations of nature flowed through it, led by a creature with six spider legs, goat hooves, bison fur, a doglike face with scorpion fangs, two insectoid arms with three small mantis claws at the end of each of them, and six rat-tail like tentacles on his back and shoulders.

The mercenary was crying pure blood. 'The hell is that.... some fancy mind trick?' TalonFyre thought, horrified by the creature.

The demonic being then spoke, "You foul Idiots, you were supposed to kill those people AND rape them. Not slash their heads off outright!" his foul voice like the cracking of bones. "And you - that slave... bring her to me," he continued. The man ended the vision before his nemesis had a chance to do anything to the un-shown female.

TalonFyre got up stunned. "No, I can end this right now..." he mumbled, grabbing his sword and cutting his neck in an attempt to end his life a second time.

The stranger was tired of this game, and decided to use his most terrifying power. "Nightmare Eternity Vision..." the man growled, one eye turning to a blue upwards pentagram, his other to a red hexagram. TalonFyre passed out after he said the words in a pool of blood.

The two were alone in a place that looked like hell. "Heh, looks like I've been here before. Don't know why..." the mercenary said with a grin.

The man spoke, "I'm healing you as we speak, but this is where you *are* headed if you keep this up."

TalonFyre smiled at the words. "Well.....nice and warm. Wouldn't need my powers. Yeah...I've seen it before when I was told to smash that unborn dragon. It hit me like a smack to the ribs. That's why I never went with it. Besides, wouldn't want anyone but me ending up here. Besides, what dad would I even be....? Same as mine...." the mercenary sighed in a hurt voice as he said the last words.

The man pointed his hand to the vats of boiling blood, and spoke again, "This is part of the circle of wrath, where those who cause harm to others through their own actions go," his voice emotionless.

The mercenary was sure this was where he was going in the first place. "Oh great - well then - guess I'm staying.....maybe," he grumbled.

The stranger dipped TalonFyre in the boiling blood, causing him to roar in pain. This however did nothing to deter the mercenary, "Heh, I like pain - makes me feel alive. *Pour* it on fancy pants. Only makes me stronger," he grunted through clenched fangs as he glowed red.

The man realized this was getting him nowhere, and decided there was only one way to make it worse. TalonFyre had betrayed Electus, who was the benevolent ruler of the kingdom. He had done so by working for Rayburn. That meant he would be somewhere worse – much worse. "Do you know where they send people like *that* then?" he asked him, once again emotionless.

"Well since I'm stuck here you'd better talk," the mercenary scoffed.

The man then warped to the ninth circle where it was constantly below freezing. "Aw hell..... heh, I'm gonna' be a popsicle," the mercenary joked.

The stranger wasn't laughing, however. Instead he cut out the part the mercenary's brain that could cause him to feel any enjoyment whatsoever, proceeding to contort TalonFyre in unimaginable ways as the dragon cried blood.

After about two minutes, TalonFyre had had enough. "**FINE**! **FINE**! Even *I* have *limits*.....!" he cried out in agony.

The man looked him in the eyes. "In fourth round of the ninth circle, the part of your brain that can feel happiness is removed, and your body is contorted in unimaginable ways. Be glad I

didn't freeze you too," he said coldly.

The mercenary could only whimper, "Yeah......don't like it too much..."

The stranger called in the big guns after this. Once again, before TalonFyre was his mother. "YOU COMPLETE FOOL! YOU THINK I'D WANT THIS!?" she screamed, eyes full of tears. The man knew it was time for the final touch.

Chapter 18

Purification

    THE stranger warped his agonized "prey" to a field of flowers with a vision of him with his future family. He gagged at the sight of the flowers. "Too damn... pretty," he grumbled.
    In the vision, TalonFyre was playing happily with his daughter and two sons.
    "You see you could bring happiness and you'd rather end up tortured in hell? Do what you wish with him!" his mother wailed, vanishing.
    The mercenary was now crying actual tears. "Nothing hurts like being abandoned...." he sobbed.
    The man gently put his hand on the dragon's forehead. "This is your subconscious desire, Talon," he said, this time with an extremely tender and kind voice.
    "....It's....." TalonFyre tried to speak, but fell over crying.
    "It's beautiful isn't it?" the man remarked sweetly.
    "You could say that... your words not mine..." the mercenary replied softly as tears escaped his eyes.
    It was then that TalonFyre's mother reappeared, speaking in a loving voice, "You think I'd let you be the last of your kind son? You got your hard-headedness from your father."
    "And your kind heart from her," the man added, finishing her statement.
    "You do this, your legacy carries on," the mother dragon sighed happily. TalonFyre hugged his mother, eyes full of tears. After this, the mother dragon did something that surprised both the stranger and TalonFyre - she revived his ability to mate.
    "Well.... now we'll see who was right," TalonFyre sighed as his mother vanished.
    "Nightmare Eternity, cease," the man whispered.
    With this, the vision ended, revealing the man next to TalonFyre. The mercenary stood up, as the stranger helped him by lifting his paw. "Uhh - my head. I feel like a golem stomped my head in," he groaned.
    It was done. The man did what he came to do. Still, he had a strange feeling like his work wasn't done. He had to stay to be certain that Hikari would be together with TalonFyre.
    The mercenary began to walk outside with the man, tripping over everything in the bunker. When he finally got himself outdoors, he stumbled again. "Dammit... Uh oh- crap, ants!" he gulped, finding his nose in a fire-ant pile. He then sneezed, resulting in a ruptured nest and both of them covered by ants.
    Instead of panicking, the stranger telepathically controlled the ants to go back into the nest. "Show off," TalonFyre growled as he rose, shaking the leftover dirt off.
    "You have no idea," the man laughed.
    "No, I'm pretty clear on the....." the mercenary started, but ended up tripping on a rock once more. "Forget it, I'm staying here," he grumbled.

The man helped him up again. "In this one universe I restored a destroyed city in seconds," the man said smugly.

TalonFyre rolled his eyes and merely replied, "...yup, total one-ups."

Ultimar knew TalonFyre would be dizzied for an indefinite amount of time after a mental vision followed by his least favorite ability. As such, he placed his hand on the dragon's forehead. Upon his touch TalonFyre snapped at his new "acquaintance". His teeth connected and he felt them stop upon the stranger's skin – with no damage.

"How the hell... You should be burning! What the hell?" the mercenary ranted.

The man smiled and gave a warm, "You're better now."

It was true, TalonFyre's headache was gone. But he couldn't imagine a mere human being able to withstand dragon teeth, let alone his! "But... How in the... You...."

The stranger merely laughed, "My skin is harder than you can imagine," as he took his hand off the dragon. TalonFyre was taken aback by his sheer power – how could anyone be so strong?

"Fine, I'm hungry," the mercenary scowled, storming off. He chased after a nearby deer, eating it like a slob. At this, the man warped a gourmet meal out of a wormhole. "No, too fancy. Besides... No, I figured out how wrong that would sound and I'm *NOT* saying it," the mercenary said, hiding a smirk.

The man smiled, "Hahahahahah! You do know I'm psychic, right?" he asked, laughing.

TalonFyre put his paw to his face embarrassedly, "Aw, hell... You know they need to fix that so it doesn't sound so loaded," he groaned.

This made the man laugh more, "Heh, don't worry I won't tell," he then shrugged.

TalonFyre then let out a burp loud enough for every creature in the vicinity to hear. "Good - hate to have to go all crazy again," the mercenary replied with a smirk.

The man's expression turned serious. "Your inner darkness - I could take care of it if you want," he offered in a kind voice.

TalonFyre shook his head, declining in a serious voice, "No, it's part of my life force. Any of it goes - it all goes. No replacement parts either."

"I meant I could seal it," the man continued.

Even with the offer to seal the evil within him, TalonFyre declined once more, "Nah, we all have our dark sides – it's what makes us living creatures," shrugging.

The man drooped his head, "I know that - all too well," he sighed.

TalonFyre thought about the vision, "Yeah, I know - I saw it. Not bad - more hate-filled but less rage. Mine - all pure rage - for those who have died wrong deaths caused by others. That was only a taste of what Rayburn did," he growled.

The man shook his head, "That was Sbarre - he's my nemesis. He's the worst the multiverse has to offer - besides Satan I mean," he explained with a grimace.

The whole Idea of hell made the man think of something. "I need to take you somewhere for repentance. Here..." he opened up a wormhole after he said this.

TalonFyre was confused by this statement. "Re-what? Some kind of festival? I don't do big crowds," he grumbled.

The man went on, "It's a draconic ritual called the Natorkia, or Purifying Method. How long can you hold your breath?"

The mercenary was unsure of what he meant. "Uh - never tried. Lava is my breath, which is why I'm able to sleep in it," he replied unsurely.

TalonFyre's nose twitched. "What the hell is in the air?" he snorted. He proceeded to pull a slimy, mouse-sized Vespatite from his nose. "Nope just nose Vespatites. They seem to like it in there," the mercenary joked.

The man decided tell him about the method he was using. "With this process, I put in some sacred herbs, mix them in holy water and dunk you in. You hold your breath under the liquid until you're purified. Oh, and it hurts a lot - of course nothing like I've already showed you," the man explained.

"Well, I'm keeping the black fire and glowing claws. It's my signature style," TalonFyre scoffed. He then sneezed, sending Vespatite into the man's face. He gave a guilty grin after this.

"Like I said, let's go," the stranger ordered.

Another sneeze was coming on, but the man used telekinesis to remove the Vespatites, crushing them into a ball. "Ahhhhh..... Ah...man holy crap - I can think straight, and I don't smell rotten Vespatite!" TalonFyre exclaimed.

The man showed him a pea-sized ball. "There they are," he smiled.

TalonFyre ate the creatures. "Hey, food is food," he shrugged. It was a disgusting display, but the stranger had seen more horrific things in his lifetime.

TalonFyre followed the man through the wormhole to the pool. He looked at the water that seemed bottomless. "If that's water, you're trying to kill me. Could've done that myself," he scoffed.

The stranger shook his head, "There's see-through fiberglass Adamantite, at the bottom. It's not endless."

The mercenary peered in, accidentally falling face-first into the water. "Oh crap - huh not melting...." he whispered.

"Hold your breath and go under," the man directed him.

Three minutes later, he came up covered in falling black clumps, gasping for breath. "Get up," the man ordered, giving him his hand.

"Man, I feel like I'm tripping..." the mercenary said, eyes spinning. "Feels.....good.... Oh man this is cool..." he laughed. The man used his telekinesis to lift him out after this. "Aww - party pooper..." TalonFyre moaned.

"Put your hand in," the stranger ordered.

"Uh which of four..." the mercenary asked, seeing double.

The man grabbed his paw and stuck it in without a single word. It didn't burn, which it would have if the treatment was ineffective. "You're purified," the man said happily.

TalonFyre was still dazed. "Puri- wha.....? Hey, look, a deer...... It's so pink....." he said, his eyes turning wide. "Man I should've done this ages ago. This is fun shit!" he yelled, chasing after it.

The man used his psychokinesis to give the mercenary's lungs oxygen. TalonFyre blinked. "The hell was I after...." he murmured.

"You were asphyxiating," the man answered as he rolled his eyes.

The dragon shook his head. "Asphi- what?" he asked.

"You were suffering from lack of oxygen," the man explained.

"I mean, I feel normal, just… weird. Oh well, it was fun chasing a pink flying deer….I'm losing it. Now what…" TalonFyre went on.

The man knew he needed more oxygen. "Let me work on that," he sighed, giving him more CPR via his psychic powers.

A yawn was heard from the mercenary so large it unhinged his jaws. He was tired – so tired that he couldn't stay awake. He lay down, falling asleep within seconds. "(Later… I feel like I haven't slept before,)" he murmured as his armor fell off, disappearing. "I'll make more….zzzz…" he snored, rolling on his side, nearly falling into the pool. The man stopped him from falling using PK. He knew it was time to take him back to meet Hikari again - which he was very intent on doing.

TalonFyre's ability to mate was restored, but after his experience with 'her' he didn't want to do anything. Hikari was the only dragoness he would ever consider mating with, ever. Still, what would happen when she went into heat? Would she try the same thing? Could he trust her to resist her instincts? She was only at most 19, and dragonesses could be very hormonal at that age. Still, she wasn't a monster, unlike the last dragoness he knew. Whatever the reason, he really did want to see her again. He loved her after all.

Chapter 19

The Nightmare

THE man took TalonFyre through another wormhole which led back to the family. TalonFyre was still asleep, but the man didn't care. He stepped through, carrying the mercenary via telekinesis.

Hikari was sobbing uncontrollably, but a single glance at the two caused her face to light up. She darted toward them happily, "Talon! You're back!" she cried out in joy, tears in her reddened eyes.

"(Mind keeping it down? I haven't slept this good in ages...)" the mercenary said telepathically as his snoring cracked a rock.

Standing, or crawling, next to her was the strange creature that had come through the wormhole with the man. "You gave him the Natorkia Method, didn't you dear?" the snake lady asked in a sweet voice.

The man answered, "You bet," in a happy tone.

Hikari walked up to him and sensed something. "His aura... it's much more benevolent now," she whispered. The dragoness lay down next to her beloved, falling asleep within seconds.

TalonFyre woke up later that night with a yawn. "Damn, that was great," he moaned. He then looked to his side to find that Hikari was next to him. "**GAH!**" he jumped back in surprise at the dragoness.

"Sorry - I couldn't resist," she giggled.

He turned away, almost at the point of hyperventilation. "What was I doing......I was trying to kill him...." he gasped, taking off.

The dragoness looked up sadly, "What the heck? ....Was it *my* fault...?" Hikari whispered, tearing up again. She needed to see what was making him so uneasy, but she couldn't let him see her. There was only one thing to do, stay out of sight.

This stranger, whoever he was, would help her love come to his senses. She could tell by the look in his eyes that he wanted them to be together. What she couldn't believe is that snake-creature was his wife. How were they supposed to have a child if they were two different species? Maybe they were content with being together, like she was with TalonFyre. Whatever the case, they both wanted to help. Why, she didn't know.

Landing in a cave a few miles away, TalonFyre began sealing the door.

"(Bad dream?)" the stranger asked through telepathy in a concerned voice.

"No.... I saw what I was - I went *primal* on you.... Raising a kid like that......*no* father should. That was primal rage, a last resort to survive. And I can't be around her.....I'd scare her off," the mercenary went on in a fit of anxiety.

His concern heightened beyond words at this, "(I need to see what you saw.)" He then looked into TalonFyre's mind. "(I can see into someone's mind from miles away. And I can avoid memories if I want,)" the man continued. "(Show me... show me what you saw in your dream when you flew away from the one you loved...) he went on until he finally found the memory.

The dream showed a child-like TalonFyre, crying. "That's me....." TalonFyre gasped sadly. His mother was by his side, long passed from cardiac arrest as the adult version of him was behind watching. "No idea why both versions of me were there."

A figure then showed up behind the young TalonFyre. "Your fault kid....." the figure spoke in a cruel voice.

"No - no it's **not**!" the young version wept.

His mother appeared in front of him and walked away without a word. "Mom! No mom!" the young TalonFyre wailed in misery. The older version of him was immobile as his mother then turned to dust. He started crying again with tears of lava. "Man.... I need to quit being so damn sensitive," he sobbed.

"(Women look for that in a man,)" the stranger corrected him.

"The guy behind me... I ate his face. Only time I've eaten dragon. Worst food ever, but he *deserved* it. Rayburn's second in command. Had me recruited to survive - said I wouldn't last - heh, I proved him wrong and ate his ugly ass face. Had me murdering unborn hatchlings - never did it. Just stood up to him, five times my size at the age I was. Drew my blade and stabbed his chest and used it as a step. Gnawed his face off while he was alive - talk about vengeance for many," the mercenary growled, ending the story.

The man sighed at this. "(I don't wish *death* upon anyone... I just can't *bring* myself to... not anymore...)"

The mercenary's face changed to a serious expression after he heard this. "Well either you end up doing it or someone else pays the ultimate price, and that isn't good."

The man frowned as the mercenary said these words, as he knew it was true.

The vision shifted to the encounter at the bunker, showing the scene that ensued with TalonFyre's dark side. This made him uneasy about staying with Hikari. Would he attack her if she made him angry? He couldn't bear the thought! This was why he couldn't be with her, she'd be in danger!

"You wouldn't do anything to hurt her. You know this," the man said softly. TalonFyre looked down, unsure of the stranger's words

"Talon... LISTEN TO ME! You wouldn't hurt her. Your heart won't allow it. Please... just go back to her," the man pleaded.

Uncertain the words were true; TalonFyre opened his mouth to say something but the man went on with a serious look on his face, "She may even try to end her *own* life if you decide to leave her. You don't want that – I know you don't."

This made TalonFyre rethink the idea of keeping his distance. He couldn't bear the thought of Hikari killing herself! His face turned to a look of horror as he contemplated it. "Now you understand," the man stated. The mercenary nodded.

"Well any more mind-rape or you done?" TalonFyre asked with a grin. "Kidding, of course."

The man smiled slightly at this. "(Yeah, I know,)" he replied.

TalonFyre unsealed the cave after the conversation and the man exited his mind. "She loves you, you know… darkness and all…" the man said in a soft voice.

"Yeah, I know," the mercenary snickered, mimicking him.

It was true – TalonFyre knew Hikari would love him unconditionally. Why she did, he had no idea. Maybe it was due to the fact that he allowed her to bear a child. No, she loved him before that. And he didn't want to admit it at first, but he loved her – as soon as he found out about her crazy attitude and sad past he had a strange feeling for her. Now he knew what it was – love. She was perfect. Her personality, her looks, the fact that she was so close to him in age… everything about her was perfect. He needed her. He wanted her, albeit not sexually, but romantically. She was the only dragoness for him, and the idea of her ending her own life was something he couldn't bear. He had to go back, if not for himself, for her.

Chapter 20

It's Not Overrated After All

THE man decided to tell TalonFyre something to ease his anxiety about Hikari. "Did you know that Mian and I... in the five decades we've been married, we've never once.... you know..." he was going to say it, but ended up cutting himself off.

"Well, you could've just said *not* to. This all could've been simpler," the mercenary replied in a casual tone. TalonFyre then shook his head, "Dammit I'm still scatterbrained..." he whispered to himself falling silent afterwards.

My name is Ultimar by the way - I run a Multi-Dimensional hospital," the stranger explained in a kind voice.

"Please stop the sneaking, Hikari - I *know* you're there," TalonFyre called out to her. He opened the door for the dragoness and lay back down.

"I can't get past you can I?" Hikari asked warmly, walking in. Mian slithered along beside her.

TalonFyre glanced at the snake-lady. "Eesh and I thought *I* was creepy," he cringed. He then realized what he had just said. "Sorry," he quickly apologized.

Mian put her hands on her snakelike hips at this. "Well, I suppose I *am* creepy... but Ultimar loves me all the same," she said in a strangely calm and kind voice.

"Yeah..." TalonFyre sighed with a smile. Hikari looked at him and smiled as well.

"Actually, was chasing a pink flying deer.... Wonder where he went," the mercenary said out of the blue with a yawn.

Ultimar rolled his eyes and decided to put this to rest, "You were hallucinating from lack of oxygen. It wasn't real." After Ultimar had said this, he walked up to Mian and kissed her on the lips.

Hikari saw this and looked at TalonFyre. 'I wonder if he'll ever do that to me,' she thought.

The mercenary yawned once more, his jaw becoming out of line with a crunch-like pop. "I'll get that..." Ultimar stated as a green light surrounded TalonFyre's jaw and it moved back into its original place.

The mercenary sneezed again. "Man stupid sneezing..." he grunted.

"I'm going to check that out and see if I can stop that sneezing," Ultimar said, folding his arms.

"Yeah, don't go sticking your claws in there - I can still bite. But there wouldn't be a point... you'd just dodge it," TalonFyre sighed in a strangely annoyed tone.

"Analysis gaze!" the doctor yelled as his eyes turned from rainbow to green.

"The hell is he on?" TalonFyre laughed.

Mian put her hand on her forehead. "He's trying to check what the sneezing is caused by," she explained with a sigh.

Ultimar's eyes turned prismatic again. "Vespatites must have gotten in there again. Let me see your nose," the doctor requested in a calm voice.

"Fine...." TalonFyre growled.

The dragon's muzzle was cupped in the doctor's hands. A few seconds later, the Vespatite was pulled out using psychokinesis. This in turn caused TalonFyre to sneeze out a large amount of mucus that the doctor had to dodge. "Wow, I can smell normal again now..." the mercenary gasped, amazed.

The doctor wasn't through though. He approached TalonFyre's muzzle again and put his hand on his nostrils. "Life-form wall – Insect," he murmured. A barrier formed outside the dragon's nostril, then dissipated. "They won't bother you anymore," Ultimar said with a thumbs-up.

"Man, thanks... Ugh, nasty," the dragon sniffed.

"Anyway, where to next?" the mercenary asked the group.

"Well, I think... would you like to marry Hikari officially? I can take you to the chapel where we were married and Ultimar could make you look human like he did me," Mian suggested.

TalonFyre shook his head no. "Nah... keep it quiet maybe," he answered. He stood still. 'Why do I feel like snuggling up to....Hikari.....' he thought to himself.

After a minute of thought, TalonFyre had decided. He pointed to where the scar had been - it was gone. He gave a semi-sarcastic, "Well, I'm normal again - I liked being a freak."

Mian slithered up to him and put a hand on his front paw, speaking in a tender and sweet voice, "Her name means light you know. She's the light of your world..."

"Yeah..." he nodded.

The mercenary hesitated for a second at what he was about to do, but got up his courage and braced himself. He walked up to Hikari and took a deep breath. "I never did this before..." he whispered. He got his muzzle close to hers, stopped for a second, and then kissed her.

Hikari looked at him in surprise. 'Yes... I can't *believe* it, but he did it... he really did!' she thought happily as she turned from white to bright red.

"Well, maybe love ain't so damn bad," he sighed, rolling his eyes.

Hikari was overjoyed at him saying this. "You really... you mean it?" she whispered in pure joy as her eyes closed slightly.

He nodded, "I guess so." He couldn't stand it anymore - he had to let it out. He fell into a hug with her, crying. Hikari began to shed tears as well when he did this.

"I don't care... I don't *care* if we never mate... I love you all the same..." she sobbed.

TalonFyre was completely overtaken by joy. "Wow, happiness isn't overrated....." he sighed lovingly. Ultimar and Mian smiled brightly at this.

The orb of energy emerged from Hikari and TalonFyre realized something. "Hey, I didn't fix you....my mother did...." he said with a smile. He decided on what to do with the orb after this, handing it to Ultimar. "Keep it, it's the most pure energy I have - *had* anyway," he shrugged at the last two words.

"I can give it back if you want... and purify it fully," the doctor offered.

TalonFyre shook his head, declining once more and taking a casual tone, "Nah, you keep it and use it. The lock is disabled on it - it's no longer a part of me, or us."

"For what?" the doctor asked ponderingly.

"Well, anything healing wise - even revival," the mercenary answered. In a kind voice.

The doctor however had another plan, but wasn't going to reveal it yet. "Well, should we head in or not dear?" he asked his love, cringing at the word 'dear'.

Hikari nodded. "Yes, I'd like that. Please don't be embarrassed," she replied, nuzzling him. He nuzzled her back and walked back into the cave, side by side with new beloved.

TalonFyre knew it now. He knew it with all his heart and soul. He wanted to be with this dragoness for the rest of his days. The kiss he gave her – it felt... right somehow. It felt warm, like a fire had lit in his chest. His heart raced as his muzzle connected with hers – It felt so passionate, even if had lasted for less than a second. It was baffling to him how a simple thing like that could make him feel so amazing. He said love wasn't bad, but his true thoughts were that love was the best thing that ever happened to him in his life. She was his world now. No, more than that, she was the light of his world. When he placed his muzzle on hers, his heart raced.

Although strange, Mian was very kind and wise. The same could be said about Ultimar. One thing irked him though – why did he come to their world? Whatever the reason, he was glad about it. He made him realize that he was meant to be with Hikari. This doctor was interesting. He hated humans, why did he have a feeling that being human wasn't exactly the case with Ultimar? His name certainly brought up questions about his parenthood, unless he gave the name to himself. This was beside the fact that he was ridiculously strong – too strong to even possibly be human. If anything he was a dragon that looked like a human. Still, not even dragons were that strong – nothing was! Deciding not to dwell on the subject, TalonFyre would continue his life with Hikari, and forget his past.

Hikari was overjoyed that TalonFyre was staying, overjoyed he admitted his love, and most of all – overjoyed that she could be mates in more than just name. When the time came, she would give herself to him. She would allow him to take her and become her mate. She was sure that no matter how much physical pain it caused to her at first, the emotional and mental pain would be greater if she were to keep herself from allowing TalonFyre to do such a thing. Until that time came, she would enjoy every minute with her new mate to be – her beloved TalonFyre.

Chapter 21

Gifts

WHEN they reached the cave entrance, TalonFyre took Hikari's paw and held it out, dropping a necklace inside it. "Yeah, my mom had a spare. You keep it, I don't like jewelry."

Hikari knew it now - he really *did* love her. "Thank you…" she sighed gratefully.

"Meh, doesn't look like a weapon but whatever," the mercenary shrugged, taking a casual voice once more.

TalonFyre put a hand on his forehead. "Aw hell, the ballista - forgot to fix it!" He ran into the cave, continuing until he reached the device, Hikari following him. "Darastrix Charis property - it's, well - busted."

"I got it," the doctor shrugged, giving another thumbs-up as he walked towards it. He stretched his arms in front of him and opened his hands, creating a strange wave of blue energy leading up to the ballista and the machine mended itself. "It's fixed."

Whatever the doctor's method was, TalonFyre had never seen anything like it. Still, questions aside, it was one less problem.

"*Good*, I almost lost an arm getting it here - gear trapped my arm, that's why it's bent," the mercenary explained, his tone still casual.

Ultimar smiled. "Was bent… was…" the doctor corrected him happily.

"Also did this," TalonFyre pulled a bit of his skin away, showing a cracked rib. "And don't - I'm fine," he added nonchalantly, putting a paw up.

"Okay, if you say so," Ultimar sighed, rolling his eyes.

"Oh, here… help Darastrix Charis so the place doesn't run out," TalonFyre instructed, handing Ultimar a map showing his family's mines.

"Once again, I got it," the super-powered gave another shrug as he opened a wormhole to Darastrix Charis, closing it behind him.

'Wonder if he *ever* does ANYTHING with manual labor?' TalonFyre thought to himself.

Mian had accidentally read his mind, however. "You have no *idea* what he does," she replied. She was somewhat insulted, but still had a kind tone.

The mercenary wobbled. "Well, I'm…" he was going to finish with "tired" but ended up falling onto Hikari, snoring. Mian picked him up with one hand and moved him to the side. The mercenary grunted a bit, then continued snoring.

'What a heavy sleeper,' the snake-lady thought to herself.

A wormhole opened up again showing a newly-restored Darastrix Charis and Ultimar walked out. "It's fixed, better than new!" the super-powered being exclaimed with a smirk.

"(Ultimar, take whatever you need from my father's treasure cave - money doesn't buy happiness…)" TalonFyre said through telepathy.

Ultimar had forgotten to tell him that his work was free. The doctor shook his head and replied, "I have no need for it."

Mian was irked by the mercenary's earlier statement about him not doing anything on his own, and decided to hit them with some truth. "Did you know Ultimar does do *operations* manually? He can't cure cancer, or any serious disease. Physical wounds maybe, but things like AIDS... no... He needs to *create* things for that," she informed them, shaking her head.

TalonFyre had rolled into a hole in the floor, lying on top of it. (Hey, that reminds me...) he got up as he began talking. "My mother had an alchemy cave," he continued, this time actually speaking with his mouth. He took a step, resulting in him getting lodged inside of the hole. Ultimar was interested in this, but decided to wait until the mercenary got out of his current predicament.

After a few minutes had passed, Ultimar removed him using PK and figured it was time to show him another power. "I want to give you something.... watch this - my biggest specialty - Ki creation. It's what I used to fix the canon – the hand-spreading was just for show."

A giant-sized bed materialized in the cave, followed by pillows. TalonFyre merely gave an unimpressed, "I like the floor."

"Heh, this bed is special. It adjusts to your personal preference on contact - for every sleeper," the super-being informed them with a grin.

TalonFyre walked up to him. "Anyway..." he handed Ultimar a simple key, "It's to an alchemy lab. Never been in but I've seen it. Same size as the treasure caves and full of, well - potions and weird-smelling crap, so check it out and whatever you need take. Stuff just stinks to me."

Ultimar was grateful for this. "These things I cannot create. Thank you," he replied with a thankful bow.

TalonFyre walked over to the bed, poking it and then sniffing it. "Smells weird," he snorted.

"I can adjust the scent," Ultimar offered.

"Nah," TalonFyre replied, stepping on it. "What the....." he started, but stopped short as he fell over sprawled on the bed. He moved over a bit, and then was quickly sound asleep.

"I think I did well," Ultimar stated proudly.

"(Yeah, show-off,)" TalonFyre grumbled telepathically. "(A nice show-off though,)" he added, softening his tone a little. He was sleeping silently for the first time.

"In all honesty, I only created the lower area. The mattress was enchanted somewhere else - specifically a universe from a certain role-playing-game a lot of people used to pass their time," Ultimar admitted.

'Wonder where Flare and Angel are....probably asleep,' TalonFyre thought. "(Hikari, you coming? This is great!)" he remarked happily.

Hikari got on the bed and was shocked. "It *does* feel great!" she exclaimed.

TalonFyre hugged her while he was asleep and smiled. This made Hikari blush, but she was more than happy to snuggle up next to him. "Night love..." the dragoness whispered.

"(Night...)" he whispered, although telepathically. 'Well, eventful day,' the mercenary thought as he fell further asleep.

A drawer then opened and a spare glowing claw floated to Ultimar. "(My life force - see if you can do anything with it. I've got loads of them because I take them off now and then,)" TalonFyre said, falling asleep completely afterwards.

Ultimar sensed the claw was still connected to the dragon's very being. Having been given the ability and right to do so by the pope in a peaceful alternate version of Earth, the doctor decided to say a prayer for TalonFyre's happiness. He began to speak in Latin, "Bless the life force of this dragon. May he live happily and love happily for the rest of his life. May evil's grip never again taint his heart, mind, body or soul. Grant this; oh lord to the newly cleansed TalonFyre." He put the claw down after this, back in the drawer.

Chapter 22

A New Wormhole, a New World to Cherish

TALONFYRE woke up next to Hikari. To his surprise, he actually *enjoyed* it. "Hey, didn't scare me that time," he whispered to the dragoness.

He got out of the bed, but ended up falling on his face again. "...ow...." he groaned. Hikari got up as well, and with better luck than her beloved TalonFyre.

"Good morning, my dearest Talon," she yawned.

"Morning. By the way Hikari - I really hope nothing happened last night...." he sighed, shuddering at the thought.

Hikari was deeply hurt by this statement. "I didn't do *anything*...I would *never*..." her voice trailed off. She was near the point of tears at the fact that he would even think that she would betray him like that.

"Good to hear - me either," he replied in a somewhat regretful tone. Hikari then realized that he must have had a bad encounter in his past, which would explain a lot of the events that had transpired. This, more than anything else, made her feel better. She didn't want to pry, so she kept it to herself.

Having stayed the night as a witness, Ultimar walked up to the two, arm-in-arm with Mian. "I'll have to put some cushions down there," he stated.

TalonFyre was surprised the doctor had stayed. "Hell man, you *still* here? Wow."

Ultimar just shrugged, but he was thinking something else, 'I wanted to make sure you didn't jump to conclusions about Hikari's intentions.'

In a joking mood, Ultimar decided to mislead the mercenary. "Mian and I slept on air together," he said with a semi-smile.

"On...air... Meh...." the mercenary whispered to himself, disturbed by the image in his mind.

Mian decided to end the joke after seeing this. "He can use PK in his sleep, so he meant we were *literally* floating in the air next to each other," she explained. TalonFyre gave a sigh of relief at hearing this.

'Kinda' wanted to do this again,' TalonFyre thought as he placed his muzzle upon Hikari's, who once again turned red. She nuzzled him affectionately, causing him to cringe a bit. It wasn't something that he liked, but he didn't necessarily dislike it either. He sighed and softly nuzzled her back.

A rumbling was heard from TalonFyre's stomach. "Is it time to go kill us some prey?" Hikari asked menacingly with a smirk. TalonFyre nodded. The two walked out of the cave to look for food, Ultimar and Mian following.

Once outside, deer were spotted and the two gave chase. TalonFyre ran after one, grabbing it by the neck in his jaw. Ultimar looked away from the sight. "You want this one?"

the mercenary asked, tossing it to Hikari without an answer. Hikari wanted to kill her own meal, but decided to accept nonetheless and started devouring it - once again sloppily. TalonFyre chased down another and started eating as well.

TalonFyre finished first, once again choking on bone, and once again the lava melted it. "BUUURRP! Ahh..." he sighed, licking his muzzle.

Hikari had finished as well by now. "And... Cover your ears - fire in the hole!" the mercenary called out jokingly, covering his earlobes. He counted down, "Three... two... one!", and an enormous "**BUUUUURRRRRRRRRRPPP**!!" was heard from the tomboyish dragoness, causing them both to laugh. Ultimar smiled, knowing that they both enjoyed these kinds of jokes.

After a nod from doctor to wife, it was settled. "If you're ever in danger or need help - go through the wormhole here," the doctor informed them as he opened a portal of glowing light leading to a strange room, which was in actuality Ultimar's first office.

"...what?" the mercenary asked, puzzled.

"This is a permanent link to our hospital in case you need us," Mian explained.

"(Yeah, just make sure it covers burp insurance,)" TalonFyre said sarcastically via a three-way psychic link between the doctors and himself as he pointed to Hikari.

"You don't need insurance at all," Ultimar replied shaking his head, obviously taking him literally.

"From her burps maybe - she outdid *me*," he laughed. Hikari just smiled proudly, which caused Ultimar to give a chuckle while Mian just put a hand on her snakelike hip. "But yeah, you guys get going. I'm sure you've got stuff to do," he continued.

"We have billions upon billions of rooms and doctors," Ultimar replied with a shrug.

"(I get it, thanks a lot, I understand,)" TalonFyre said gruffly.

He then realized he had just snapped at the very man who talked him into finding happiness. "Sorry, I'm a bit cranky," he apologized. He walked to the lava pit and lay down in it. "There, that should fix it...." TalonFyre gurgled as he submerged himself in the lava. He sighed at his earlier action, which he regretted.

Ultimar had taken no offense however. "My hospital is as big as a large galaxy - see you guys later... but first, I have something to show you," he grinned as he said this.

TalonFyre automatically jumped to a conclusion, "what... let me guess - egg right? I knew it..." he grumbled, diving down into the lava. Ultimar was a bit depressed when TalonFyre guessed this. He and his wife were two different species. Therefore they would never be able to conceive. He shook his despair off as he had done for multiple decades, in order to show the two one of his many abilities he had be created with.

"**Ultimation- Alpha**!" the super-powered doctor cried out. TalonFyre came back just in time up to see the doctor's transformation. His hair turned white and he sprouted angel wings, followed by his hands turning to pearly dragon claws. "This is my first level of power increase," the doctor stated proudly.

It was true TalonFyre was impressed, but didn't let them see it. "Heh, like I said - show off - but a nice one," he said with a smirk. "Yeah I don't need to see more, I get the picture... about five levels or ten or something," he went on, rolling his eyes.

"I have many more - but later," the doctor shrugged, powering down.

"Wonder where your parents went to anyway...." the mercenary mumbled.

Ultimar turned silent at this. TalonFyre was a bit confused. "He never had any..." Mian sighed sadly, putting her hand on her husband's shoulder.

"No I mean Hikari's. Same here by the way - well, mostly," TalonFyre corrected them.

Ultimar was lost in thought however. "I was created in a lab I mean," he went on, sounding a bit sad.

At this TalonFyre scratched his head, giving a surprised yet understanding response, "Oh well, there's a reason for it - reason behind everything."

Mian hugged Ultimar when she saw him start to tear up and quickly whispered, "He doesn't like to talk about it..."

TalonFyre knew this feeling all too well. "It's fine..... I don't like my past that much either," he said, sounding a bit sad also.

An intercom went off at this time saying something incomprehensible, taking Hikari and TalonFyre by surprise. "The *hell*? That you they want?" the mercenary asked.

"I know all about your past. Let's go Mian dear. Oh, and if you're looking for Flare and Angel - they're off on a flight," the doctor laughed the last sentence.

"Ohhh......" the mercenary grinned a bit and shuddered at the thought. He composed himself, waving goodbye, "Well best of luck guys."

"Goodbye, my friend. I have to attend to a Gigas - she's in labor so I have to hurry." The doctor walked through another wormhole as he said this, this time taking off flying after he got through.

TalonFyre didn't notice the flight part however. "Yeah...do that...." he gagged. "Never liked the thought really but....whatever. I know *she* heard me too.... great I'm in trouble. Well, then again, I'm not on the worst side of it am I," he rambled. He looked around for Hikari, and was glad she was eating another deer instead of listening to him. 'You know, I never realized how happy I could be with a dragoness. Still, I'm just not ready for *that* yet,' he thought as he walked over to her.

TalonFyre knew this dragoness wanted him, but he also knew one thing in his heart - she would never force him to do anything. She may be tomboyish, but she wasn't a monster. His mind however, was another story. He was disgusted by the idea of mating, which made him wary of her. He was especially worried of what would happen if she went into heat around him. It wasn't as if she was an animal – she wouldn't jump on him as soon as he showed interest. Still, he couldn't shake the feeling of unease about it.

This was a situation that was alien to him. His heart knew, but his mind didn't. This meant although he was conflicted about staying because of his fear of her, he couldn't bring himself to leave her because of his love for her. It was strange - in only a few days, he had gotten closer to her than he had anyone in his entire life.

A/N: Dragons tend to mate mid-flight, but not always. This is why TalonFyre was disturbed by the phrase, "They're off on a flight". If they don't mate mid-flight, the male usually places himself on top of the female or vice-versa in a human-like fashion.

Chapter 23

Uncertainty

HIKARI had eaten two deer by now, and was starting on a third. "(How much deer did I give you? Yeesh,)" the mercenary said telepathically as he got out of the lava. He then thought to himself, 'Did she mate with me when I was asleep?'

Hikari looked at the second deer and her eyes widened. "I *didn't* eat that deer..." she replied.

"Oh..." TalonFyre turned it to ash, figuring it had died of disease or starvation.

"Well, your parents must be happy we were away from them for a while," he laughed. After this he approached her and pulled her into an embrace, a happy sigh emitting from his mouth.

"You're the only one for me..." she whispered.

TalonFyre smiled at this. "Yeah... funny how that works," he sighed, kissing Hikari. She blushed again, a small amount less than before, but blushing nonetheless.

"Well, I guess happiness isn't so bad," TalonFyre said once again, this time with more feeling.

"If you're happy... then I'm happy," Hikari replied, nuzzling him.

The mercenary decided to contact Hikari's parents, although he was unsure about doing so. "(Flare - you guys done yet, or am I *INTERRUPTING* something?)" he asked, grinning as he talked. Flare and Angel come down from the flight upon hearing him.

"Enjoy yourself Flare?" the mercenary asked with a wink. Flare gave a shrug and a nod.

Hikari giggled at this. "....ok....ok.... don't need details... yick," the mercenary gagged, shuddering.

Flare answered, "We wouldn't give them anyway," rolling his eyes.

Wanting to reiterate the situation to Hikari, TalonFyre stated, "Well, anyway.... I'm all fixed up, but we aren't going to mate so no worries," with a serious expression.

Hikari decided to remind him of her own resolve in turn. "Only when you're ready," she assured him in a kind tone, nuzzling him.

He stared at her blankly. "Yeah......that whole entire mind-trip kind of put me off for a while."

"So, now what? I'm bored," he looked at the dragoness next to him. "**Don't** suggest it Hikari. It's kind of off-putting when it's my end... on my end, whatever." he groaned as he corrected himself.

Hikari was hurt again. "Do I look like a *slut* to you?" she asked angrily, finally having enough of his distrust.

TalonFyre became ashamed at this and sighed, "No...." as he kissed her. 'Ugh I still hate that,' TalonFyre thought, lying to himself about the feeling inside him when he touched his muzzle to hers.

After the kiss, TalonFyre pulled a ring from one of his satchels. Attached to it was one of TalonFyre glowing claws. He handed the ring to his beloved Hikari with a smile. Hikari was dumbfounded at this, but at the same time her heart was filled with joy. "Made that in my sleep - or maybe I just forgot when I did it," the mercenary said, grinning. Hikari was bright red by this point, but TalonFyre had turned to her father before he could see.

The doctor then spoke, "(That claw you gave me - touch it - it's been blessed.)"

The mercenary walked into Flare and Angel's cave, opening the drawer that contained his talons. One of them was glowing golden, so he surmised that it was the one he was talking about. He poked it, which resulted in a small stun.

"(The whole stunning thing is just a small side effect. You'll have a good, happy life with Hikari and her family as long as you're willing to work towards it,)" Ultimar explained happily.

"Ugh- well...anyway thanks again," the mercenary replied.

"What did he say?" Hikari asked ponderingly, confused about the turn of events.

TalonFyre shrugged. "Something about happy life or something – well, he's right on with the happiness," he said with a smile, putting his foreleg around Hikari.

The entire situation with the doctor made Hikari wonder, "He seems wise... He looked in his twenties but I think he has to be a lot older," the dragoness remarked, a bit confused by her own words.

"Still...he looked a bit flashy... Well, I'm sure he has his reasons," TalonFyre remarked in turn, shrugging at the last sentence.

"So then Flare, what's going on today?" TalonFyre yawned, turning to his love's parents.

"Nothing... Ultimar told me Angel wasn't gravid," Flare replied.

TalonFyre was confused at this. "Wasn't...what?" he asked, unfamiliar with the term.

"(It's this world's term for being pregnant,)" Ultimar informed him.

TalonFyre cringed a bit at the word, "Ok...didn't need to hear that!" he gagged, proceeding to vomit a little.

"Sorry." Flare apologized embarrassedly.

"....yeah.....try to keep it quiet next time. Don't need to know that," TalonFyre growled as the vomit melted a hole in the floor.

"Again, sorry," Flare sighed, turning a bit red.

"Well... besides that nice detail, what's today's plan?" TalonFyre quickly asked.

"Well, we could always explore a ruin," Flare pointed out happily.

TalonFyre however, was a bit dazed with thought. "Talon? Talon?" Flare shook him, snapping him out of it.

"Sorry my mind is getting....images...." the mercenary winced.

Flare looked at Angel and slunk back in an embarrassed fashion. "Not all bad but that's the complete me talking," TalonFyre went on, winking at Hikari. This caused her to flush once more.

"Now, what was the plan again?" the mercenary asked once more.

Flare looked at him to make sure he wasn't spaced-out again and saw he was listening now. "We were going to explore a ruin," he repeated.

This caused TalonFyre to nod. "Sounds good to me," the mercenary agreed happily. The four walked into the cave once more to search for a site to explore.

TalonFyre was more confused than he was before. Not about wanting to be with Hikari - he knew he wanted to do that. What he was confused about was his emotions about mating. The very idea disgusted him. The images that flashed through his mind mostly involved 'her' and the dragonesses that made advances on him. However, the ones that involved Hikari – he actually *liked* them. Was it just because he could mate again, or was it because he actually *wanted* to take her? He was more conflicted now than ever except about one thing - he wanted to be with Hikari forever, whether they ever mated or not.

Hikari was crushed when TalonFyre had suggested that she would want to mate immediately. She wanted him to know that she trusted him. In turn however, she wanted to *be* trusted! She would never ask for him to mate with her – she wanted him to say the words "I'm ready – I want you to be mine" to her. She wanted him to ask her to mate before he took her as his own. She didn't want to use her wiles to make him want her. She didn't want to do or say anything to sway him to take her. She could wait. She wanted him to finally break her wall, but she wanted him to do so out of his own decision.

A/N: Ultimar has psychic abilities and multiple other attributes. He can see things over distance with telepathic visions, erect psychic, spiritual and/or elemental barriers, create permanent objects out of his own chakra, speak to animals and perform a multitude of obscenely superhuman feats including ascending in power through an ability he has dubbed "Ultimation".

Chapter 24

The Second Adventure, Part 1

THE four walked to the map room and started to look for potential spots. After a few minutes, they came to a decision. "I was thinking we could explore this one," Hikari suggested, pointing to a mark on their map.

"So, where is the ruin Flare?" the mercenary asked casually.

"Two miles south in a valley, or somewhere around the area. We don't know the exact location, but we *do* know it houses a jewel called the Dragonheart Sapphire," Flare replied, hiding a grin.

"Wow, how original..." the mercenary sighed with an eye-roll.

TalonFyre started to get images again, but quickly regained his composure. "Yeah.... I'm happy now..." he sighed, nuzzling Hikari, who smiled, nuzzling him back.

"We may have to do a bit of digging to get to it, as the entrance is buried beneath a few feet of ground," Angel added.

The words caused TalonFyre to give a smug response, "Well... if you need explosives - you saw the crater." Flare nodded at this.

"Well, let's go. I can pick it out in the lava nearby the ruins anyway," TalonFyre shrugged as he grabbed a strange, conical object. "Yeah, getting my head stuck gave me an idea," the mercenary continued as he strapped the cone onto his snout. "It looks stupid at first," he added with a muffled voice. "Well, shall we get going?"

They walked outside to depart. Flare however, had one last piece of information. "There's also an artifact there called Heaven's Charm. It may look like a stone feather, but it can give a powerful speed boost when put into a bracer or a necklace," he continued, giving a grin to his daughter.

TalonFyre declined nonchalantly, "Nah, I don't need speed." With this, the mercenary took off leaving a gust behind him.

"Yeah, I've held back," TalonFyre laughed as he hovered above the family, his wings making large gusts of air.

Hikari looked at her mother and father. "Let's go!" she yelled eagerly, taking flight after him. Angel and Flare took to the sky upon hearing this.

The family was having trouble keeping up with the mercenary, which worried Hikari a lot.

Knowing he needed to lay his beloved's fears to rest, TalonFyre spoke in a kind tone through is telepathy, "(I'll meet you there. I already have an idea of a location.)"

Hikari sighed at this. Due to the fact that he couldn't bear to see her upset, TalonFyre teleported her next to him mid-air. "Yeah, you're a bit slow," he laughed.

Hikari looked at him and scoffed, "A little *warning* next time, maybe?" putting on a fake frown.

"Fair enough," TalonFyre replied, smiling at her false anger.

After they had flown for a few minutes, TalonFyre's earlobes twitched, sensing lava. "Right....." he whispered, diving down, landing in a valley. Hikari followed him, unsure of what he was doing.

"This isn't the ruin site. What are we doing here?" Hikari asked with slight impatience, turning her head to the side.

"Around here I can pinpoint it when I get in the lava. Move back a ways," TalonFyre answered as he placed his coned snout into the ground, motioning her to step away. Hikari did as she was told and leaped back a few yards.

Taking a deep breath, TalonFyre released a black fireball from the cone, creating a half-mile deep hole filled with lava. "Well, it looks stupid but works," he shrugged. He then proceeded to sniff and taste the lava, after which he was able to pinpoint the locations of the artifacts they were seeking. "Right - in there," the mercenary pointed to a large mountainside. "I'm not sensing any dragons or remains down there but just random junk - a few artifacts, maybe a bit of jewelry," the mercenary reported after taking his snout away.

Flare and Angel had seen the fire even though they were a bit behind, deciding to fly in the general direction of the blast. They arrived just in time to see TalonFyre and Hikari flying off into the distance towards the ridge. "They're leaving us behind, I suppose," Angel sighed.

Flare shook his head, "What am I going to do with that girl?" he asked himself, sighing as well. He then motioned for Angel to come with him.

A few minutes later on the mountainside, both Hikari and TalonFyre were looking for a suitable area to start the excavation. Less than thirty minutes through, TalonFyre's patience had worn thin. This caused him to decide to improvise. He looked at Hikari with grin.

"I can do a blast, clearing it as far as a few feet from the gem - but it's a blast for sure. I'd give it half a mile to be safe," TalonFyre remarked happily, his grin growing wider as he started to glow.

"You might destroy the Heaven's Charm in the blast though!" Hikari protested.

TalonFyre merely grinned larger. "Nope.... I've got that thing shielded. That lava gave me an outline, and I just made a shield to fit it," he replied smugly.

This caused the dragoness's concerned expression to become one of pure excitement. "Go for it then!" she yelled happily as she took off a mile and a half into the air, rubbing her paws in anticipation.

The mercenary's body started to flame, a blaze emitting from his body. Fire burned from his very core as the blast began to take shape, growing in size each passing second, finally detonating with a thunderous boom, taking a sizeable amount of land out of the area.

"Totally freaking KICKASS!!" Hikari yelled in enjoyment as she closed her paws and held them up as she flew back down, ready to claim the spoils with her family and beloved TalonFyre.

Chapter 25

The Second Adventure, Part 2

TALONFYRE picked up a feather-looking rock from the pile of debris as the dragoness walked up. "Hikari you wanted this, right?" the mercenary asked, holding it up to her.

"Hell yes!" Hikari exclaimed as he handed it to her, "Screw bracelets or necklaces - I wanna try this *now*!" With this, she took off at Mach 2.

"Daayum - Now **that's** fast!" TalonFyre shouted, amazed at its power.

While Hikari darted around, TalonFyre was looking about in the rubble. On the other hand, Flare and Angel were only just approaching the blast site. The mercenary spotted what he was looking for as they landed. "Flare, I found the gem!" TalonFyre called out, unaware that they were right behind him.

Staring at the huge gem embedded on the pedestal, TalonFyre slowly walked up to it. He then placed his nose upon the jewel, sniffing it. "Wow, smells great!" he exclaimed. After this he couldn't help himself and began to lick the deep-blue piece of rock. "Tastes great too!"

"Do you want it?" Flare asked in a kind voice as he walked up to TalonFyre.

The mercenary shook his head and answered with a mere, "Nah..."

This caused Flare to roll his eyes and ask another question, "You realize why I wanted it, don't you?"

TalonFyre's own eyes darted to Angel. "Yeah - suck up," he replied smartly as he used his lava claw to cut it out perfectly from where it stood.

"It's not for that reason. This gem gives water resistance," Angel explained in motherly voice.

TalonFyre pulled it out of its resting place, grabbing it with both paws. Unfortunately it ended up pulling him over due to its weight, trapping his arm. "Woah - talk about heavy rock," he laughed, knowing full-well that this was no dilemma.

"You wondered why it tasted good, right? Go on and eat it," Flare offered with a smile.

TalonFyre sniffed it again. "Well.... I guess." With this, he bit it in half, his eyes widening. "Wow, what flavor!" he exclaimed, eating more.

A tooth broke off of TalonFyre as he chewed, which caused a bit of blood to drip. "Ow..." he groaned.

Flare looked at his mouth and asked, "Will that grow back?" slight concern in his voice.

His question was answered immediately as the tooth was replaced by a brand-new one. "Again - made of hardened lava... plus bone," the mercenary mumbled, mouth full of gem as he ate the rest, burping blue smoke at the end.

Hikari was amazed at this. "You can *regrow* bones?" she asked in awe.

TalonFyre grinned. "If I want – watch," he growled, tearing a leg bone off. The bone regrew instantly, and the old one shattered. Hikari looked at him with awe, while Angel and Flare were disgusted.

The unwillingness to see any more dismemberment caused Angel to change the subject. "If you could give a percentage, what was your weakness to water?" she asked intently.

TalonFyre looked at them a bit confused. "Never tried to test it," he replied, shrugging. He burped blue smoke again after this.

"That gem was powerful. I think you could even swim in water now," Angel remarked with a smile.

Flare looked around for his daughter, who was nowhere to be found.

"Hikari has the stone somewhere. Didn't see her take off - it was that fast," TalonFyre stated in amazement as he reached down to the ground, picking up a pure white gem the color of Flare's scales. "This was in there too," he went on, handing it to the two light dragons. Flare looked puzzled as to why TalonFyre did this. "It's light dragon property - only one I sensed. No clue what it is apart from that, really old too, like around the time when they started to build all those dragon holds."

Upon examination of the stone, Flare found writing upon it. "It seems like the stone says something in ancient Draconic - thankfully I know it," Flare looked for a few seconds, deciphering the code. After he had, he was confused. "All it says is - to a pure heart, this will give untold power."

This gem wasn't for TalonFyre - his heart wasn't completely pure even though he had gotten Ultimar's treatment. "Nope not doing it, I've taken too much anyway - besides I have enough power as is."

"What did I miss?" Hikari asked with a smile as she landed by her beloved.

"Well, water isn't much of my issue anymore," TalonFyre replied, burping blue smoke.

Hikari gave a smug reply, "I knew you'd love my idea." She was glad to have helped her love overcome his weakness.

"Yeah, well it gave me indigestion," TalonFyre replied with a grin and false anger, causing Hikari to laugh.

After this, Flare handed Hikari the stone he was holding. "Eat this, Hikari. You may be tomboyish, but your heart is as pure as can be," he said kindly. Hikari looked at the stone and took it in her paws and licked it.

"Heh, at least it's not me being told to eat a rock for a change. Yeah, give her half a second it'll be down," the mercenary laughed. He was right - Hikari bit into the gem three times and swallowed the rest whole with a large gulp.

Something happened after this that surprised them all - Hikari started to glow gold and her forehead began to move a bit. Then a golden mark appeared upon it saying "Light" in ancient draconic. After this, her wings turned feathery and angelic. "Wh... feathers?" she gasped in an odd tone as the mark disappeared, confused at what had happened to her.

"You never needed a mark to look beautiful - or those," TalonFyre commented lovingly. His eyes then widened as he realized what had just came out of his mouth. "Chicken wings!" he laughed, trying to cover up what he had just said. Hikari grinned at this.

Knowing he couldn't hide the truth from her or his words, TalonFyre reiterated in a kind voice, "Anyway, it makes you look even prettier than before."

Hikari was taken aback by his comment, and in her shock could only say one thing. "Thank you," she whispered, nuzzling him.

The mercenary smiled. "Well, you were a jewel anyway," he whispered back.

As he got close he sniffed her, realizing something. "AW GOD- You **stink**! The hell was that thing, a dirt magnet!?" he both yelled and gagged at the same time.

Angel sniffed her as well. "Ugh! Even to a light dragon it smells bad!" she coughed.

TalonFyre ran to a nearby bush and began to vomit. "Hey blue barf - cool!" he said, wiping his mouth with his paw.

"I think the smell will go away in time," Angel sighed, looking at both of them.

"(It will. I took a few glimpses every few hours in case something went awry in my time away. That smell is from the feathers having newly grown. They have pus on them from growing from the scales so quickly. It's not visible, but it's there. A bath will do you some good,)" Ultimar spoke through telepathy.

"Yeah, bath *isn't* in my vocabulary. So, I stink - big deal," the mercenary shrugged.

A small wormhole opened up, dropping a can of spray out. "(Use this then. Spray it on the dirty areas,)" Ultimar sighed.

"Didn't say I didn't want a bath, now did I? Never had one - and hey, if I'm with her that's even better, we can both reek," TalonFyre laughed, walking over to Hikari with a crinkled nose.

For the first time, TalonFyre heard Flare speak in a parental voice, "You're going to be staying with *all* of us, so you're getting one."

Chapter 26

The Spring

TALONFYRE knew Flare was right, but there was one thing he didn't know. "So, what the hell is a bath anyway?" he asked. This made the entire family laugh. "Yes, I'm asking that," the mercenary grumbled.

Hikari smiled at this. "It's where you get in *water* to clean yourself Talon," she explained with a chuckle.

This made TalonFyre uncertain whether the gem he ate was intended for this reason, or if it was just coincidence. "Oh, I've never been clean anyway - never needed to be," he shrugged, shaking off dust, "just ash - and who knows what else."

Knowing there was no getting out of this, TalonFyre decided to state the obvious, "Hey, I'm immune to water now."

By this time flies were buzzing around them. The mercenary followed one with his eyes as it landed upon his nose. Hikari sniffed herself again, almost vomiting at the stench. "I'll *need* a bath to get all the grime off my wings," she gagged.

"Well, I've never *had* a "bath" and it seems fine now that I'm resistant. Why not now?" the mercenary asked rhetorically, shaking soot out of his ear.

"(There's a hot spring a little ways down the mountain. The best of both worlds,)" Ultimar informed them.

TalonFyre was glad he didn't have to use cold water. "Fine by me - I know where it is anyway," he shrugged in a semi-uncaring tone. Hikari and her family followed TalonFyre, wondering what the spring would look like.

After a few minutes of walking, they arrived at the hot spring, which turned out to be two-hundred feet in diameter. Although the water was heated, there were multiple lotus pads and cattails scattered about. The mercenary had only one thing to say, "Wooow!"

TalonFyre's armor dropped off, apart from one on his lower belly. "Yeah…. that's a safety net," he said seriously. He leaned over the water, sniffing it. "Huh… not that bad but it's not lava," he said uncertainly as he stuck one of his claws in.

"Huh… well who's in first? Well, I'm the dirtiest," TalonFyre began to talk to himself, lost in thought. Hikari jumped into to pool of heated water before he had a chance to say another word. After this she spat out water playfully at the mercenary, smiling.

"Oh well then - I don't know," TalonFyre whispered, hesitating.

"(Do I really need to slap a water-resistance Omamori on you?)" Ultimar said impatiently.

TalonFyre rolled his eyes and grumbled, "No."

The mercenary got a little closer and ended up falling in. "Wah!" he yelled as the water around him turned black with ash and dirt. This caused him to sigh in relief.

His protective armor began to fall off. "Oh no you don't!" he growled as he grabbed it and put it back on. "Yeah, that's *staying* on.... maybe latch it to my bones," he grumbled. Hikari was a bit afraid he was serious, but decided to brush it off as a joke or a heat-of-the-moment thing.

"Not bad really - I feel clean in places I didn't know I had - well have now but didn't," he said with a grin. This caused everyone to laugh.

This made Hikari afraid they might have offended him. "Sorry," she apologized.

TalonFyre was a bit uncertain what she meant. "What? Oh, it's fine," he replied, diving down.

Hikari gave out a sigh of relief. 'That's good. I thought he would be mad we laughed at that,' she thought.

After about ten minutes, TalonFyre started swimming very well. "Yeah, it's called practice," he said smugly.

Hikari swam up to him and nuzzled him, speaking in an impressed tone, "You're a fast learner."

TalonFyre smiled back, relying with a grin and a smug, "Yeah."

Roughly five minutes later the two got out as Flare and Angel looked at them. "The hell... **Yuck**," the mercenary said softly as he looked at the filthy water, shaking off. The spring was completely covered in dirt and ash.

"At least it's a big pool," Hikari pointed out with a shrug.

TalonFyre looked into an untainted portion of the pool and was surprised at what he saw. His scales were iridescent and shining, his horns polished, his claws gleaming. "Heh, wow," he chuckled, surprised at his appearance.

"You look... amazing..." Hikari whispered in awe.

TalonFyre turned to her. "Yeah, guess I was really dirt..." he began but instead gawked at the dragoness. "Well, you're probably better," he replied, looking away as she blushed.

One of Hikari's feathers went into the mercenary's nose, causing him to sneeze. "Sorry..." she apologized once more.

TalonFyre shrugged. "Well, at least it's not Vespatites anymore," he said with a smile.

"(You're welcome,)" Ultimar butted in.

"Yeah, by the way I hear some really creepy noise - must be you. Don't tell me I'm not bothered," TalonFyre said back.

The mercenary's eyes were now visible - black with a red pupil. "Hey, anyone see this great? Weird - probably all that crap in my eyes," he laughed.

"What happened to your eyes?" Angel asked in wonder.

TalonFyre shrugged again. "Oh, just weren't clean- I think. Or maybe it's this happiness junk. Either way I can see way better," he replied nonchalantly, albeit with a smile.

Hikari walked up to him and nuzzled him again. "I don't care what your eyes look like," she said kindly.

TalonFyre also noted that his wings were shiny and leathery. "Ok yeah, I was a walking dirt pile," he chuckled, earning a giggle from Hikari.

"By the way..." the mercenary whispered mischievously. Hikari was confused, only to be taken aback when the mercenary disappeared, teleporting behind her, shoving her in and laughing.

"What was that for?" she asked with a grin.

"No clue!" TalonFyre replied. They both laughed as he helped her out.

They left the spring, and after a bit of hunting and eating they decided to go back to the cave.

TalonFyre was confused again. Why did he push Hikari in for no reason? Did he want to get a rise out of her? Did he know she would think it was funny due to her attitude? He wasn't sure. He knew one thing - she was beautiful when he looked at her, he even gawked at her figure! He despised the idea of mating, but now he wasn't even sure of his own hate for it. He almost *wanted* to have her, but was conflicted about the past. Either way, whether he wanted to mate with her or not, he loved her with all his heart and soul. There was one thing that was bothering him, though - did she know how to defend herself if he couldn't? He wanted to make sure she could, but didn't know how he could train her. He knew that he could, but would there be enough time before someone came for them?

Hikari was completely taken aback by TalonFyre's playfulness. She supposed he had a fun side too, but not this much. When he did that it made her so happy. She was happy he was finally letting go, happy that he would trust her not to be angry, and most of all – happy that he's finally allowing himself to enjoy his... no, not his life. She was happy he was allowing himself to enjoy *their* life. Spending time with TalonFyre was the most joyous thing she had ever done. She had only one thought right now – 'This is what love feels like.'

Chapter 27

Training, Part 1

THE family arrived back at the cave with TalonFyre, stomachs full. "Well now what?" "Hikari needs to train for one - I need a new blade," the mercenary rambled, showing them the shattered blade.

"(Train? I can help with that. I have a room for training,)" Ultimar offered helpfully, once again butting in.

TalonFyre's brow furrowed. "Yeah, well you touch her I'm back to kicking that fancy tail of yours - and I **will** find a way!" he growled defensively.

A wormhole opened up next to both of them. "Yeah, well, I'll be watching. Get going dear, training awaits," TalonFyre stated as he kissed her, enjoying it this time.

"*You're* training with her smart guy, not me," the doctor corrected him, talking in in a tone of false annoyance through the rift.

"Oh - well I was gonna' kiss you anyway," TalonFyre added happily to his beloved as she flushed slightly.

"You wanted to train, right? This is the perfect place," Ultimar asked then remarked in a kind yet eager voice.

TalonFyre put a claw up in the air, suggesting for them to wait. "Hang on," he mumbled, teleporting to the weapon stash in the cave. "Ah, here we are - my spare golem buster pure!" he exclaimed happily, pulling up a golden sword.

TalonFyre appeared once more, holding the golden blade. He gave a smug grin, stating, "It's my only spare."

Hikari, loving weapons, grabbed it in her tail, giving an eager, "Thanks!"

Although he had meant it for himself, Hikari was more important to TalonFyre than using a sword. "Hey - aw fine. I'm tired of blades," he grumbled in defeated tone. Making his love happy was more important than holding a weapon.

Ultimar laughed at the situation, taking a proud tone, "I can teach you both my techniques. Well, one of them for each of you. You won't need weapons when I'm through."

After hearing this and trusting Ultimar's judgment, TalonFyre opened a lava pit at his workspace, sucking in all the metals and equipment. "I'm done with that stuff," the mercenary stated with a shrug.

TalonFyre turned to Hikari. "By the way - that's a light blade, golem infused. I made it for you ages ago," he said happily.

Hikari was amazed by this. "Ages...? Really?" she asked softly.

"Yeah... when we met, something somehow lit up and I just made it. It's inscribed with your name," TalonFyre replied as he blushed slightly through his black scales.

Hikari started to cry tears of joy as she read the inscription: *To one heck of a gal – Hikari*

"I knew it - I knew you were a loving dragon," she sighed in content happiness as she shed tears.

"Yeah, and this can go," TalonFyre said with a smile, grabbing a loose scale, ripping it off along with some of his skin. He showed them what it was - his mercenary ID. TalonFyre smirked as he floated it in his hand and torched it with his black fire. "Yeah much better," he said, keeping his smirk.

A smile was on Ultimar's face as he looked through the wormhole. All he could say to this was, "I like the fact that you're giving up on that life, Talon."

"The past can bite my scaly ass!" TalonFyre exclaimed in a mixture of false rage and joy, continuing with the destruction of is old identity.

"Yeah, they even got me branded," he continued as he grabbed a horn, snapping it off. "....ok *that* hurt..." he growled as a new one replaced it.

"Here, it's got the ability to regenerate - use it. If you notice the lack of blood, that part of my horn was hollowed out," TalonFyre informed the doctor as he threw it through the wormhole.

"Heh, you don't think I have that ability already?" Ultimar rhetorically asked in a smug voice.

TalonFyre rolled his eyes. "Oh well, **sorry** for trying to help," he replied sarcastically.

"It's fine," the doctor chuckled.

The mercenary was almost finished. "One last thing - might want to look away Hikari," he warned. The dragoness did as she was told and turned her head. TalonFyre grabbed a dagger, cutting a small chunk of heart out. "This is the last of what they have to track me," TalonFyre grunted as he crushed it. "There, now my bunker and every archive are gone. So... now what?" he asked, wondering what his life would be like now.

"Come through the wormhole," Ultimar instructed. TalonFyre did as he was told, walking through the wormhole next to Hikari, who was beaming with happiness.

They ended up in a gray-tinted, nearly endless room with a golden square floor in the center and an odd ceiling with a small sun and moon slowly rotating on a few panels with an arrow on one side. It also had downwards staircases on each side of the square leading to four separate bunker rooms below the surface. It was slightly late so the gray represented afternoon in this place. This of course was something that escaped TalonFyre. "Well this is bland. Must be storage - or modern art," TalonFyre jested.

"Well, it's kind of something I got from my old job. Don't ask," Ultimar shrugged, appearing in front of them out of nowhere. TalonFyre jumped back, startled.

"God, I'm sick of being spooked by my own tricks," he growled.

"You're going to be in here for two years. But it's only going to be two hours outside. I call it the Temporal-Defiant Study. It can be set to any kind of time-manipulation within reason along with multiple other functions, but if you don't know how to work it properly it can have bad consequences. This is why I have it pre-set to this and never touch the controls at all," the doctor explained, wiping the sweat from his brow. He then thought to himself, 'I wonder if my old pals at the Federation could teach me how to use this better. I don't miss those days but sometimes I wish I could ask for more of their training equipment to help out with my hospital. I heard you can even change the appearance of this place to a forest. Even so, thank goodness for anime. ...I really need to be more creative.'

"Ok - you *stink* buddy. Don't tell me why either," TalonFyre grumbled, wrinkling his nose.

"I was training, Talon," Ultimar answered, rolling his eyes.

TalonFyre's nose wrinkled even more. "For what, the non-bathing marathon I would've won?" the mercenary asked sarcastically, gagging.

Ultimar smiled. "No, for four years. I've been training here for four years, equaling four hours outside," Ultimar answered.

TalonFyre gagged again, "Ugh, no *wonder* you stink!"

He showed Ultimar his shining scales and clean eyes. "I feel great!" he exclaimed out of the blue. He then realized he was still bleeding from when he cut out his heart. "Ok, must've forgot about that," he stated, filling the gaps with lava, closing the wound.

"Hey, by the way, I left something by the hot spring.... thing was a bit cold. You just drop it in and it gets twice as hot," TalonFyre stated, once again for no reason.

Ultimar started to glow, amazing TalonFyre. The doctor's stench was gone, along with the sweat. "That power is used to clean the body. It's much easier than a bath," the doctor explained.

TalonFyre rolled his eyes. "Yeah, and some places I'd rather clean *myself* anyway," he replied with a grin.

After laughing for a few seconds, Ultimar's expression turned serious. "Enough crude humor, it's time to train," he ordered.

TalonFyre looked disappointed, but understood. "Aww- fine..." he sighed, annoyed.

It was then that TalonFyre looked around and realized his love was missing, "Wait, where did Hikari go? I don't see her!" he gasped in a worried tone.

Ultimar put his hand to his face. "She must have found the fridge," the doctor sighed.

TalonFyre laughed at this. "Yeah, just follow the burp. I swear she has some sort of gift."

They did as TalonFyre suggested following the sound of scarfing and belching until they got to a mammoth fridge, which Hikari was eating from. TalonFyre tapped her foreleg. "Busy eating? Yeah, as usual," he laughed. She turned towards them and TalonFyre grinned at her face, which was covered in pie crust.

Ultimar rolled his eyes. "Now that you're stuffed, the first thing you have to learn is to use Ki, the universal life force that flows through all things," the doctor informed them. He turned away from them. "Like so." With this, he shot an energy blast out of his hand towards the nothingness.

"Wow - well I thought this training was for weight loss. I see weight gain...oh now I've done it!" TalonFyre moaned as he ran off, hiding behind the wall.

Chapter 28

Training, Part 2

HIKARI walked behind the wall, smiling. "You *really* think I'd take offense to that?" she asked with a laugh.

TalonFyre scratched his head with his paw. "Well... no clue. Again, still not the romantic type," he answered with a semi-sheepish look. "But it wouldn't piss me off - you maybe," he continued.

Hikari rolled her eyes. "Heh, call her "angel food cake"," he went on. Hikari **smirked**. "Yup, she heard it....." TalonFyre groaned once more, putting his paw to his face. He vanished, embarrassed by his comment. "(I'll be in the next room, hiding under the floor,)" he said, the embarrassment showing in his telepathy. This actually caused Hikari to start laughing.

After hearing her laugh, TalonFyre was glad that he didn't make her upset. Unfortunately, he ended up running his head into a panel, the bang resonating around the halls. "OW, GODDAMMIT!" he growled, rubbing his head.

"Holy crap!" Ultimar shouted, knowing full-well the panels were extremely hard.

"I'm fine - just...a bit...dazed... I'll ....just...sleep," TalonFyre grumbled, falling asleep like he said he would. A panel landed on him, but he ignored it.

Ultimar was frustrated by TalonFyre's lack of resolve. "Well, looks like **someone** doesn't want to protect his lover," he said in teasing tone.

This caused TalonFyre to angrily appear between the two, grabbing the doctor by the throat. "You touch her I'll skin your ass alive!!!" the ex-mercenary screamed at the top of his lungs as his head tilted sideways.

"I have a wife, moron," Ultimar sighed in annoyance, unfazed by any of it.

TalonFyre dropped him. "Well sorry," TalonFyre grunted cruelly.

"That really hurt... Ooh man," TalonFyre groaned, rubbing his snout. He turned to Hikari. "Well, whatever, get training "precious"," he grumbled. Hikari looked down, a bit hurt.

TalonFyre then realized something – although Hikari may be tomboyish and violent, she was still a dragoness, and dragonesses can get upset when talked to cruelly, especially if it's the one they love doing it.

"Ok yeah that - yeah that's mean – sorry," he said, hugging her and kissing her in an apologetic manner. Unfortunately his nose ended up touching her too. TalonFyre jumped back, holding his nose.

Hikari smirked. "I see how it is - you want *me* to protect *you*," she said slyly.

Ultimar decided to add to the ruse. "You can teach him if you want," he suggested in the same sly tone.

Angered, TalonFyre walked up to Ultimar, stealing some of his Ki and giving it back. He then walked over to the corner, lying down. "I know damn well how to protect her. Ow – great, nosebleed. I stick to *my* powers, not using anyone else's," he grumbled.

"What do I do, Ultimar?" Hikari asked excitedly.

The doctor put his hand to his face sighing. "The first thing you do - relax... Ki flows through the body of every living thing, but few know its full potential. Use your psychic powers to feel the energy inside of you, find your center, bring it through your body to your front paws and let it out," Ultimar instructed.

Hikari closed her eyes and did as the Ultimar told her, feeling her own energy. She felt a slight tingle in her paws, and an orb of energy appeared in them. TalonFyre fixated on it, following it with his eyes.

"Good. Now send it forward into the nothingness," the doctor continued.

Hikari threw the orb as he said, sending it into the void. For a reason he didn't know, TalonFyre chased after the glowing orb. 'Wait why am I chasing it?' he thought to himself.

"You're a fast learn - oh dear," Ultimar groaned as TalonFyre grabbed it.

Staring at the blue orb, he sniffed it, and as soon as he did it exploded, throwing him into a hallway. "Dammit, just got cleaned," he groaned.

Ultimar put his hand to his face. "Yeah, I figured that would happen," the doctor sighed.

TalonFyre got up, stumbling over. "Damn that smarts... Yeah, **not** doing that again," he grumbled, lying down and falling asleep.

"The Ultima-Blast can only be used by a pure heart," Ultimar informed them, looking at Hikari.

"What, her burp? That's a damn blast," TalonFyre laughed, proceeding to yawn.

Touching Hikari's head, Ultimar began feeding her knowledge of every Chakra points in a dragon's body. "Didn't I say *no* touching!?" TalonFyre growled. He then looked at Hikari, who was unharmed. "Meh, I'll let it slide - this time," he said begrudgingly.

"First, concentrate your Ki into your crown chakra," Ultimar instructed. He turned to TalonFyre. "Also, I was giving her knowledge of the Chakra points in a dragon's body so she could use this power, Talon," the doctor added.

Hikari concentrated, as she did so the top of her head between her eyes started to glow violet. "Next, focus it into the form you want in the mind chakra," Ultimar continued. Hikari's head glowed indigo between her eyes and she began to rise a few dozen feet in the air. "Now release it through your breath, Hikari," Ultimar said, finishing his instruction.

"Not a burp - God, she'll kill us *all*," TalonFyre laughed. This earned an eye-roll from the super-powered doctor. Hikari shot out a large energy blast shaped like TalonFyre. "Figured that would happen," the ex-mercenary chuckled.

Seven seconds from its release, the blast exploded five miles away in a kilometer-wide eruption. TalonFyre was shocked at the spectacle. "Yeesh - makes mine look crap," he said in awe.

Ultimar was concerned, and with a reason. Hikari started to fall, her eyes closing. "*Be careful*! You *don't* want to put too much energy into or - Talon, catch her!" the doctor yelled as she fell.

TalonFyre grabbed her in his forepaws five feet above the ground, heart beating fast. "Damn close," he sighed in relief.

Ultimar walked up and put a hand on her crown, then nodded. "She's just a little dazed... good," the doctor said, sighing in relief as well.

"So where do I put her, just anywhere?" TalonFyre asked with a laugh. This earned him a glare from Ultimar. "Kidding!" the ex-mercenary said anxiously.

Ultimar looked at him seriously and gave the normal response, "That's enough for today - for her at least,"

TalonFyre groaned. "Fine - again where do I put her?" he asked once more.

The doctor pointed to a hallway. "There's a bed down the hall," he answered.

TalonFyre placed her gently on his back, walking toward the hall. After a few seconds he found the bed and placed her gently down kissing her. "You did good, Hikari...." he said kindly. He walked out looking back at her sleeping body. 'She looks so peaceful... and beautiful,' he thought. He then realized he had seen a part of her he felt he shouldn't have – or possibly one that he should have seen earlier. He shook his head to clear his mind of distraction and left the room, taking one last glance. What he didn't notice was the plethora of books on the wall – at least one thousand. If he did he would have realized this place wasn't just for training. There was a reason it was called a study. That reason was due to the fact that many doctors had come here to learn what it took to cater to every type of specie in the multiverse. The more longevity and youth a specie had, the more time it had to hone its skills to be a proficient doctor.

After putting his love on the bed, TalonFyre walked back out, looking at Ultimar. "Well, now what?" he asked, wondering about the training.

"You, my friend, are learning a different technique," the doctor answered.

TalonFyre smirked. "I have one held back, it's just never used - kind of a secret. I could show you if you want," he said smugly.

"I'm going to show you all the chakra points first. Do you mind?" Ultimar asked politely.

TalonFyre blinked. "Hey, you already handled my brain, so I have some *reasons* to be worried!" he replied with a grimace.

Ultimar looked at him curiously, his face matching his expression, "You said you have a technique you wanted to show me?"

TalonFyre looked at him with a cruel smile. "Well, I do have *one* thing - but to make it happen... you have to make me mad, and I mean *worse* than earlier. It's not evil anymore, but I kept it locked away...." TalonFyre answered with a grin.

"Ah, the Nuclear Blast thing?" Ultimar asked, sure that wasn't the case.

TalonFyre grinned even more. "Oh no, for close combat. Well, give me your best...and I'll do the same," he said cruelly.

Ultimar created pair of blue and red goggles. "I need my combat gazer on," the doctor stated as the goggles clasped onto his eyes.

Ultimar wanted to see TalonFyre's resolve. This is what drove him to train Hikari as well as her love. It was true, the doctor was glad he decided to copy his old mentors' training equipment, but he still hated the fact that he used to be a heartless vigilante. He wasn't technically a criminal. In truth, he was an asset to the Federation for a long time. He had friends in a lot of places there, most of them living longer than he would. He was eventually taken into their ranks and considered a Substitute General as well as a first-class warrior. Still, every time he remembered all the creatures he killed, his heart ached. He had to make sure he remembered what he was, in order to stop him from becoming such a thing once more.

Chapter 29

Where True Power Comes From

TALONFYRE began to glow. "Yeah....that's a taste - but to get it through the roof... I have to hurt - both spiritual and physical. Then.....well I suggest you close the doors so she doesn't hear," the ex-mercenary said, unsure if he wanted to do this. Ultimar on the other hand, wanted to see it very much

"There's a reason I crack my bones so loud. It's......very...terrifying - even scares me. Used it once on Mr. "High and Mighty" Rayburn. It's why he's scraped up," TalonFyre went on, starting to glow deep red.

"Okay, Combat Level at normal... 1500 physical, 3000 spiritual. Mine in normal form is five-hundred million," Ultimar said.

TalonFyre was surprised. He was already starting to transform, and without any anger at all. "Well... looks like the whole "mad" thing was the old me," he said with a grin. Ultimar smiled at this.

TalonFyre's eyes rolled back, his jaw unhinged, his teeth started to move as if they were a band-saw, his tongue becoming a blade. His tail transformed into the shape of chainsaw, and his spines began to erupt in flame. He then turned neon red with his spine dislocating. "Well...power up I guess...." he said as he transformed.

Ultimar decided to push him with, "Keep going, I need to be impressed."

TalonFyre's muscles grew to ten times the size along with his body, his heart beating faster by the second.

"Combat Level 40,000 to 80,000, enough to crush a small dirt hill with a single punch. You've *already* eclipsed Rayburn," Ultimar stated happily.

TalonFyre lit up in black flame, his roar cracking the panels on the wall. "Yeah, just watch..." he growled in a demonic voice as his claws turned into volcanic swords.

Ultimar counted once more, "75,000 to 150,000, enough to destroy a small boulder with your Ki."

TalonFyre's armor reappeared as massive black panels. "Remember when I said that it reflects heat? I can turn it around," he growled as the room rose to the temperature of his lava-like blood.

Ultimar put up a weak barrier around him at this and spoke in an ordering tone, "This barrier is Combat Level 500,000. I want to see you break it."

TalonFyre had to show Ultimar that he could protect his mate. He had to prove that he could defend her! He *would* show him.

"Fine....but I *wasn't* gonna' do this," TalonFyre growled as his scales glowed golden, flashing red. His power became double, then quadruple. "This......is my bloodline..... *And* why I never die.... I'm linked to the earth's core," he said proudly as the barrier broke.

"Good, your spiritual energy broke it," Ultimar said happily.

TalonFyre drew energy from the core of the planet as his eyes rolled into place filled with flaming magma. "I am the earth's core. This world dies....I die," he said, with even more pride than before.

"Your power is 500,000 over 1,500,000, enough to level a twenty-foot dirt hill with your fire," Ultimar said, continuing to tally TalonFyre's power.

TalonFyre's wings grew massive, forming into blades covered in smoldering lava. "This is.....where it gets scary," TalonFyre warned as his eyes disappeared.

"1,000,000 over 2,500,000 - you're getting to about one-hundredth my level," Ultimar said, hoping for more, which he would get.

TalonFyre's skin and scales disappeared completely, leaving only lava and a heart.

"Your power is 5,000,000 over 15,000,000, enough to destroy a 50-foot slab of soft rock with a head-butt. I like where this is going," Ultimar said, crossing his arms.

The panels ripped off the wall, placing themselves over TalonFyre's body, which he turned into pure power. "Did I say the earth? Oh sure when I *need* to stay here. But that big yellow star - the sun - is my true heart," TalonFyre said with a smirk, growing to ten times his current size, snorting black fire that melted his armor.

Although he was impressed, Ultimar wanted to know TalonFyre's resolve. "*I'll* transform now," Ultimar said, shifting into his Alpha form. "Five Billion - you're at 250 Million over 750 Million, which is enough to level a 200-foot slab of concrete if you could use Ki," he said, ready to see more of what the ex-mercenary had to offer, 'Even though you'd have to use all of it.' he thought.

"My mistake... you know why I picked today? All the hot planets align," TalonFyre said smugly as black flame covered the whole room. "Well..... I am the heart of the universe's heat," he said in the same smug tone.

"Ultimation - Beta!" Ultimar yelled as his angel wings turned gold and his feet turned into pearl-colored dragon talons. "500 Billion - you're at Ten billion," Ultimar said, hoping TalonFyre could push a little more, and that he did.

The ex-mercenary forced himself to grow ten times larger stopping at that, a flame version of Hikari appearing by his side. "And she.....makes me....hot," he laughed in a semi-smart manner.

These words caused Ultimar's eyes to grow wide as he burst out in joyous laughter. TalonFyre began to glow with blue flames. "Wasn't a joke..." he growled, the flames turning into clear fire.

Ultimar shook his head. "You've *finally* realized it... protecting others – that's what makes you *TRULY* strong!" the doctor said in proud joy.

TalonFyre smiled kindly. "Yeah..." the ex-mercenary agreed.

"You're at 100 billion now," Ultimar said, still wanting more power to be shown.

"Well, one more thing - we need to go outside," TalonFyre said teleporting into an empty part of space.

"*Now* I'm impressed... You've actually *eclipsed* my Alpha form!" Ultimar said happily.

TalonFyre wasn't done however. "Ahh, perfect," he said as versions of Flare, Hikari, Angel and his parents showed up beside him flaming. He grinned. "Well...last push," TalonFyre grunted.

"Ultimation - Mega!" the doctor yelled as his wings turned white again and split, then grew to twice the size of the original. He then grew white, fur-like feathers.

TalonFyre in turn grew to the size that one of his eyes could have been the sun. "I **AM** THE UNIVERSE!" he boomed, his roar breaking the sound barrier.

"50 Trillion all around. It's enough to destroy large mountain range with a single Ki explosion. Yours is the same. Also, I put up a barrier to keep us alive," Ultimar stated proudly. He then thought to himself, 'Once again, you'd have to use all of it – that means you'd die.'

"Well, I'm tired as hell......but for them I'd do....." TalonFyre whispered, cutting off as his heart disappeared.

Ultimar became concerned at this. "Are you okay?" he asked, looking at the spot where TalonFyre's heart was.

"....more than...ok." TalonFyre sighed happily. He then uttered a deep, guttural roar, fearsome beyond words.

"Ultimation - Omega!" Ultimar yelled. His four wings turned gold, his fur-like feathers glowing blue with Ki, and his eyes turned pure prismatic "5 Quadrillion," Ultimar said, this time a bit sadly.

TalonFyre was breathing hard. He stopped growing and shrank to normal size, floating in the emptiness of space. "(Yeah - I went...too...far....)" he said through his telepathy, his body unconscious.

Ultimar flew after TalonFyre, gently catching him in his arms with ease as he blacked out. "(Crap... heh - held it just long enough....for them.....)" the ex-mercenary said softly as his eyes rolled back, his claws ceasing to glow.

"I'll heal you - Stamina Palm!" the doctor yelled, slamming TalonFyre's head with a prismatic, glowing hand, waking the unconscious dragon.

"Yeah, knew I'd go too far..." TalonFyre chuckled with a sad smile.

"(Can't... breathe...)" TalonFyre communicated through telepathy. Ultimar knew the barrier would keep TalonFyre from dying in space, but all the oxygen had been burned away by the flames to a point where the ex-mercenary could no longer breathe on his own. The genetic alterations given to Ultimar allowed him to survive in almost any environment, but TalonFyre didn't have those.

"Hang on!" the doctor said in a panic, opening a wormhole back and flying through with TalonFyre in his arms.

They arrived back at the main room of the training chamber, and the doctor set TalonFyre down. "(I swear - if she sees *any* of this... she won't want me,)" the ex-mercenary communicated sadly, not wanting Hikari to hear.

This caused Ultimar to sigh, "She loves you no matter what," in an assuring tone, giving him CPR with his psychokinetic powers once more.

TalonFyre gasped, air coming back into his lungs. "By the way, keep my heart - the sun is my life source. That - it's just a toy. Piece of ancient rock from the sun when it was a star," TalonFyre said, his air supply replenished.

"I hate to tell you this, but I have four forms beyond that. I'm sorry, but there's no way you can eclipse me," Ultimar sighed regretfully, looking down at the floor as he gave the information.

TalonFyre merely smiled and coughed, "Yup, I figured." Ultimar smiled back, glad that the ex-mercenary wasn't envious.

"Well, anyway keep the thing it's no use, all an act. Just wasn't before. Now I'm fighting for them. I need all the power I can get... and, well, the sun is the only thing hot enough besides Hikari," TalonFyre said chuckling at the last few words.

An idea came to Ultimar after hearing him say this, "I'll tell you what, *all* of my nurses and doctors have some of my own power. I'll give you some, as well as the others," he offered.

"Nah," TalonFyre shrugged, declining.

"God, I hope she didn't hear me say that about her," the ex-mercenary mumbled, looking at the room Hikari was in.

Ultimar shook his head no and replied, "She's still out cold."

The ex-mercenary looked up and sighed in relief, "Oh, thank God."

A/N: Ultimar is very intelligent, but for the most part un-creative due to his Ultimate Copy and dominant left brain, leading to him to trace, modify and re-name other techniques and technologies from earth or other planets. He has created three signature techniques – The first is the Ultima-Blast, which is an energy burst that can be modified into any shape or form. The second is the Nuclear Vulcan, a volley of pea-sized energy bullets that explode on impact based on the amount of power condensed into each of them. The third is Nightmare Eternity Vision, which gives an evil person a vision of Hell, followed by a vision of what could be.

Chapter 30

Love Knows No Limits

TALONFYRE had an idea of his own. "Well, one thing - hand me my old heart," he requested with a smirk. Ultimar did as he was told. At this TalonFyre transformed it into a pure white version of itself. He spoke in a kind voice, "This revives anything - give it to her if she needs it."

"It only works once, am I correct?" Ultimar asked in a serious voice.

TalonFyre nodded, "Yeah. It's got no trace of me anymore - it's the purest of pure."

Looking at the heart, Ultimar wavered. "With all my power, there is one thing I cannot do - revive the dead," he stated with a frown.

TalonFyre on the other hand, was smiling. "Well.... *there's* the ticket. You absorb it, you **get** that power. Hey, you did me a favor I do you one," he shrugged, taking a kind voice.

Ultimar looked at TalonFyre with a serious face. "That's why I give my power to others. And I... no, I don't want that power. Only *God* deserves it," the doctor continued with a tone as serious as his face.

TalonFyre sighed, "Aw, whatever, fine."

It was then that the ex-mercenary smirked, "Well, it can also... how do I put it..." he mumbled. He smiled, and whispered the second function in Ultimar's ear. "No clue why... either way it's yours. Besides the thing wouldn't work on me, I designed it for you," TalonFyre said, his smile growing wider, knowing the doctor would accept.

Tears welled up in the doctor's eyes. "You mean... Mian and I, despite being different species... can conceive?" Ultimar asked hopefully.

TalonFyre's smile grew wider still. "Yup - breaks all barriers," he answered in smug happiness.

At this, Ultimar dropped to his knees. "Thank you... Thank you *so* much!" he exclaimed, his eyes flowing with tears of joy.

TalonFyre's look turned a bit serious, though keeping a smile. "Well, don't tell her outright and keep that telepathy off buddy. Don't want to hear a thing," the ex-mercenary ordered. He gagged a bit after this. "Sorry, reflex," he apologized.

This caused Ultimar to smile, his eyes still tear-filled, "Trust me, I will," he chuckled.

TalonFyre looked at the doctor with a serious face, "Yeah, you leave it on and I'm done with kids. Sorry, not trying to sound awful. Love is what love is regardless of species I'm sure," he went on with a strange mix of coldness and empathy. "And if you decide to have children, it can sense that urge and act upon it. So, it's a gift as thanks," he finished.

Ultimar nodded. "Now if I die, my children can carry on my work, even stronger than me," the doctor stated confidently. This wasn't the only reason, however. Since he married he had always dreamed of having a child with his wife. Now it was finally coming true.

"Now, where the hell is Hikari?" TalonFyre asked as he looked around, having forgotten she was asleep in the bedroom.

As if on cue, Hikari spoke, "Talon, are you here?" she yawned.

Hearing this, TalonFyre walked off to the room she was in to find her getting up. "Yeah, I'm here - just... training," he half-lied. He put his paw on hers and kissed her. "Sleep well?" he asked as he drew his muzzle back. She smiled lovingly.

One thing TalonFyre hadn't realized is that his eyes were still rolled back. "Hey, anyone else not see anything? Oh crap, right!" he gasped in a semi-panic, rolling his eyes back to normal. He then spoke in a loving voice, "Ah, there's my reason for life, as beautiful as ever."

Ultimar walked in with a smile. "I have an idea in case you're always afraid to mate and still want to have a child," the doctor stated.

TalonFyre shook his head. "Nope. Well, not afraid - of you maybe, just not that soon - and you have "business" to attend to," he replied in a semi-rant.

Ultimar shrugged. "It's a medical procedure. If you ever want this procedure, you're welcome to it," the doctor offered, proceeding to whisper in his ear what it was.

"Uh..." TalonFyre was about to talk, but vomited instead. "**God no**!" he screamed, wiping his muzzle.

At this, Ultimar placed his hand behind his head in an embarrassed fashion. "Sorry... forget I mentioned it," the doctor apologized.

TalonFyre put his paw to his face. "I was feeling pretty hungry but now... Great, now I have an image in my brain," he growled, glaring at Ultimar.

"Again, sorry," the doctor apologized once more.

TalonFyre's eye twitched. "Yeah... that image, ugh - can't you get it out... it hurts to watch... being as you planted it," the ex-mercenary went on. "I'll just have to live with it. Well, you need to get busy anyway," he sighed, finishing the rant.

It pained Ultimar to do this to his friend, 'Please stop lying to yourself Talon. You want Hikari, she wants you. Just accept it and allow yourselves to become one. If not, I'll have to pressure you harder than I just did, and I don't want to do that,' he thought regrettably as he walked to the side of the bedroom.

Once Ultimar had reached a fair enough distance away from the bed, he was ready to show his true power, "If my child is to have any chance of being stronger and protecting this place... Warp Ultimation - Sigma!" he shouted. The doctor sprouted six wings, one set gold, one set silver, one set bronze. His eyes glowed pure heavenly white. He grew glowing, fur-like feathers, each changing colors every second like a prism. His hair turned prismatic as well. His hands became dragon claws and his feet talons once more, but this time they were gold. Finally, a feathered, birdlike dragon tail formed from his tailbone, completing the transformation. The only thing that remained the same is was his face and that he stayed the size of a human.

'Aw, can it, man.' the ex-mercenary thought.

TalonFyre walked up to his beloved. "...Hikari, you ok to travel?" he asked softly, his concern showing in his voice.

"Yeah, I am," the dragoness answered.

Hearing this, the ex-mercenary teleported home, bringing Hikari with him. "(Now, go get some,)" he communicated to Ultimar, teleporting him near his wife and cutting the telepathy off. Ultimar put up an impassable barrier, impairing all spectrums of vision. "Heh - yeah...he's gonna' have fun..." TalonFyre laughed.

The teleportation landed them at the hot spring, TalonFyre catching Hikari before she fell into the pool of boiling water, placing her on the ground.

"(No one, and I repeat *no one*, will see this or hear it,)" Ultimar stated assertively.

TalonFyre grinned. "Yeah, he's happy," he chuckled.

After this, the ex-mercenary then turned to his love. "Well, you feeling ok?" he asked.

Hikari nodded, but something else was on her mind. "What did you do for him?" she asked.

TalonFyre looked to the side uncomfortably. "Well... Let's just say something he hasn't done before is now possible. Love is love, not held by species. It can cross the world," he answered in a kind voice.

"I get it. I'm happy for what you did," Hikari said, smiling broadly.

"Which reminds me..." TalonFyre mumbled, unstrapping his only armor. "Yeah, let's keep this hidden awhile," he went on, smiling romantically. "Well... You ready?" he asked, turning a bit red, barely visible through his black scales. Hikari, however turned as red as a rose.

"I'm not in heat..." she whispered.

TalonFyre stepped back at this, placing his armor on once again. "Oh...well... How damn awkward. F.....no better not say that," he stuttered.

Hikari turned redder, to the shade of a ripe tomato. "It doesn't mean we can't, you know," she replied, whispering even more.

TalonFyre scratched his head. "Oh - Yeah, I'm still a bit unclear," he murmured, unstrapping it again. He looked at the armor. "Hell with this thing!" he yelled, tossing it in the spring. He looked at Hikari longingly, and decided. He *would* mate with her, here and now. They didn't need to fly in order to mate. He wanted her too much to bother with it. She saw this and lay upon on her back with her wings spread upon the ground, ready to for him to place himself on top of her. He obliged her.

Hikari's blush made it evident that she had never mated before. It was the first time for both of them. They were both nervous to be sure, but it didn't matter. The only thing that mattered to them is that they were both ready.

The reason Hikari had never mated before wasn't just the fact that she never found the right dragon before, but it was because she had heard from her mother how painful it was the first time. She only was willing to go through that kind of pain for someone who would be willing to be with her for life. That someone was TalonFyre.

TalonFyre, on the other hand, used to be disgusted by the very idea of mating. Now, with this dragoness, Hikari, it was the most wonderful feeling in the world. He never dreamed he'd *ever* mate, but now, here he was enjoying every moment. It was magical, and neither one of them wanted it to end.

The reason behind Ultimar's reluctance of this until now – he didn't really know. He had never really seen his wife without clothing. Now that he laid eyes upon her figure it became clear that any male of her species would have killed for her. She was beautiful. He knew that it was a mistake to wait until now. It was their first time, but they both wanted a child. It didn't matter how long it lasted. The wanted to become parents, and that's all that mattered.

The only thought on Mian's mind was to finally conceive by the man she loved. Still, she was surprised by what he looked like. His appearance was... amazing – perfect in every way. It dawned on her that he was genetically engineered, which was why he looked so... she didn't have words to describe him. Transfixed is the only word that could describe how she was feeling.

It was done. Hikari and TalonFyre were one for life. On the other hand, Ultimar and Mian – they were going to have a child after at least five long decades.

Chapter 31

The Third Adventure, Part 1

"MAN, what a night..." TalonFyre yawned. He got up, blinded by the sun. He smiled. "Hey, looking at my heart. Heh - Well....better stay here a bit," he sighed happily, sniffing himself. He hopped in the spring to get clean after the whole ordeal. 'That was just happiness incarnate,' he thought, a loving smile on his face.

Meanwhile, Flare and Angel were on their way up to the spring, and nearly there. "I wonder where TalonFyre and Hikari are. Ultimar said he'd train them, but I expected them to be back by the way he said it worked," Flare said worriedly.

His mate nuzzled him. "I'm sure they're both fine. Ultimar is not a cruel person, dear. He would never hurt them or make them train for years on end. They're just resting up somewhere, I'm *certain* of it. TalonFyre is a loving dragon, as well. He would never hurt her; if anything he would protect her with his *life*. You needn't be so concerned," Angel assured him in a kind tone.

Flare nodded, nuzzling Angel back as they walked up the mountain, unaware of what had just transpired with their daughter and the former mercenary.

Back at the spring TalonFyre decided to see if Ultimar wanted to talk. "(My telepathy is back on. Also, I wanted to play something for you through PK,)" the doctor said, unaware of what had happened between the two.

TalonFyre looked disturbed. "No, *don't* - I've done it already myself. Don't need to hear a replay!" he yelled, shaking his head in protest.

"(I wasn't going to play - WHAT THE HEL- ...*Seriously*?!)" Ultimar stuttered a bit, surprised by TalonFyre's actions.

"What...?" the ex-mercenary asked in a confused voice. He then realized why the doctor was in so much shock. "Well, the whole training thing... kinda' got me in the mood. Don't know how," he corrected himself in a happy tone. What he didn't tell Ultimar is what he saw after he had placed his new mate on the bed.

Back at the hospital, Ultimar was smiling brightly. "(Heh, I guess the song won't be necessary,)" the doctor chuckled.

"Nope," TalonFyre answered in matter-of-fact tone. The ex-mercenary's smile turned mischievous, as his tone became sly, "Well, I'll take it *you* enjoyed yourselves."

"(I'd say the same for you, judging by Hikari's expression,)" Ultimar answered in a smart voice.

TalonFyre nudged his mate. "Hikari, you up?"

The dragoness opened her eyes. "Yeah..." she moaned, a content smile on her face.

TalonFyre looked at her, "I didn't end up hurting you last night, did I?" he asked, concerned.

The dragoness shook her head no and replied with, "I told you not to worry. I knew it would be a bit painful for me at first. I'm glad you listened, no matter how scared you were for me," She nuzzled him after this and continued, "What about you? Did you like it?" Her voice was soft and affectionate, but had a slight sly tone to it. The thought 'I know you did' entered her mind at this time.

"W- Well..." TalonFyre stuttered, at a loss for words. Hikari blushed again due to being unable to hold up her façade. This time, TalonFyre did as well and visibly, "Uh, what – whatever, let's keep it quiet. Well, I will," he finished with a slight stutter.

Hikari looked away, still a bit embarrassed. "Uh... anyway, what do you want to do today?" she asked quickly.

TalonFyre looked her. He knew she wouldn't keep it a secret. "You tell them if you want," he sighed in defeat, grabbing his armor from the water.

Flare and Angel, however, had just arrived at the spring for a bath. "Tell us what?" Angel asked curiously.

TalonFyre put his armor back on and vanished, embarrassed beyond words. Hikari turned bright red. Not just her face, but all the way down to past her neck. Hikari's parents looked on in shock when they saw her.

"Oh dear..." Angel whispered, putting a paw up to her muzzle.

A sly smile crept up on Flare's face, "I *knew* the guy had it in him!" he exclaimed in a tone that could only be described as a father who was proud of his shy son for having intercourse on the first day of his honeymoon. In this case however, it was the son-in-law who had just become mated to the daughter of said father.

This was more serious however – The first mating between a draconic pair was the absolute equivalent to matrimony between two humans. The two were officially a mated pair for life in the eyes of the world they lived in.

TalonFyre appeared behind them. "I heard that! Well...it was..." he started to stutter again as he looked at Flare's smile.

Although Flare was about to say the word 'amazing' or some variation of it, but Angel decided to keep the two from making the moment any more awkward. "Alright, I know you're embarrassed so let's get off that topic," she said kindly.

TalonFyre was glad she had stopped Flare before he had made it any worse. "Yes, let's," the ex-mercenary quickly agreed, running after a nearby deer.

After a few seconds of chase, TalonFyre grabbed the deer, tossing it to Hikari. "Yours - mine is over here," he shrugged, taking a casual tone. He gave chase to another deer after this.

Hikari, once again, wanted to catch her own prey. She loved the way deer squealed when she shot them with light bullets and devoured them. However, after what TalonFyre was willing to do last night, she couldn't care less.

TalonFyre grabbed a deer, eating it alive, which made Hikari smirk. He did it once more, this time with more voraciousness. Once the ex-mercenary had finished, Hikari ate hers. She ate sloppier than before, wanting to "outdo" TalonFyre.

"Well, she has an appetite too!" the ex-mercenary laughed. Hikari let out a resounding belch again. "Forget I said that," TalonFyre gulped uncertainly.

The words caused Hikari to be uncertain as to if her beloved thought she was gravid or not. "Don't worry, I wasn't - y'know…" she assured him, blood on her mouth.

TalonFyre gave a shrug and a nod, "Yeah, just forget it."

"Well, what's today's plan?" TalonFyre asked casually as he approached his new parents. An image then flashed in his mind, causing him to smirk.

Even knowing what his son was thinking of, Flare decided to keep it to himself and answer the question. "Glad you asked. We've looked up somewhere called 'Heeka di wer Siksta' or 'Temple of the Sun' in modern terms. It came from an anonymous letter saying it's got something to give a boost to solar powers," Flare replied in an eager tone.

TalonFyre wondered if Ultimar had let word out about his new heart after hearing this.

"(I gave it to them. Trust me only you can hear this,)" Ultimar informed the ex-mercenary.

"(Well fine, as long as I don't go in. Been in a few too many caves recently,)" TalonFyre grumbled telepathically. He then realized the inappropriate irony of what he had just said. "(Oh, man - sorry,)" he apologized.

Ultimar was unfazed by the comment, and wanted to get his point across. "(Do you really think she'll be scared?)" the doctor asked rhetorically.

"(Well since I'm fighting for them no,)" TalonFyre answered with uncertainly.

The ex-mercenary decided to try to tease Ultimar. "(Anyway, you enjoy yourself or are you still busy?)" he asked in a telepathic snicker.

The doctor answered in a nonchalant tone, "(No, I'm not.)"

"(What, tired already? Hahaah, man I'm terrible!)" TalonFyre laughed.

"(I'm not Feodor Vassilyev. I don't want over 36 children!)" Ultimar retorted in an annoyed tone.

"Who the hell is Fedora Vissilyiv?" the ex-mercenary asked in a confused voice, not sure if he wanted to know.

Ultimar took a casual yet smart tone for the explanation, "(I'll put in simple terms - he was a Russian man who had the most kids with a single wife.)"

This was greeted by an uninterested "Oh," from TalonFyre.

Still a bit uncertain of what the reaction of Hikari's parents would be, TalonFyre reluctantly agreed, "(Well, anyway I'll play along, but I go in there - I… well, they'll see it,)" sighing through the telepathy.

Ultimar was certain of what would happen though. "(Flare and Angel see you as their son, and love you as such. I checked their minds,)" the doctor assured him. TalonFyre cut off the telepathy, ready to find the temple and reveal his true form to the three.

Chapter 32

The Third Adventure, Part 2

"WELL, let's go guys. Where is it, I can't sense it for some reason. Minds a bit foggy - didn't sleep much... And, I *keep* bringing it up," TalonFyre sighed in self-annoyance, putting his paw to his face at the last five words.

Flare chuckled at this. "It's a while away from here, twenty miles south," Flare replied, still laughing a bit.

TalonFyre was still a bit embarrassed about mating with Hikari, but decided if Flare and Angel were actually happy about it, he was fine. "Well, anyway, let's go. Flare, you lead - I'll stick by Hikari," he stated, looking at his beloved. Flare took to the sky with Angel and TalonFyre with Hikari - after kissing her of course.

They soared through the clouds, each pair of mates side by side. TalonFyre thought about Flare and Angel's cave. "I don't know - that place is.... not hot enough," he mumbled. He then glanced at Hikari and smiled. "Well, she is one place I can always be hot," he whispered under his breath in a humorous and sly fashion.

"Hmmm? Did you say something Talon?" Hikari asked curiously, looking at him.

TalonFyre looked away. "Nothing," he yawned. How could Hikari have noticed he was talking about her? Whatever the case, she would have found it funny, if anything else.

Hikari smiled lovingly at him. "You know, by draconic law, we're one for life now," she pointed out, her voice as loving as her smile.

TalonFyre made the same face. "Well, why would I go anywhere else when I have my world right next to me?" he asked, knowing what his beloved would say.

Hikari's smile grew. "You wouldn't," she replied.

He chucked, "Nope," at this.

Having seen such an answer coming, TalonFyre was relieved. She trusted him fully, and that was assurance that was needed. They flew for about ten minutes, and eventually came to a stop, landing by a glowing temple.

The moment had come, but TalonFyre was having second thoughts about showing the three. "Uh, I'll stay outside... Try and catch up on some rest," he lied nervously. He walked into a nearby cave, lying down and closing the entrance behind him.

Ultimar was tired of TalonFyre being so distrustful of the three, especially Hikari, who he had *mated* with just last night. He didn't want to be forceful - it wasn't his way in the first place. "(It's going to be alright... they won't be afraid,)" he communicated in a kind and reassuring voice.

"Sorry, just remembered I slept," TalonFyre mumbled, lying once more as he held his head low. Hikari looked at him uncertainly. She could already tell there was something making him upset. "Anyway, I think I'll lead," the ex-mercenary said in a disheartened tone, his body already glowing a shade of gold. He walked up to the door, opening it without a word. "Come on then," he sighed in anxiety.

At this point Hikari's worry had increased drastically, but she didn't know what was wrong with her mate. 'Talon, please let me help you,' she thought as she and her family followed him through the yellow-plated square tiles and copper-colored pillars that made up the temple.

The ex-mercenary walked up to an altar. To his surprise, it was shaped like him. He fell silent, staring at the statue. 'He looks so handsome, glowing like that,' Hikari thought.

"Go if you want. The sun, well... the sun *is* my heart," TalonFyre admitted sadly, opening his heartless chest. Hikari's mouth hung open, and his own hung down in shame. 'She'll never speak to me again,' he thought, a tear about to form in his eye.

Hikari's mouth closed as she shook, causing TalonFyre to panic more, but then she said something he didn't expect. "That's so… **Awesome**!" she screamed happily.

This reaction was the exact opposite of what TalonFyre expected. He thought Hikari was shaking out of fear, but she was actually trembling in excitement. "Yeah, it is," he sighed happily. He had an idea of how he could make Hikari even happier. "(Mind showing them the training Romeo?)" he asked Ultimar.

"(I would be glad to, Talon,)" Ultimar replied, beginning to show them the vision.

The training played in the family's minds. "This may freak you guys out," TalonFyre warned as it got to the part where he transformed.

"**AMAZING!**" Hikari screamed in excitement as she saw the transformation.

"Well, not Hikari anyway. Can't scare her – impossible," TalonFyre laughed.

When the vision had finished, Angel and Flare were speechless. "Basically, I am the sun. And, sorry for this but - Hikari you make me *hot*. Yeah, cheesy," TalonFyre chuckled.

Flare looked at his new son-in-law with amazement. "Your power is *stronger* than Ultimar's in his first transformation!?" he asked in a surprised tone.

TalonFyre nodded. "Well, guess so," the ex-mercenary replied, a bit uncertain of what he meant.

Angel, although a bit shocked about the whole scenario, was impressed nonetheless. "You… you now have our utmost confidence TalonFyre," she said, a bit shaken.

TalonFyre was glad they weren't afraid, and was now proud of his form. "All that play before, with the attacking him - child's play, like a drop on a rock. Or should I say planet," he laughed.

Hikari smiled, looking at him with amazement. "Ultimar may be stronger, but he had to transform *three times* to match you!" she exclaimed.

TalonFyre was even prouder hearing that from his mate. "Yup - I passed out though. But you guys… you're what I was fighting for," he said with a loving smile.

"(It will become easier. Don't go too far until it does,)" Ultimar warned, once again through telepathy.

"(Too far? Oh, too much at once you mean,)" TalonFyre replied, realizing what the doctor meant.

"(I can show you how to control that power,)" Ultimar offered in a kind voice.

TalonFyre knew that he would need help, and Ultimar was the only person that could offer it. He gave an understanding response, "(Later maybe.)"

Ultimar knew he meant it. "(Indeed. You have all the time in the sun anyway. Mind the cruddy pun,)" the doctor laughed.

TalonFyre smiled. "(Yeah, I've been doing the same puns all morning - well, innuendo, so we're even,)" the ex-mercenary replied, laughing as well. This caused Hikari to begin to giggle in turn.

The ex-mercenary had some information to relay while he was at it. "(Oh, also, every time that heart I gave you is used; it recharges a year later. Sun power,)" he explained.

This caused the doctor to give him a reproductive fact of his wife's species in a nonchalant voice, "(That's great, but Nagasapiens have a 2-year gestation, so that's something we'll have to wait on.)" TalonFyre was surprised by this, but figured it would be best to make sure Mian wouldn't get pregnant too quickly.

"(Ah fine, I'll adjust it,)" he mumbled as the heart made a humming noise. "(There - go nuts. ...Forget I said that,)" TalonFyre groaned, now embarrassed at his own words. Ultimar merely gave a chuckle. Hikari however, was on the floor in a fit of laughter, her parents looking at her like she was insane.

"(Well, she's snooping in on the conversation again. Hikari, you *know* I could tell before I started taking,)" TalonFyre said in a tone of false annoyance as he gazed at his love. It was painfully obvious that she was listening due the fact that she was on the floor, crippled by her own laughter.

"Well, miss nosy, let's get going - oh hang on," TalonFyre said, about to leave when he realized he forgot something. Flare and Angel realized why Hikari was laughing when he said this.

"(Also, here's some trivia - Nagasapiens, unlike Nagas, don't lay eggs, that's all I'll say,)" Mian informed them, cutting in.

TalonFyre was disturbed at this. "(*Ok* thank you,)" he replied sarcastically, cutting off the telepathy.

Raising his closed paw, TalonFyre smashed the altar, causing a door to open. "Secret button. Yeah, I'm full of surprises," he said with a grin. He turned to Hikari, who was smiling as well. "Where do you think I trained? It's a training room, an archive and basically an armory. Plus accommodations, enough for all of us," he finished.

"This is our home now, huh?" Hikari asked in a mixture of curiosity and happiness.

TalonFyre nodded. "Yup, beats that old cave – sorry," he apologized, hoping he hadn't offended Flare and Angel.

"It's fine. I'd say it's an improvement," Flare corrected him in a matter-of-fact tone, smiling.

A press of a button opened another door revealing a white and yellow room. "This is a room for the light dragons. Everything you need - training, archives, rooms," the ex-mercenary said happily. Flare and Angel nuzzled each other at this, certain about what TalonFyre would say next. "You guys have your room, Hikari and I have ours," the ex-Mercenary continued with a smile. He looked at Hikari uncertainly. "Of course.... if she wants to opt out…" he went on, looking down.

Hikari approached him and put her paw on his, "This is our happily ever after, Talon. Of course I won't opt out," she assured him lovingly.

TalonFyre looked at his mate sadly. "Well, you guys check out whatever you want. I'm gonna' head off - no clue where," he sighed, looking more distraught.

Hikari looked at him concernedly. "I'll come with!" she exclaimed, looking him in the eyes intently.

TalonFyre's head drooped. "Ok, I expected that," he sighed. He saw Hikari's expression. It was one of sheer sadness. He knew he couldn't hide it. "There's - well - someone I have to deal with," the ex-mercenary continued, even more distraught than before.

TalonFyre's past had caught up with him, and now his family was in danger. However, with his new power, he could defend them. Ultimar had helped him reach his potential, and now he would use it.

Chapter 33

A Threat Arises

"WHO could that be?" Hikari asked seriously.

TalonFyre looked at her sad eyes. "Well... he's one of my mortal enemies, and... he's... after you guys so... well, I got a call from my ex home and... he's looking for me. He's the one who designed the heart of the Thantaos Golem to be my mother, and he doesn't know me. I managed to hide this long and I'm *done*," he finished, growling at the last few words as his eyes narrowed.

A wormhole opened next to TalonFyre, Ultimar walking out in his Sigma form, in which he was his strongest. "I won't let you do this alone," the doctor said in a somewhat sad voice, a bit uncertain of his own resolve.

"Yeah, I figured," the ex-mercenary sighed.

TalonFyre looked at the doctor, who had a look of sadness on his face. "Well, the thing that worries me most – he... he eats dragon eggs. Anything not pure he eats when it's an egg," he said distastefully.

Ultimar couldn't believe this, and couldn't hold back the anger. "**OH, HELL NO**!!" the doctor screamed, his resolve strengthening.

"Yeah, calm down fancy pants. He has a bead on everyone but me. He has an army around the size of Rayburn's, maybe smaller. I knew that bunker was a mistake making," TalonFyre sighed at the last words again, a look of regret on his face.

The doctor was thinking about the idea of eggs being devoured, and it sickened him to the core. He became embittered and his old self was awakening. "I'll wipe them out with **one** blast. *Screw* pacifism!" he screamed in rage.

Hikari was stunned at Ultimar's face - it was cold, spiteful, cruel, wrathful, and clearly full of murderous intent. It was one she didn't ever think the kind-hearted, loving doctor could ever wear.

At this, TalonFyre handed the doctor a small, round, glowing object, "Yeah, about that..." he began, his eyes fixated on the doctor's hate-filled expression.

Ultimar looked at it, his eyes widening. "What's this?" he asked, his face and voice now filled with worry. He knew this technology.

TalonFyre shook his head in sadness. "It's a tracker. It was in my bunker when it was made," he replied, already sure that the doctor knew.

"His?" Ultimar questioned in denial.

The ex-mercenary nodded, "Yeah, but he can't get a bead on my life source. Ha, it doesn't work in space," he laughed cruelly.

Even after this, the doctor knew that TalonFyre was leaving something out, and he was certain of what it was. "Anyway, if you guys go charging in, well he... he has a room of dragonesses - dozens of them apparently, and you wonder where the eggs are from. He sees you guys... everything in there is dead in a second. That's why the dustbowl never had kids running around. My plan is to go "merc" again, join his army and sneak in, and well I - I have to disable his tie to the dragonesses first. Meaning - I have to "fix" him with no notice," TalonFyre finished his story with a grimace.

"Hmm... what if I made ten thousand of me?" Ultimar asked, wanting to try out one of his powers he copied.

TalonFyre shook his head, "No, he knows your signature, one of them shows up, everything dies," he sighed, tearing up slightly.

"What about my doctors?" Ultimar asked, only half-hoping what the answer would be.

TalonFyre began to cry. "Same deal. He has a bead on everyone," he sobbed.

The doctor fell silent, only to say one word, "Shit!"

After this, TalonFyre's sobbing became a smirk. "He targets the heart - heh, I don't have one on me," he pointed out smugly. His expression then quickly darkened. "And, unless you know... I don't know how, he has Mian. You go running in, she goes down too," he added, a look of worry on his face.

At this point, it hit Ultimar like a bolt of lightning darker than the shade of purest black, as his eyes narrowed in a mixture of rage, bitter sorrow and regret. "I can only think of one way he could do that - SBAAARRRRRRE!!!!!" he screamed, the fierce reverberations of voice rocking the temple at its very foundation. TalonFyre smacked him at this, knowing if he kept going it would bring the building down.

Who was Sbarre? TalonFyre had never heard that name before. Was he someone the doctor knew beforehand? Was it someone that he could have hurt? Then it struck him. He remembered that name – the doctor's nemesis. The demon of the multiverse. The very opposite of what the Ultimar had become – a being like the devil incarnate – a monster through and through.

"Calm the hell down, I know what to do!" the ex-mercenary yelled. Ultimar was panting in fear and anxiety after he did this.

"I've seen the solar eclipses around here. If I go when it's dark I can go powerless - meaning as long as it stays eclipsed he can't tell who I am. But, I'll have my normal heart back, meaning when it ends he knows... but I'll be done by then," the ex-mercenary said, sounding extensively cruel at the last words.

TalonFyre turned to his new family, "Oh, before I forget... Hikari, Flare, Angel - you guys stay put. He won't kill the dragonesses if he sees you but he will kill you," he said worriedly.

Hikari looked down. "I couldn't do anything anyway," she sighed.

It was true; she couldn't do anything – not now at least. However, TalonFyre had a remedy for this, handing her an orb of light, a sly smile on his face, speaking in a tone that matched, "This is actually able to make your powers ten times the strength... but unstable as hell," looking at his love seriously as he said the last words. "Hang on....." he mumbled, motioning for Ultimar to follow him outside alone.

"How long will the instability last?" Hikari asked intently as the two walked out the door.

TalonFyre turned his head back and answered, "A few hours. The orb's powers only last a few hours too," as he walked outside with Ultimar.

TalonFyre knew he had the power to face this threat, but the question was – would he get everyone out in time? Mian was someone he knew could handle herself as long as that monster didn't power up, but the dragonesses were defenseless. That was what he worried about.

Chapter 34

Readying for Combat

ULTIMAR followed TalonFyre outside to see what he had to show him. "Well Ultimar, you know when I got a taste of that Kai, that ultra-ma-whatever-you-did?" the ex-mercenary asked.

"The words are Ki and Ultima-Blast," the doctor corrected him, rolling his eyes.

TalonFyre just grinned. "Well, I know it too," he said smugly.

Flying two miles up in the air, TalonFyre readied himself. "You *might* want to stay back," he suggested, keeping his smug tone as his eyes started to glow a shade of bright red.

"Solar Ultima-Blast, right?" the doctor asked curiously.

TalonFyre replied with a muffled, "Yeah....improved," as his jaw unhinged.

A small ball of energy appeared in TalonFyre's mouth, pulsing black. "Might want to go inside for this one," the ex-mercenary laughed.

Ultimar just rolled his eyes. "**Shoot da' woop**!" the doctor yelled, knowing his draconic friend would need to have it explained.

"The what?" TalonFyre asked, puzzled.

Ultimar smirked, "Just an old earth meme."

TalonFyre looked uninterested. The doctor thought that would be for the best, since the most possible and well-known origin of the joke was very offensive to him in the first place, as a person that ran an inter-dimensional hospital. A lot of his employees felt he same way, save a very select few. 'I've been hanging around that dragon too much for my own good,' he thought.

The ball tripled in size, growing bigger with each second up to six times the original. "Ok, this is gonna' be *cool*. Hikari will like it as usual, little miss violent," TalonFyre chuckled. He then roared, the power of the sound-waves shaking the walls. He yelled out a powerful tone, "Ini wer vers di wer siksta vur wer regipreic tiichia acht ve, si drevab malsvir mojka ekess uoinota coinah!" as the orb of energy began to glow a deep gold.

"Cover your ears guys, this is gonna' be **loud**!" the ex-mercenary warned. Ultimar created barriers around everyone's ears as the ball was fired at a mountain making a five-mile-wide hole. "New pool, I guess. Oh man, that was *fun*!" TalonFyre laughed as he landed.

"Awesome as hell!!" Hikari exclaimed happily, her eyes lighting up.

TalonFyre smiled at this. 'I knew she'd love it. She's a real prize. Maybe when this is all over we can finally have a...' his train of thought was cut off as he saw the sun begin to black out.

"It's time to go and meet the egg eater," the ex-mercenary growled. He stopped glowing, turning jet black, "Oh man, what a hangover feeling. I can't use the same portal or a wormhole, he has them all marked," he sighed.

Ultimar was pondering upon a thought – one that worried him. "I don't know how Sbarre intervened without breaking the pact, but I need to be more careful from now on," he grumbled, clearly worried about his wife.

TalonFyre knew what he had to do at this point. "I'll get Milan out first. I can sneak her out quick - my bunker is still standing. It's clean now too - no *way* they can find her. I'll take her there, give "him" the snip snip - then you guys get in there and rip **everything** you see apart!" he finished with a menacing one.

Reaching into his armor, Ultimar pulled out a vial and handed it to TalonFyre, "A paralyzing poison made of concentrated draconic blowfish venom. Take it, it leaves the pain receptors fully intact and causes paralysis," the doctor offered.

TalonFyre drank it, letting out a burp. "Tastes like ass and sweat!" he snapped.

This caused Ultimar to put his hand on his face again. "That was for the egg eater, Talon," The doctor sighed, surprised it didn't cause the volcanic dragon to fall over in palsy and die.

TalonFyre gave an embarrassed grin, "Oh… oops."

Ultimar then handed him another, sure that he wouldn't make the same mistake twice. TalonFyre shoved it away. "My mom taught me all I know; and that lab I said to go to? Crates of it," he declined nonchalantly.

It was blatantly and painfully obvious to Ultimar that TalonFyre was lying through his teeth, and it showed in the dragon's expression, as well as his eyes. The latter was a telltale sign for the doctor, who was very good at reading people.

Having no desire to bring up his friend's sad past, Ultimar decided to merely inform him of the effect, "Nothing like this. It causes ten thousand years' worth of paralysis in a normal dragon. I've been saving it since…" he cut off, not wanting to remember what he used to do. TalonFyre took it, knowing full well that the doctor was having regrets.

He didn't know too much about the past in Ultimar's case, but the ex-mercenary knew one thing – neither of them was proud of it or what they did in it.

"Anyway, when I tell you guys, go through a wormhole into the bunker. Wait till I finish getting Milan out then *let loose!*" the ex-mercenary instructed.

After remembering his past, Ultimar was having second thoughts. "Okay… and it's Mian," he sighed. TalonFyre couldn't see the doctor's pained expression, but his voice made him quite wary of his resolve.

"Oh, my mistake. Wish me luck. Oh, and take any armor or weapons you need," TalonFyre finished with a grin.

Ultimar sighed, "No problem. Good luck, my friend," as TalonFyre disappeared through an unmarked portal.

Ultimar turned to Hikari after the entire ordeal and looked at her intently and began to speak in an adamant tone, "Hikari – I want you to listen. Ki is not something to be used like a normal weapon, nor is your psychokinesis. I understand you're a psychic dragon and this is an inherent power for you, therefore can be used without consequence. However, Ki is called 'life energy' for a reason – in truth, you can even die if you use too much of it. There is scientific reasoning behind what you did, but I fell explaining it in spiritual terms would be best for now. All I can say is it can cause your body to shut down if you use too much. In closing, only use Ki if you are completely and utterly out of options." With a nod from Hikari, Ultimar finished his speech.

    TalonFyre was unsure if the doctor could go through with it. The look on his face before was so determined, but his look now worried him. Ultimar was back to his pacifistic self, which wasn't good for the scenario at hand. Still, the ex-mercenary knew one thing, and that was that he needed to kill his enemy.

A/N

1. The incantation used by TalonFyre is, "By the power of the sun and the gifts blessed upon me, I blast evil away to hell itself."

2. I have revised the book series to approach Ki from a quasi-scientific viewpoint, as opposed to most genres that see it as a spiritual ability. In this series, Ki attacks will be described as positive, negative and neutral plasmas, the fourth type of matter. I feel this would both be an interesting new frontier to explore and add to the sci-fi aspect of the Chronicles.

Chapter 35

The Rescue, Part 1

TALONFYRE stepped through the portal, flying over the dusted landscape. 'Can't say I miss this place anymore,' he thought as he landed in the camp. "Well...here goes, I guess," he sighed. "(And yes, you guys can listen in if you feel like it. He's not telepathic,)" the ex-mercenary communicated.

He looked around until he saw his nemesis, Hrothgar. The dragon had orange-red scales and a dark red underbelly. His upper spine was covered in odd, needle-like spikes like that of a hedgehog. His tail had a spear-like tip to it, whereas most dragons have a lizard-like tail without any appendages on it. His eyes were dark red and he had two crescent horns on each side of his head. He also had an additional two straight horns in the middle his snout.

After composing himself for his trickery, TalonFyre walked up to the monstrous fiery dragon, hiding the distaste in his eyes. "What do you want you fool, I'm busy?" Hrothgar boomed.

TalonFyre bowed, "I'm here to offer my services your lordship," he lied in a respectful tone.

Hrothgar was none too bright, so the ruse worked. "Very well, watch over the eggs," he ordered, pointing TalonFyre in the direction of the caves.

TalonFyre bowed again saying, "Yes sir!" walking in the direction pointed. 'Yeah, not happening' he thought cruelly as he entered. "(Just an idiot,)" the ex-mercenary laughed through telepathy.

The cavern was filled with a sickening odor. He sent Ultimar a whiff, just to show him what Hrothgar was doing. "(The *heck*!)" the doctor growled.

"(Yeah, rotten eggs mixed with dead flesh,)" the ex-mercenary replied in distaste.

Upon walking into the cave the doctor's wife was visible, chained by her upper tail and arms, eyes filled with fear.

"Son of a *bitch*, there's Mian," the ex-mercenary growled softly, proceeding to walk up to her. Her eyes widened in hope at this. "Shh... he *doesn't* know me," the ex-mercenary whispered. Mian nodded and remained silent.

Getting close to Mian's earlobe TalonFyre whispered, "I have a plan." However, he was cut off when he saw his so-called "boss" rounding the corner. "Oh shit, here he comes!" he growled as he walked behind to the cave tunnel.

Hrothgar walked up to the young alien woman and put his paw to her chin, "Well my special snack - you shall soon be mine..." he said in a sweet, sickening tone, laughing afterwards.

"(*Don't* go crazy!)" TalonFyre warned the doctor.

"(I'm meditating to make sure that doesn't happen,)" Ultimar replied calmly.

"Anything I can help with? Eggs look fine," TalonFyre asked, walking up to the monstrous orangish-red dragon.

Hrothgar nodded, "Yes, follow me - I need to prepare."

TalonFyre followed Hrothgar into a dark, dank cave. "You see.....I can't stand these **impure atrocities** walking among us and they need to be erased. That "thing" over there... well, she is the *very* embodiment," Hrothgar growled, lying down. "Now, I need you to guard me while I sleep before the big meal," he instructed.

TalonFyre nodded. "Yes sir, I won't move," he replied, while thinking, 'Yeah, I will and so will Mian.'

After the conversation, Hrothgar lay down and began to snore. "(Ok, phase one…)" TalonFyre began communicating as he pulled out a tiny, needle-thin blade. "(Thanks to your image Ultimar, I know where to cut. He won't notice until it's too late,)" he continued with a cruel voice.

Carving into Hrothgar's side, TalonFyre began to cringe. "(GAH, *man* this is... *Uugh*,)" he telepathically groaned as he reached the needed area and cut Hrothgar's unmentionables out. "(There done. He has no connection to them now,)" the ex-mercenary sighed, pulling the knife back.

"(Good,)" Ultimar communicated back.

The draconic puffer venom was then poured into Hrothgar's snout. "Heh, idiot," TalonFyre laughed.

"WHAT - WHAT HAVE YOU **DONE**!?" Hrothgar boomed.

The ex-mercenary looked at him with a cruel smile and narrowed eyes and growled, "I've given you the works, you old piece of trash," still wearing the same face.

A glow started to radiate from TalonFyre once more as the eclipse faded. "Yeah, I'm the one that got away," he said hatefully.

Hrothgar began to get up, "BUT, HOW..?" he asked, starting to sweat.

"(He should feel it right…)" TalonFyre said, purposefully cutting off when Hrothgar let out a scream of pain and fell over.

The plan was now in motion. TalonFyre ran over the Ultimar's snake-like wife and broke her bonds. "Ok Mian, let's get going - looks like the bunker is safe now," he said hurriedly.

TalonFyre knew he had to kill Hrothgar, but he had another mission. "Yeah, he needs to be finished off for *good,*" he said with a cruel tone. He turned away and teleported to his bunker with Mian.

Chapter 36

The Rescue, Part 2

THE bunker was in disrepair, but as far as a safe house it was the best that the ex-mercenary had. "(Now guys, she's safe – Ultimar, she's waiting,)" TalonFyre said proudly as he lit the room.

TalonFyre heard his enemy approach. "Well... now it begins," he growled, clenching a paw. In futility, Hrothgar attempted to open the door. "He can't get in," TalonFyre laughed. Hrothgar then attempted to slam it, screaming in agony as the barrier took effect. TalonFyre smirked, "Hey, call me a sadist but that's music to my ears!"

"(You guys ready or not?)" TalonFyre asked impatiently.

"(Yes, I am,)" Ultimar replied.

The ex-mercenary opened up a door, "Mian, go to the adjoining room, it's spell protected," he instructed. The serpentine woman did as she was told, heading through the doorway.

Grabbing a sun-bright sword and a weight device, the ex-mercenary began to head for the door. However, he stopped when he remembered a critical part of the plan. He turned to the snake-like woman. "Oh, and Mian - you have to free the dragonesses. You can "slip in" unnoticed," he said with a grin. He then realized he may have made a racist joke about the serpentine woman's species, and if she *was* pregnant that would be one of the worst things he could do. "Ok, sorry," he apologized. Mian didn't seem to take offense however.

"How can I get in unnoticed?" Mian asked curiously.

TalonFyre handed her a simple crystal. "The alarm system is able to detect pure breed dragons - mainly him. Hold this up to it and it shuts it down. Then you get the dragonesses and any live eggs out," he instructed.

Mian was confused. "I'm not a dragon... not even half. I'm an alien!" she protested.

TalonFyre grinned again. "That's why it *doesn't* detect you. Why do you think he wanted to eat you?" he asked.

Mian thought for a minute, then came to the only logical conclusion. "He thought I was part dragon..." she whispered. TalonFyre nodded at this.

Once Hrothgar had departed back to his cavern, the plan was in action. TalonFyre teleported them to the entrance, with the guards none the wiser.

"When you're ready Ultimar can warp you, the dragonesses, and the eggs to my place. I have enough rooms for an army. Plus a hatchery and nursery," the ex-mercenary said happily. "It came that way...maybe. Anyway, when they get here... you go and I'll take of Mr. "egg-breath". He can in fact... get to *my* Combat Level," he continued. He grinned fearlessly, "But I have a bit of help from the family and you two, so I should be fine," he finished.

They began to hear screaming. They knew what that meant - the plan was falling apart. "Oh crap, he got to them!" TalonFyre yelled. They rushed into the room. "No time to waste Mian, save the rest…..that one is….gone," he sighed, his voice filled with regret.

(What do we do?") Ultimar asked, unnerved by the casualty.

"(Wait till he unleashes the horde, then cut loose,)" the ex-mercenary replied.

Mian and TalonFyre walked into the room to see Hrothgar eating a dragoness and her unhatched egg. "No more… It ends *now*," TalonFyre growled, his voice filled with as much rage as his eyes.

"You guys ready? I don't see you," TalonFyre asked, worrying Ultimar had lost all resolve.

The ex-mercenary then remembered his backup plan. "Oh Ultimar, that orb - balance it for me so she's safe using it. It's unlocked now," he half ordered, half instructed the doctor. Ultimar concentrated on the orb, focusing it with his chakra.

TalonFyre powered up, this time with pure rage. "**HROTHGAR, YOU DIE TONIGHT YOU UNHOLY BEAST!**" he screamed at the top of his lungs.

Hrothgar, however, was unfazed. The monstrous fire dragon looked at him with a smirk, "So where's your mate then? She must taste divine," he sneered.

TalonFyre grabbed Hrothgar's neck with his forepaws as soon as he said this. "You even lay a *claw* on her and you are **beyond** hell - ninth circle my friend!!!" the ex-mercenary screamed, this time louder than before.

While Hrothgar was distracted, Mian was busy cutting the chain of the dragonesses with her claws. She didn't want to stress herself by moving at her top speed. She *was* pregnant after all. It was true, her Combat Level was ten billion thanks to her husband, but she didn't want to miscarry. After about two minutes, she had them released, and used her teleportation to escape with them.

Chapter 37

A Battle With A Monster, part 1

A snapping of Hrothgar's claws signaled the release of the army. A large pack of dragons, wolves, and other beasts came into the cave from all sides, while he ran through them towards the exit.

"Guys, GO – *NOW*!" TalonFyre yelled, this time in a fully ordering tone.

"(My time?)" Ultimar asked uncertainly.

"Yeah, go nuts but leave some for the others," the ex-mercenary replied. Ultimar appeared bringing Hikari, Flare, and Angel, all glowing with power.

Thinking he had escaped through his horde, Hrothgar put his paw up to his ear, waiting to hear TalonFyre scream, only to have the ex-mercenary appear in front of him instead with a glare as cold as ice.

The turn of events confused Hrothgar, but he was about to find out the reason behind it. "Yeah....you should've checked my mother beforehand," TalonFyre spat as he began to glow.

Hrothgar realized what this meant, "So *you're* the one that escaped death....well no longer," he growled as he took to the sky, TalonFyre giving chase.

Back at Hrothgar's hideout, TalonFyre's new family was facing the army with little difficulty. Hikari picked up fifty dragons, crushing them with telekinesis in seconds. Flare created a twenty-foot photon tail-blade and spun through the wolves, cutting them down like they were nothing, coating the room in a crimson tide. Angel however, was reluctant to fight. In her hesitation, she was picked up and carried to the corner of the room by an ogre-like lizard-man, who stuck a needle in her neck covered in a paralyzing venom. Hikari and Flare were too busy fighting to notice this, so Angel was on her own.

Looking at Angel, the lizard-man smiled, "Well, look what I found... don't worry, I won't kill you. We're going to have *fun*, you and I," he said in a sadistic tone.

Angel was horrified at the thought of what he meant. The lizard-man stuck out his tongue, his eyes glinting. "Eeny-meeny-miny-moe, I wonder where my tongue will go?" he laughed.

At this point Angel was in complete panic, "Please, don't..." she whimpered. The lizard man only sneered as his head lowered. Angel looked up to avoid seeing him.

Angel felt something hit her chest, but it wasn't a tongue. It was a sticky fluid, and there was a lot of it. She looked down and saw the lizard-man in shock, his tongue gone. The lizard-man was too fixated on Angel to realize Ultimar had just hit his tongue with a series of half-millimeter-thick bo-shuriken with a minuscule amount of gunpowder in their tips, and had paid for it dearly.

He dropped Angel and fell over, convulsing from blood-loss. Ultimar then threw a syringe in his neck filled with sedatives, knocking him out. It was followed up with a flat 3-inch-wide kunai covered in a strange substance with a burning 1x20-inch silk cloth tied to the end, which was aimed at the base of the lizard-man's now-gone tongue. The goo lit ablaze upon the full incineration of the cloth, searing the wound shut. Angel had never seen things like this, but was glad the doctor had them.

The doctor walked up to Angel, his expression serious, "You *know* what he would have done if I hadn't have blown his tongue off," he said to the dragoness, his tone in a strange mix of empathy and cruelty.

He then inserted a needle into her neck, neutralizing the poison. After this, Angel rose to her feet and nodded, a tear forming in her eye.

The army had been decimated completely by this time due to Hikari and her father. Flare had a gash on his left side and some large bruises on his back, forelegs, and tail. His tail was also drenched in blood. Hikari, however only had a few minute cuts distributed across her body and small bruises on her forepaws, the latter from slashing her photon claws against armor. Unlike her father, she had blood spattered on her from head to tail.

The two saw Angel weeping in the corner and ran up to her, wondering why she was in tears. "What happened, mom?" Hikari asked in concern, putting her paw on Angel's neck.

Angel cried even more at this, "That lizard-man… he - he tried to…" she stopped short.

Hikari and Flare were able figure out the rest by the lizard-man's missing tongue and Ultimar's expression. "Take care of her, I have to give Talon some help - *and* Hrothgar some payback," the doctor said, growling the last three words.

In the sky, two figures were visible. One belonged to TalonFyre, the other to Hrothgar, the latter transforming into a monstrosity. Instead of his scales being orange-red, they were dark red. Instead of a crescent, his horns were goat-like, resembling Rayburn's. His legs and paws turned into buzzard-like feet and legs. His eyes were pitch-black, almost like sockets. The end of his tail became like a pitchfork, as black as his eyes. Finally, his muzzle no longer resembled a dragon's but that of a snapping turtle with jagged edges on its beak.

This didn't surprise TalonFyre; he knew full well that Hrothgar could do this. "Well, not bad old man," he mused.

This infuriated Hrothgar, "I AM THE PUREST OF THEM ALL - YOU SHALL DIE!" he boomed. TalonFyre just smirked, matching his level easily.

Ultimar appeared before them, ready to fight if needed. He was still uncertain if he wanted to kill Hrothgar, but he kept thinking about the monstrous dragon's deeds. He got angrier and angrier until he was ready to tear him apart. However, like in every battle, something held him back, the one thought that always crossed his mind in combat - 'Mian would be heartbroken if she found out I killed again.' This was all it took to keep him in check. He loved his wife, and would do anything for her.

Pointing to the bright spot in the sky, TalonFyre's smirk became even wider, "You see, you "fool" - the sun there..." he cut off, waiting for Hrothgar's unwitting response.

"What of it, it's just a star!" the monstrous dragon scoffed.

The ex-mercenary looked him in the eyes. "No... It's my heart," he said cruelly.

Hrothgar was speechless at first, but managed to get out three words, "But, that's... impossible."

Chapter 38

A Battle With A Monster, part 2

TALONFYRE grabbed Hrothgar by the wings and flipped him in the air, tearing them off. "It happened because of something *you* cannot know," Ultimar said, his loathing evident in his voice. Hrothgar glared at him.

"You think it would be that simple.....fool?" the monstrous dragon scoffed, somehow still flying.

The doctor looked at him with a look of contempt. "You don't deserve to be named after a benevolent ruler. Come at me. If you think you can cause me any harm, then perhaps you haven't realized why I am named after the word... **ULTIMATE**!!!" he screamed.

The very idea that there was someone stronger than him filled Hrothgar with rage. He doubled his power output, growing to twice his current size.

"Ok, now see what you did!? Great, last time I did this I passed out but, oh well..." TalonFyre sighed in an annoyed tone, once again turning into his solar form and matching Hrothgar in size.

Thinking about dragonesses being violated and eggs being devoured, as well as his wife suffering the same fate as the eggs, Ultimar began to seethe with anger once more. This time, however, he couldn't keep it inside. He fired 10-Kilometer-wide blast at Hrothgar in pure rage. The blast, however, didn't connect, as it was blocked and thrown to the side by TalonFyre.

"Butt out! He's mine!" he growled, looking doctor in the eyes.

Ultimar sighed in relief at this. 'It's a good thing that blast was low-powered and dispersed,' the doctor thought.

It was then that TalonFyre took a look around and spotted a figure further up in the sky. "Oh, and someone looking like that thing you showed me just popped up over there," the ex-mercenary said, pointing to the abomination above them. Ultimar took off after hearing this.

TalonFyre received a slash across the face while he was distracted, causing a bit of blood to trickle down from his muzzle's side.

"What is this!? You should have had your face torn off!" Hrothgar screamed, shocked at his attack's lack of damage.

TalonFyre looked at him coldly. "You see, love makes someone even more powerful - making you weak," he said with a smug tone, "Yeah, cliché I know. Still true."

A look of horror was plastered upon Hrothgar's face as he saw the black fire start to build up in the ex-mercenary's mouth. He was outmatched, and he knew it. "And now... DIE!" TalonFyre screamed as he unleashed the inferno at the monstrous dragon's face, melting it.

The victory was short lived however. TalonFyre saw the monstrous dragon glow with a black light.

"You see, when I was young I met a Demon Dragon named Rayburn. He gave me these powers.... I am immortal," Hrothgar laughed, his voice sounding like a demon's.

TalonFyre was unfazed. "Yeah, well, immortality bites," he scoffed.

The two started their second bout. TalonFyre slashed at Hrothgar's chest, making a scratch. He was met with a closed buzzard-like fist to his left side, sending him flying over a few feet. It was then that Hrothgar let loose a stream of green fire at him, burning his chest. TalonFyre grunted in pain, causing Hrothgar to fly at him, his talons pulsing with green fire. The ex-mercenary had the tops of both his forelegs pierced as Hrothgar looked at him with a triumphant glare.

TalonFyre wasn't done yet, however. He bit into the monstrous dragon where he had made the scratch before, causing a bit of flesh to be removed. Hrothgar let go of the ex-mercenary, screaming in pain as the skin came off. TalonFyre was a bit closer to his goal, but knew he needed to keep his enemy in the dark. TalonFyre connected a punch to the monstrous dragon's upper forehead, causing him to lose balance. Even so, he was able to regain composure and strike TalonFyre in the gut, causing him to cough up bile.

TalonFyre then dodged a blow to his left wing and used a back-paw to the side of Hrothgar's head, disorienting him. The ex-mercenary then performed a mid-air flip, bringing his scythe-like tail-tip down on the Hrothgar's head. The monstrous dragon was reeling, but pulling punches wasn't something to be done in a battle like this. TalonFyre slashed at his target further, tearing away at the monstrous dragon's chest bit by bit.

In a last ditch effort, Hrothgar bit down on TalonFyre's chest, trying to reach his non-existent heart, which was a large mistake. TalonFyre, though in an immense amount of pain, plunged his paw into Hrothgar's chest, tearing away the final piece. A roar of agony was heard for miles as the monstrous dragon writhed in pain. TalonFyre then sank his mouth into the opening, biting Hrothgar's heart.

"GAAAHHH! BUT HOW!?" the monstrous dragon screamed in pain.

"Idiot, Rayburn is long gone. Electus burned his soul to a *CRISP*!" TalonFyre laughed, ripping Hrothgar's heart out. "And now, since you're immortal..." he continued, a sinister grin on his face. Hrothgar looked in terror as TalonFyre pulled a blood-red crystal out of his chest. "Know what this is you sick piece of trash? It's an eternity crystal. Traps you forever in suffering!" the ex-mercenary said sadistically as he threw the ancient device.

It was too late for apologies, too late for regrets, and too late to dodge. The crystal flew into Hrothgar's chest and sucked him inside as he breathed his last breath of fresh air.

Meanwhile, Ultimar was busy staring down his own nemesis. The creature looked exactly like what he had shown TalonFyre. His body was that of a muscular human's, but covered in black, bison-like fur. His lower half was that of a six-legged spider with hooves like that of a goat. His arms were like that of an insect with three claws like that of a praying mantis on the end. His face was like that of a wolf with scorpion-like mandibles to the side of it. He also had six tendrils on his back that were each like a rat's tail. Six legs, six claws, and six tendrils – in other words, he was the physically embodied representation of evil in the multiverse. He wasn't exactly the devil, but as close as a living being could get to him.

After TalonFyre had imprisoned Hrothgar the doctor finally spoke, "Don't you remember the pact magic deal? You intervene in a world directly, you die. So, what will it be? You touch anyone here and you croak worse than a bullfrog in a desert, Sbarre. I can't hurt you, but you do it to anyone else... well... you know..." he mocked.

Sbarre looked at him curiously. "You won't fight me, even after I helped Hrothgar try to murder you pregnant wife?" he asked, mocking him back.

Ultimar just looked at him with disinterest and went even further, "If you think I'm that foolish, you must have taken some medicine of your own that you prescribed to yourself. Also, it was likely made of wendigo crap, which you most likely eat on a day-to-day basis. Oh, and you might want to take a bath in a septic tank, it would make you smell a lot better. In closing, **bite me**!"

Sbarre closed his six mantis-like claws in anger. "You dare mock me, the most evil living being in the multiverse?" he growled. Ultimar nodded with a grin.

It was then that TalonFyre set his sights on the hideous creature. Before he could do anything, however, Ultimar warped back to him. "What now?" TalonFyre groaned.

The doctor looked at him seriously. "I can't hurt him, but his combat power is ten billion. He can transform once, reaching exactly six-hundred and sixty-six trillion. He's too much for you," he warned.

TalonFyre sighed in defeat. "Oh, Well **** me," he groaned. He then realized what had come out of his mouth. "Oh god, I hope she didn't hear that," he gulped.

Ultimar decided to continue, "The bright side is that he can't *hurt* anyone directly or else he'll die. All he can do... is watch," he said, smiling cruelly as the last words escaped his lips.

TalonFyre looked at the abomination. "Well, what a damn miserable way to exist," he remarked. His gazed turned to the imprisoned Hrothgar, "Well, not as miserable as him."

It was then that TalonFyre remembered what he said earlier. "I hope she didn't hear that," he whispered, blushing.

"Don't worry, she didn't," Ultimar laughed.

"Oh, good," TalonFyre sighed in relief. "Well, now everything is safe. What the hell now?" he pondered.

There was something Ultimar wanted to do for a long time – rub the pact in Sbarre's face. He teleported to his nemesis and looked him in the eyes. "Scratch someone, I dare you. What's wrong, are you a buffalo-furred chicken? Are you a wuss?" he asked cruelly, patting his rear. Sbarre disappeared after this, roaring in fury.

"Ha, what a bitch!" TalonFyre laughed.

This was the first time in decades that Ultimar had ever been so cruel to someone verbally, and it was bitter-sweet. It was true he hated Sbarre, but at the same time he felt pity for him. Sbarre was a monster to be sure, but it wasn't his fault he was made like that. Ultimar knew he was created to be almost demonic, both in nature and form. Nothing could change this, not even his Nightmare Eternity Vision. He was the one creature the doctor wanted to die, and he didn't have the ability or the will to end him. All he could do is make sure his minions didn't attack any more universes by sealing them. The problem with this one was that for some reason, his seal didn't work. TalonFyre was the last line of defense against Sbarre's monstrous army, and Ultimar himself was the first. The one thing Ultimar wondered was how far his friend's power could go.

Chapter 39

Ready to Begin Anew

"SHALL we go see what happened at home?" TalonFyre asked rhetorically. Ultimar nodded. "Oh, and Mian 'wants treatment'. I kept getting that signal, so you'd better get going," TalonFyre added in a sly voice.

Ultimar looked puzzled, "We already..." he cut off as he realized what was happening, warping to his wife. TalonFyre in turn teleported to his cave, laughing.

As he had expected, when Ultimar arrived at his bedroom Mian was on the bed with a romantic look on her face. "I know what's going on, but it's not good for our child. I'm sorry Mian, we can't risk it," Ultimar said, with an understanding yet firm tone in his voice.

Mian looked at him with a puppy-dog expression. "But..." she was about to protest when Ultimar put his hand on her stomach.

"Mian, please listen to me. We *both* know what's going on because we're *both* doctors. Just let it go, because in two years we'll have a beautiful child. After that I'll give you as much as you want. Just wait until then," Ultimar went on with a soft tone, a loving look on his face as he rubbed her stomach.

Mian smiled. "Alright dear. I'll wait," she replied lovingly, kissing him afterwards.

TalonFyre walked up to the cave after returning to his normal size. "Well, that was fun," he casually stated, grinning.

Hikari ran out at full speed, hugging him with both her front paws. "Well, enjoy the show?" TalonFyre asked, figuring she would say she did.

Instead Hikari kissed him, nuzzled him, and put her neck around his. "You **moron**! I was worried *sick*!" she yelled angrily.

This behavior puzzled TalonFyre. He looked at her. "You...didn't hear anything....odd - did you?" he asked, trying to hide his embarrassment.

"No, why?" Hikari asked back, her anger diminishing.

TalonFyre sighed, "Nothing."

A strong, odd scent filled TalonFyre's nostrils at this time. It was sort of like succulently fragrant cheese and honey – one he couldn't put his finger on. He wasn't around any kind of honey or cheese factory. They didn't even exist in Treskri di wer Zezhuanth Qarocuirar.

"Hey, you smell something?" TalonFyre asked, sniffing around. "The hell is it? Makes me feel energized," he went on.

He then sniffed the dragoness next to him and realized the smell was coming from her. "Oh man, bath time... Wait, I thought you were clean..." he continued, puzzled.

"(Ultimar, why does she stink?)" he asked. He then remembered he had cut off the telepathy due to Mian's statement. Why did Hikari smell so odd?

"Dammit, what smells? Isn't me is it?" the ex-mercenary asked himself, sniffing his back.

"(Do you really want to know?)" Ultimar asked semi-rhetorically in a smart tone.

"Oh..... Uh....well....that's....." TalonFyre began to stutter again.

"(It *is* Hikari... and for a reason,)" the doctor said happily.

No more words needed to be said. TalonFyre began to speak in a nervous yet loving tone, "Uhhh....I think I know what I'm doing now - I mean plans anyway." He smiled broadly at the last four words.

Hikari looked at him lovingly. "What is that?" she asked with fake wonder.

TalonFyre looked at her with the same loving expression. "Well... remember last time how it didn't do anything? I think it can now," he answered romantically. With this, he teleported to the spring with is beloved.

This time was better than the last. Hikari didn't sound like she was in pain, which relieved TalonFyre of an immense amount of guilt and worry. It wasn't just because of this, though – Hikari was in heat, and they both knew she would most likely become gravid from this. They would have a son or daughter to call their very own. This, more than anything else, made both of them happy beyond words.

TalonFyre swore to himself an oath this day – he wouldn't be like *his* father. He would be there for his children *and* his mate forever, and nothing could convince him otherwise. This new life was something he could never repay Ultimar for. The doctor had given him true purpose, as well as true happiness. TalonFyre had given Ultimar the power to have a child, but he knew that he could never repay him completely. Even so, the ex-mercenary was glad to have him as a friend.

A/N: Treskri di wer Zezhuanth Qarocuirar means "World of the Ancient Overseer" as this planet is called for reasons unknown.

Chapter 40

The Aftermath

TALONFYRE yawned, waking up in a heap. "Man, what the hell....happened?" he mumbled. He then proceeded to sniff himself and realized he was covered in Hikari's scent, "Aw, man..." he groaned, diving into the spring.

Hikari then walked up to her mate. "Uh... you don't remember?" the dragoness asked in a tone of fake wonder.

It was then the ex-mercenary did remember – and clearly. "Oh......how the hell am I forgetting the happiest moment of my existence - being with you!" he replied lovingly. Hikari smiled happily upon hearing this.

Another yawn came from TalonFyre as Hikari joined him in the spring and swam beside him. "Yeah, didn't sleep much again," the ex-mercenary chuckled, blushing. Hikari nuzzled him at this.

It was then that TalonFyre heard a voice he never had before making musical noises that sounded like something out of a dirty movie through Telepathy. "AW, *HELL NO* -**SHUT UP**!" TalonFyre screamed.

"(Sorry, that was one of my doctors,)" Ultimar sighed in annoyance.

TalonFyre rolled his eyes. "(Yeah, sure...)" he replied sarcastically.

"(He was on my head and decided to be an ass!)" Ultimar went on, losing his patience.

TalonFyre knew the doctor was telling the truth by the tone in his voice. "F........nope - not saying that," he muttered.

"(Dammit Kaze, get off my head before I throw you off!)" the doctor yelled, his anger heightening.

TalonFyre had a look of complete and utter bemusement. "I think I've heard enough for a while..." he groaned. It was easy to see Hikari was listening to the conversation by her expression. She was actually enjoying it.

"By the way, what's that dripping noise?" TalonFyre asked. He then got an image in his head. "Wait, don't want to know," he quickly retracted his question.

Since TalonFyre couldn't actually see the doctor, he was thinking the most disturbing possible scenario. "(I was in the shower, and I'm cutting off my telepathy until I can get this 3 centimeter moron off my head!)" Ultimar answered, his anger becoming near-rage.

This caused TalonFyre to sigh in relief, "Oh good, thank God."

After the two mates had gotten out, TalonFyre ran off after a deer, biting its neck. He then cooked it with his black flames and tossed it to Hikari.

Before the dragoness started eating, he walked up to her. "Ok, no one can hear this right Hikari?" he asked nervously. Hikari nodded at this. He got close to her earlobe and whispered, "No one can beat my meat but you."

Hikari looked at him coldly. "Sorry, sorry…" TalonFyre apologized. It was then that the dragoness couldn't hold up the facade anymore and started laughing. TalonFyre joined in after he had seen that her anger was obviously false and was merely to toy with him.

Another deer was chased down and devoured by the ex-mercenary, followed by a second.

"Save some for me!" Hikari called out to TalonFyre.

"Hey, you got yours!" the ex-mercenary replied. He once again realized he had spoken with inappropriate irony and groaned, "Oh god, why do I talk."

Hikari was eating faster than usual. "FORGET IT, IM NOT HERE! Yup, I'm very awkward," TalonFyre went on, first yelling then speaking in a sigh.

By this time Hikari had finished eating and started laughing at the top of her lungs. "By the way – there's a pit in the temple full of pre-cooked deer. Go raid it gal," TalonFyre stated happily. Hikari darted off upon hearing.

It was apparent to TalonFyre his mate's appetite was because she was gravid. "(Yup, I know why she's so hungry,)" he communicated to Ultimar.

"(She hasn't eaten since you left to fight. She's going to be eating a lot more when it becomes full-swing, you know,)" the doctor warned.

Although feeling a bit guilty about causing his beloved to stop eating, TalonFyre was glad to know that Hikari was indeed gravid. "(It worked alright. Hey, I'm not *that* dumb,)" the ex-mercenary replied happily.

"(I was right all along about your subconscious desire - a family and a happy life,)" Ultimar said kindly.

TalonFyre now knew the doctor was right, and always had been. He loved Hikari with his entire being. It amazed him how a person could be that wise and kind. Ultimar was an amazing person, and someone he'd always look to if he needed help or advice, within reason.

Chapter 41

Some Doctors Are Crazy

THERE was a voice in the background when TalonFyre was talking to the doctor, so he decided to do a bit of digging. "Hey, Ultimar – open up a little wormhole so I can get a look at the other guy," the ex-mercenary requested, his curiosity getting the better of him. The doctor sighed and created a small wormhole, revealing his head and neck.

"Why is there a miniature guy dancing on your head again? And why is the guy naked?" TalonFyre asked in bemusement.

Ultimar sighed again, "He's a wind sprite, he's always like that," he answered.

TalonFyre was both disturbed by the spectacle, and surprised the doctor hadn't lost his patience by now. "What the hell am I watching? He's dancing the cha-cha on your head saying something I'm *not* repeating. Something about slime," the disturbed ex-mercenary grumbled.

A vein appeared on Ultimar's forehead. "The *only* guy... who can piss me off as much as Sbarre... **is him**!" the doctor said, yelling the last two words.

"Bleh, ok I feel sick... and I just ate so..."

TalonFyre was about to continue when Ultimar interrupted, "He just did his wife ten minutes ago and he won't stop talking about it!" he yelled, clearly out of patience by this time.

TalonFyre laughed at this. "Well, tell him welcome to the club - and also, is he sane? He doesn't sound like it," the ex-mercenary remarked with a grimace.

Ultimar picked the wind sprite up and threw him off onto a bed. "He's an asshole who decides to *act* crazy to **piss** people off!!!" the doctor screamed. TalonFyre laughed even more.

"Ever light a firecracker in his ass, just to see his face?" the ex-mercenary asked with a grin.

Ultimar shook his head no. "I'm not a monster. I was done with being that way when I met Mian," he replied with sigh. TalonFyre shrugged.

"He's going into the sanitarium to *chill*," Ultimar shrugged, his voice now collected and calm. He placed a cubic barrier around the wind sprite. He then proceeded to pick up the cage and carry him out of the room. "Now, let's see how you like it if I treat you like you really *are* crazy," the doctor said cruelly.

TalonFyre spread his wings. "Well, time to check on greedy guts – I'm off to see if she ate the cave," he stated. He then realized he had made another ironically inappropriate comment. "I really need to stop talking," he sighed in embarrassment, putting his paw to his face as he took off.

As he was flying, TalonFyre wondered what his new life would be like with a family. 'Only one I'd ever think of having a family with – Hikari. Perfect for me in every way - loving, strong, kind, *and* tomboyish. Most guys would be put off by that stuff – not me. She's a prize for sure,' he thought.

Meanwhile, Ultimar was shutting Kaze into a padded room. This kind of structure was never used unless it was for a rampaging beast that was too unstable with anger to be dealt with using normal means. He threw the wind sprite into the room and put a barrier up.

"I hate to do this, Kaze, but you've left me no choice but to use an ironic punishment," the doctor said with a frown.

Kaze pounded on the barrier. "I promise I won't act crazy no more! Pease let me out!" he yelled.

Ultimar folded his arms and turned away. "I can read eyes *and* minds, remember Kaze? I don't know why I even let you become one of my doctors," he sighed in disgruntlement. Kaze looked at him with anger, which Ultimar sensed. The doctor turned around to look at him. "Oh, and one thing you have to remember about the power I lend – you abuse it, you lose it," he warned. Kaze just clenched his fist as Ultimar walked away again.

After thinking about his new life for a few minutes as he flew, TalonFyre touched down outside the Sun Temple. "Well, she seems to be fine... heh...just follow the scarfing," he mused as he walked to the room with the deer meat.

Following the sounds of Hikari's voracious eating, TalonFyre arrived at his destination. "Hikari you finished y..." the ex-mercenary stopped as he realized a fourth of the meat was gone, his eyes widening.

Hikari belched as she approached him, covered in meat. "HOLY CRAP WOMAN - You can eat!" he exclaimed. Hikari shot him a glare. "And yeah, I know why too," TalonFyre continued, hugging her.

Hikari put her neck around his. "You're right about that," she sighed happily.

Ultimar opened up a wormhole next to them, showing Kaze in the room. "He's done this ever since he got here five years ago, and I'm through with it! I'm a kind person, but enough is enough," he said coldly, wondering what the two would say about it.

"Ever think about having him fixed?" TalonFyre asked with a laugh.

"I wouldn't do that unless he raped someone. Luckily he's married," Ultimar replied.

TalonFyre was surprised by this. "Why marry that guy?" he asked in confused voice.

He then saw a small, anthropomorphic termite approach the room. "Hello mister pingas!" she said happily.

TalonFyre put his paw on his face. "Oh god, is that her?" he asked in annoyed bemusement.

"And that, my friend, is the answer to your second question," the doctor replied in a smart tone, dropping the barrier.

The termite-woman hugged the wind sprite. "Hey, Hazel – come back to my room. We'll bang, ok?" the wind sprite said with a sly smile, getting one back.

"I'm going to go and watch some TV to get some new powers. Come through the wormhole if you want any tests done, Hikari," Ultimar said, walking away from sanitarium.

TalonFyre, in turn walked out of the cavern where the food was kept. "Anyway I'm going to go see how Angel and Flare are," she stated happily.

Chapter 42

The Effects

TALONFYRE walked into his adopted parent's room. "Flare, Angel, you guys in here?" he asked, looking around. He spotted them laying down, Angel's head on Flare's. "Oh good," the ex-mercenary sighed.

Angel and Flare stood up after this. "What is it Talon?" Angel asked curiously.

After he heard the question, TalonFyre stood still for a few seconds, bracing himself. The news he was about to give was something that he didn't take lightly, and was sure they would either. He sighed in preparation. "How's the nursery doing? We... may need it," he answered her sheepishly.

Angel looked at him, "Five have hatched, and...," she stopped as soon as she realized what her adopted son really meant when he started to blush.

"I *knew* it," Flare said with a happy smile.

This caused TalonFyre to blush even more. "Flare, shut it. You're not... helping," he sighed.

Flare put his paws on his mouth after this. Angel, however put her own paw on TalonFyre's. "We were nervous too," she said sweetly, a kind smile on her face.

It was true, TalonFyre was nervous about being a parent, but was excited as well. "Yeah... about time. All I'm saying is, it was the *single* happiest point in my whole existence," he said contently.

Smiling, Flare began to speak, "Son... I'm so glad. You've made her so happy," his tone carried more parental gladness that he would have ever imagined it would.

TalonFyre smirked at what he would say next, "By the way, she ate a quarter of the fridge - on a normal day. Yeah, I expected it too."

Both of Hikari's parents burst out laughing at this. "You'll get used to it," Flare said with a smile.

"At least she didn't find the rest," TalonFyre laughed.

The words caused Hikari walked in with a sly smile. TalonFyre put his paw to his face, "Oh great - I'm not telling." Hikari would have slapped TalonFyre at this if a wormhole hadn't have opened up revealing a giant fridge, as well as Ultimar.

"A little gift from me to you. The food re-spawns," the doctor informed them, a grin on his face.

This 'gift' warranted an eye-roll from TalonFyre. "Well, thank you fancy pants," he said with false sarcasm, grabbing a shield from the wall just for good measure.

The sound of sniffing was heard from Hikari. Knowing what was next, TalonFyre put the shield up for Angel, Flare and himself to block the multiple layers of debris that were to come.

"You guys might want to take cover," the ex-mercenary warned. They all ducked as the dragoness began to devour multiple foodstuffs, including, as the doctor expected, pickles, meat, milk, hard-boiled eggs and cake – the latter of which she put hot sauce on.

'She doesn't know that she's not actually *going* to be this hungry until she starts to produce more yolk for the eggs. This is going to be messy,' Ultimar thought to himself as he put a barrier up.

Food sprayed upon the ground and walls as Hikari began to decimate the entire fridge's supply of food. TalonFyre of course, got splattered even with his shield up. "Oh, **gross**... *Man* she can eat, and even on a normal day," the ex-mercenary said disgustedly, wiping egg off his face in a literal sense of wording.

"You do know another part of it is the morning sickness, right?" Ultimar asked, smirking at the impression he'd give.

"Oh....crap.... **RUN**!" TalonFyre yelled, heeding his own advice and running outside.

"Well, it's not your fault son," Flare said, waiting to see TalonFyre's reaction to his words.

TalonFyre smiled sadly, "Yeah....dad...."

The food stopped raining towards the three when Hikari realized that she'd eaten so sloppily that she had accidentally hit them with half of the things Ultimar had meant for her to devour. "Sorry about that," Hikari sighed apologetically, coming out of the fridge.

A rumbling was heard from her gut after this, causing TalonFyre's eyes to widen. "Arm yourselves!" the ex-mercenary warned, sending his adoptive parents a shield each.

A large, five second belch was heard from the dragoness as she let out the air she had taken into her stomach during the eating frenzy. "I hope this isn't the second most painful part," TalonFyre coughed, passing out from the noise.

"That's going to happen when you eat that fast," Ultimar laughed.

A few minutes later, TalonFyre got up from his stupor, only to see that a liquid started to drip from his mate's mouth as her head started to move downwards. "Uh, Hikari is that...drool? Cause' there's a lot of it," the ex-mercenary asked obliviously.

Flare and Angel looked at him with a blank expression as their daughter's neck and head craned and dropped to the floor. Upon reaching the ground the gravid dragoness vomited up half of what she had eaten so voraciously from the refrigerator. "Ate... too much..." she coughed sickly.

"No shit!" the ex-mercenary exclaimed. Upon saying the words he had, TalonFyre came to the realization that he might have made Hikari angry. "Sorry," he apologized, his head hung low.

This was only met with a nuzzle from her newly-wiped mouth. "It's alright," Hikari said softly.

TalonFyre put his paw on Hikari's. "About before - ignore the whole painful part. I shouldn't have said it," he sighed with an embarrassed grin.

At this, Ultimar put his hand upon the held paws of both mates. "Mian and I will be there when the time comes," he said confidently, walking back through the wormhole to his hospital.

The two mates, as well as their parents, spent the rest of the day reading scrolls and maps about the world and all the places they could visit on their adventures together once Hikari had laid her egg. When night had fallen, they went back to their separate rooms, TalonFyre and Hikari in one room, their parents in the other.

The next morning, TalonFyre awoke with a start when Hikari ran from under his wing to the bathroom. He heard her vomit repeatedly for at least a full minute. "I've set this up for her - she must be miserable," he groaned sadly.

Re-entering the room, Hikari walked up to and nuzzled her mate. "Why would I be miserable? So what if I barf a little? It's a small price to pay," she remarked, kissing the ex-mercenary on the muzzle. This made him feel much better about impregnating her.

They then heard Mian through Telepathy. "(It's all part of becoming a parent,)" she said kindly.

TalonFyre smiled at this. 'Glad she doesn't hate me for it,' he thought to himself.

The refrigerator had re-stocked itself, causing Hikari to start eating again, this time monitoring how much she consumed. After seeing this, TalonFyre decided to catch his own breakfast of deer. He walked out, taking a small look at his mate's belly, which was soon to be larger, for two separate reasons.

TalonFyre knew this was coming – Hikari would be hungry a lot from now up until the egg was laid. He wouldn't admit it, but he was more than grateful for the doctor's gift. Now he wouldn't have to hunt for his mate during her pregnancy. He couldn't wait to be a father. He would finally have a child he could call his own! His life was perfect, a mate, a mother and father that loved him unconditionally, and soon a son or daughter.

The words "I'm finally going to have his child" were all that Hikari could think about. She was gravid. She was finally going to bear a child to TalonFyre. She didn't care about the sickness, the eating, or even how much pain it would cause her. She wanted this, and she finally had it.

Chapter 43

Annoying As a Fly

AFTER eating his fill of deer, TalonFyre was about to re-enter the temple, but stopped short when he felt a sensation on his underbelly. "....The hell?" the ex-mercenary murmured.

TalonFyre decided to contact the doctor after this feeling came about. It's not that he didn't trust Hikari; she never mated with anyone before him – that was obvious, in more ways than one. He just needed to know what was going on.

"(Uh I got an 'itch' - not normal either,)" the ex-mercenary communicated as he began to scratch his underbelly. The itch intensified, so he began to scrape his belly on the rocks. "What the hell did I get into other than..." he growled worriedly.

Back at Ultimar's hospital the doctor was looking for two doctors. After he realized they were missing, it hit him. "(Oh geez... he's there isn't he?)" he communicated back.

A wormhole opened up and Ultimar walked out, furious. "KAZE! Get off him right **NOW**!!" he screamed at the snickering wind spirit climbing on TalonFyre's underbelly.

"GAH WHAT THE *HELL*! You little bastard - only one person goes there!" he yelled angrily at the wind spirit, grabbing him in his teeth.

The wind spirit snickered again. "Bleh!" TalonFyre spit him out, disgusted.

The wind spirit started to laugh hysterically after this. "**DID HE JUST PEE IN MY MOUTH**!?" the ex-mercenary screamed in anger. He was going to say more, but he began to vomit instead.

By this point Ultimar was at the end of his rope. "Okay, don't kill him, but give him what for," he said begrudgingly.

The wind sprite looked at him with a smirk. "You don't have the guts to let him kill me anyway. Bang your wife lately?" he mocked.

Ultimar looked at him in disgust. He had never seen such horrible behavior in any one of his employees.

A nod from Ultimar caused TalonFyre to smirk. "I'm not touching that creep but..." he purposely trailed off as he lit a miniscule fire on the wind spirit's backside, causing him to scrape his posterior on the dirt, attempting to put out the fire. "See, told you... funny as hell!" TalonFyre laughed.

Ultimar steeled himself for what he was about to say and do. "This is the first time I'm saying this, but... Kaze, for abusing your power- YOU'RE **FIRED**!!! And Hazel too!" he boomed.

TalonFyre was under the impression that it was a pun, "Yeah, he *looks* like he's fired up!"

This only increased the doctor's sorrow. "I can't believe it. I had to... I need Mian right now," he sighed, his voice a whisper.

The old wormhole closed and a new one opened leading to his bedroom where his wife was laying down with a smile, her scaly hand on her stomach. She got up after seeing her husband's face and slithered over to him as he walked through. "What's wrong dear?" she asked in a loving, concerned voice. The wormhole closed before the doctor could say more.

TalonFyre was confused at the doctor's reaction. Did it really hurt him *that* much just to let an employee go? It even looked like he was about to cry. The most puzzling thing is why didn't Ultimar ever cry when he was cruel to him, especially when he showed him the vision of hell? Could the doctor be softer than he let on? If so, what could be the reasoning behind his lack of emotion during that vision? It was true that Ultimar did end up looking away from him when he showed the vision of his future family. Was he crying from sorrow or joy? Was he even crying at all? These questions were things TalonFyre had no answers to, and he wanted them badly. Still, there were more important things at hand, like keeping Hikari happy during her pregnancy. This was all TalonFyre needed to think about to keep his mind off such trivial things.

Chapter 44

Shenanigans

THE ex-mercenary walked back inside the temple. However, in his haste to see his beloved he slipped, smashing his jaw on the floor. "Oh, what the hell?" he groaned.

After he had said this his jaw dropped loose, hanging by the left side of his muzzle. "I got it," TalonFyre stated casually, pulling off his old jaw, regenerating it anew.

This was when the ex-mercenary realized he had vomit on the side of his cheek. "And....it's on my face. Well, not the worst thing I guess," he sighed, walking into the main hall.

"You guys ok?" TalonFyre asked, looking at his love and new foster parents.

They looked at him strangely. They hadn't heard about the argument with the wind sprite or any of the things that had happened with him. Hikari replied, "Yeah, what's wrong Talon?"

Glad that no one was injured, TalonFyre shrugged, "I slipped and landed in barf."

"Sorry..." Hikari sighed, putting her head down in shame.

TalonFyre smiled. "Ah, it's fine. You guys get splattered or no?" he said looking at the three, noticing that Flare had a clean body.

Flare gave a half-hearted, "Not me," rolling his eyes as he knew what would come next.

"Yeah, why doesn't that surprise me," TalonFyre sarcastically replied, flinging vomit onto him and laughing, "Now you *did*!"

"And, how did *I* see that coming?" Flare asked rhetorically, rolling his eyes once more. He knew TalonFyre's jokes and attitude, and he didn't expect anything less than this. However, as long as Hikari loved him and they could be a family, he didn't care.

TalonFyre began to glow, "Hang on - hold still," he said as the ground heated up, removing the vomit. He then proceeded to blow a light flame on Angel and Flare, cleaning them off. "There."

"Thank you son..." Angel said warmly.

TalonFyre looked away uncertainly. "Yeah...ok mom....uh... Yeah still not used to it," he rambled.

Flare gave a kind smile and replied, "You will be."

Knowing Hikari would be sick. TalonFyre handed her a small, white gem. "This is an anti-sickness gem - one thing you can't puke up."

Hikari quickly swallowed it whole and sighed in relief, "Thanks - I needed this."

A sound was heard in the main hallway. "The hell? I hear screaming, but tiny - in the other room? Great, what now?" the ex-mercenary rambled.

"(Kaze, Hazel, what the F-)" Ultimar cut off before he could curse.

TalonFyre laughed at this, "Sorry, but someone didn't cut the line did they?"

~ 142 ~

The screaming intensified and Ultimar groaned, "(They're in the next room over, you moron... I'm sending them an image- NOW!)" he boomed, using his telepathic powers to send them a mental video of the Gigas's delivery, as well as other unappealing things.

The two began to become sickened after this, causing TalonFyre to laugh as they lost the contents of their stomachs, "BWAHAHAH, man, you should do a TV show!"

"(You don't want to hear what I showed them... Bad, bad, mental image,)" Ultimar said with an uncertain tone.

"I hear beeping in the room, why is that?" TalonFyre asked in confusion, walking into the room with the nauseated wind sprite and termite-woman.

Inside the room there was a recording device. "Uh, there's a camera," the ex-mercenary remarked, keeping his confused tone.

"(I sent that to tape the reaction,)" Ultimar explained calmly.

TalonFyre chuckled at this, "Yeah, show the whole staff – no, not a good idea, you'd look bad."

Ultimar replied, "(I'll show Mian, that's all.)"

TalonFyre walked into his room once more. "Well, Hikari, what's new other than the barf off?" he asked with smile. "(Yeah, she'll laugh,)" he said, communicating to the doctor.

And just like he assumed, his love burst out into a fit of laughter, which he joined.

The two passed the day looking at scrolls, enjoying each other's company, and talking with Flare and Angel, who were more than happy to give them tips on child-rearing. At the end of the day, each of the pairs of mates, one being the parents and the other being the children, lay down to bed.

Before TalonFyre could get to sleep, Ultimar interrupted. "(Can I tell you something personal?)" he asked.

TalonFyre nodded, "Yeah, sure."

The doctor took a deep breath, "(I'm a lot softer than I let on... I use my chakra to hold back tears when I hurt people.)"

TalonFyre's question was answered, and now he could say it, "Don't hold back feelings.... I did, and I'm stronger because I don't hold them back."

Ultimar knew this was true, but had to tell TalonFyre why he did, "(I need to sometimes, but I usually don't. When I showed you those visions, I couldn't look weak,)" he cut off after this; glad that he could show his true self to the four.

So that was why... TalonFyre always assumed Ultimar's emotions were strongly hidden. However, that wasn't the case at all. Ultimar was like himself – only strong when he needed to be. It was strange, as TalonFyre always assumed he had nothing in common with the doctor when it came to personality, but now he wasn't so sure. Maybe they were more similar than he thought, in more ways than just their troubled pasts.

Chapter 45

Kaze's Revenge (?)

THREE days passed, Hikari growing closer to TalonFyre as each went by. On the morning of the fourth day, TalonFyre got up with a start as he was dive-bombed by a strange creature, running outside afterwards.

"The *hell* - was that Vespatites?" the mercenary asked, looking at the creatures. The insect landed on his nose and bit him.

"The hells after me no-"he stopped as he was swarmed by large insects, almost like cicadas or locusts. "**GAH,** what *now*!? Thought I wiped 'em all out!"

The creatures circled him and proceeded to bite him. "Gh... Weird Vespatites, but oh well..." he began charging a blast of black fire as he grumbled this. He fired the blaze, burning the creatures, incinerating the ones at close range.

The creatures continued to swarm, flames charring them over and over from TalonFyre's inexhaustible supply.

"Man, there's a lot of them," TalonFyre growled.

A voice was heard after this, "Heheh... I lost my power from Ultimar, but Hazel still has her power over insects!" the wind sprite cackled.

"...Hazel? Wait...!" the ex-mercenary realized that the sprite and the termite women were the culprits in this attack.

Then, the sprite spat out, "My WIFE dumb****!"

TalonFyre retorted with a return curse, "Oh **** off numb nuts!" and a blast of black fire, albeit small. Kaze screamed in pain as TalonFyre grunted, "Piss off!" as the door slammed shut behind him.

"Okay, that's it, Kaze. Cancel the revenge plan for them," Hazel ordered.

Kaze merely responded with a weak, "Got it."

Angered, TalonFyre tossed a pebble below the sprite's belt area and growled, "Get lost," in a cruel manner.

He heard a thump as the sprite screeched, "Okaaay!" in a high-pitched voice.

Immediately TalonFyre laughed, "BWAHAHAH - Thank god mine don't show where they can be seen!"

It was then that Hikari walked out. "*That*... was *priceless*!" she laughed in a squeaky voice.

TalonFyre grinned, "Yeah, just cause' I don't have the same setup doesn't mean I don't know where it's kept!"

Hikari looked at him evilly. "Should I throw another and make him a girl?" TalonFyre asked menacingly as he looked at her. He picked up another rock the size of a pea and took aim.

~ 144 ~

"Do it...!" Hikari snickered.

TalonFyre shook his head, "Hehe, no. He has to have some happiness," he sighed, looking at her face.

"**Do it**!" the dragoness screamed angrily.

TalonFyre crushed the pebble and kissed her, "Hey, would you say the same if it was me?"

Hikari sighed, "No..." hanging her head in defeat.

TalonFyre nuzzled her and snickered, "I will do this..." throwing another, onto his backside on the left cheek. "There, now beat it!"

The wind sprite flailed and yelped, "Ah! My ass! I'm out of here!" as the two ran away, Hazel at a faster pace due to the sprite's odd stride.

"That's what his wife said!" TalonFyre laughed.

The two were laughing hysterically, only to stop as TalonFyre got up and wiped his eyes "Oh my god, man I can be funny when I want...."

Chapter 46

An Emotional Rollecoaster

AFTER the scene with the two former doctors, TalonFyre set himself upright, hugging his mate gently as not to endanger the egg inside of her.

"Glad you're feeling better babe," TalonFyre said warmly, kissing her.

Hikari smiled lovingly, "Yeah, that gem did the trick."

This caused TalonFyre to smirk, "What gem? It was a rock, painted like a gem." He then realized he had made a grave error in telling Hikari this as her eyes narrowed in rage.

"Oh......great," he grinned weakly as she approached him, "Uh – surprise?" he whimpered guiltily, looking at his mate's angry expression.

This did nothing to calm the angry dragoness, who slapped him with the full force of her paw, causing him to flinch as a red mark appeared on his face.

"Ok yeah, I deserved that," he gulped, looking at her raised claw, which slashed him as it came down upon his head. "Ok yeah, and that... Ow..." he held his left eye, which had been narrowly missed when she had cut him with her claw.

It was then that Hikari saw the blood on his face, causing her to adopt a regretful look. "Did I hurt you too badly?" she asked, putting her paw upon his lower muzzle with a look of concern.

TalonFyre shrugged, "Nah," as he put his paw to the side of his head, "What, this? Nothing I can't handle."

"Hey, that rock took a beating. I feel bad for it... And again I say it out loud," TalonFyre groaned at the last five words.

This caused the dragoness to nuzzle him. "Well, you did give me the fake gem to help, so I forgive you," she sighed, kissing his muzzle.

"No, I mean the rock by the.....oh right - Yeah that's what I meant," the ex-mercenary quickly covered up what he had said for fear that Hikari would become angrier.

Hikari nuzzled TalonFyre's neck affectionately and softly whispered, "I can't wait to be a parent," into his earlobe in a sweet tone. TalonFyre nuzzled her neck as well, causing her to flinch happily.

The two nuzzled each other for a few short minutes then lay upon the bed, fully satisfied with the fact that they were both parents-to-be.

A thought began to enter the gravid dragoness's mind after this with others following, 'I wonder if it's going to be a boy or a girl? Will it be like Talon or Me? Will it be a new kind altogether – A mix-breed? Will it be healthy? Will the child grow up strong and loving like Talon is? Is it going to find a suitable mate? Will they even love me when a mate is found? What if they move far away – What if I never see the poor thing again? What if *she* dies during a laying or *his* mate dies when she lays her egg!? What if *I* end up like TalonFyre's mother, leaving my child alone!? Talon can't raise a child by himself!!!' she began to shake.

"What's wrong Hikari? It can't be time yet!" TalonFyre gasped worriedly.

Hikari nuzzled him after this. "Talon, what if I can't make it through it and I lay early? What if it doesn't turn out right? What if I can't get it out at all? What if I get it out and don't live after I've laid the egg? What if my child grows up without-"she stopped when she began to see the look in TalonFyre's eyes. It showed horror, sadness, worry, and most of all, despair.

It was then that they heard Ultimar speak in a determined, assertive, and sure tone, "(I swear – I will not, repeat NOT, let you die Hikari, now or ever! I never wanted to save and protect a patient's life more than I do you right now. I will do all in my power to ensure a safe delivery, and I will use all in my power to save your lives if in danger – You and Talon. I give you my word that, as God as my witness, I will not allow you to die!)"

The doctor's words shocked TalonFyre. He would do all he can to protect them. Still, the question was – why? Why would he do so much just to protect them? Why would he do all this just for his mate and himself? Was it because he owed TalonFyre? No, that couldn't be it. He had paid the doctor back tenfold for training him, but the doctor had paid him forty-fold for what he did in the beginning – giving him Hikari and a chance for a new life.

Whatever the reason, he was glad to have the doctor beside him when Hikari delivered. She would need all the help in the world. It was true, Hikari was in a state of maturity where a laying may not be much of a problem, but after what happened with his mother he was nervous about any laying. Hikari was his world. Her dying would give his life no purpose. At the end of the day, she was his rock. Ultimar... this doctor... he was the only thing standing between him and certain destruction when it came to mental stability about the laying. This he was grateful for.

Chapter 47

Preparations, part 1

THE next morning TalonFyre woke up to Hikari vomiting in the toilet once more. "Why'd I have do this to her? Throwing up every day, angry one minute then crying the next... Makes me feel horrible," he sighed, thinking out loud.

After she had finished washing her face the dragoness came back into the room where TalonFyre lay, nuzzling him saying, "Talon, quit blaming yourself. I wanted this. *I* wanted a child." She saw his pained expression and put her paw on his head, moving down to the side onto his neck, "I knew this would happen, so stop making yourself out the bad guy, because you're not."

A smile lifted onto TalonFyre's face upon the words being spoken. "So, what are Flare and Angel up to?" the ex-mercenary asked as the paw of his beloved slinked from his neck and placed itself on the back of his head, slowly removing itself.

Hikari smiled, "They were in the nursery last night, tending to the hatchlings and dragonesses. They said they'd be busy trying to help them realize that it wasn't their fault they were made into..." she cut off as she clenched her paw and growled, "I wish I could have made him eat his own freaking pissworm," a cruel tone in her voice, making it obvious to TalonFyre that it was unlikely to be a joke.

The two lifted themselves out a bed and headed to the room belonging their parents. "Flare, Angel, you there?" TalonFyre asked as he knocked on the door. A creak was heard as the door opened, revealing Angel, her foreleg on her mate's upper body, nuzzling him.

"So, how're the others doing in the nursery? I could use a bit of info," TalonFyre asked.

Angel closed her eyes sadly, "They're doing alright in the physical sense despite their reproductive systems being strained so horridly. However, they need a lot of help emotionally, as Hrothgar broke their wills into..." she stopped, unable to continue.

"I can't believe that monster," Angel sighed in anger and dismay as Flare put his paw upon her face, moving it back and forth in a soothing fashion.

It was at that moment that Ultimar spoke, "(Mian and I would be happy to help. She'll be by in a bit to pick up the girls. Why don't you see them beforehand?)" His tone was kind and soft.

This caused TalonFyre to shake his head in refusal, "No they'll be scared. They saw me fighting him. Kinda broadcasted live."

It was true the fight Between TalonFyre and Hrothgar was shown upon every TV in his homeland, but the fact still stood that TalonFyre was a hero to many people, at least now.

"(Your rescued them,)" Ultimar reminded the ex-mercenary, wanting him to understand his logic.

This was met with an oblivious, "Yeah, duh," from TalonFyre.

"(That means they would actually be glad that you would want to see them,)" the doctor continued.

It was clear that Ultimar's plea fell on deaf ears when TalonFyre shook his head once more and replied, "Nah, I don't want to scare them."

At this point, the doctor gave up trying to make his new friend realize what he meant to those dragonesses, that he was their hero. He merely sighed, "Okay, Mian will get them and bring them to the hospital."

A familiar odd smell entered TalonFyre's nostrils at this time. Knowing Hikari was gravid, that could only mean one thing.

"Ok, uh Flare... How do I put this...?" TalonFyre said in an awkward tone, lifting one of his paws and slowly pointing it to his father's left and the other to his nose.

Flare turned his head unsurely. He then came to the realization of what his son-in-law meant when he saw TalonFyre pointing to his mate with a wink.

This caused Flare to give an embarrassed, "Oh," as he realized that he had failed to notice the fact that his mate had been in heat for the past few hours, despite her painfully obvious advances in affection for him.

"Hey, I pick it up once I'm used to it," TalonFyre remarked with a smug grin, "Besides, I have to take Hikari home. A real home."

TalonFyre handed his adopted father a glowing scale and gave a warm smile, "You need me, just let me know." At this he turned around and approached his beloved.

The fact that Angel was rubbing up against Flare made it apparent. She wanted to mate and her heat was exceptionally strong at this time.

"Looks like you'll have a little sibling Hikari," Flare chuckled, proceeding to give a romantic look toward his mate.

Hikari smiled at the thought of having a sibling, which she had all but given up on entirely when her mother had died. Now she was back. Best of all was the fact that her beloved TalonFyre, her mate, the father of her forming child, was to thank for it.

"Anyway Hikari, it's time to go to my real home. This is just a decoy," TalonFyre said in a kind, yet assertive, tone.

"Really?" Hikari gasped.

TalonFyre merely replied with a simple and warm, "Yeah."

Chapter 48

Preparations, part 2

"KEEP in touch guys, but not in the next twelve hours please," TalonFyre said to his new parents, a sly tone to his voice during the last few words.

The words 'twelve hours' caused Ultimar to panic, as he had just tapped into his far-sight. "(Oh crap, is it time already? Is it an early lay?)" he asked nervously.

TalonFyre rolled his eyes and replied, "Aw, shut it pretty boy," in a voice of faked anger and annoyance. This caused Ultimar to give a chuckle of relief.

TalonFyre grabbed Hikari's paw, albeit gently. "Bye, you guys! ...And Flare, go get some," TalonFyre called out as he teleported away.

Flare, who was completely taken aback by his son's bluntness, could merely give an embarrassed, "Got it," as he turned toward Angel, ready to finally let her bear another child after eighteen years.

The teleportation spell landed the two mates in an arid, sand-filled desert, life gone for miles on end. Sound was absent to the point of being deafening.

"Mind the sand," TalonFyre said with a smile. The dragoness gave a smile in return. "By the way Hikari..." he began.

"Yes, dear?" the dragoness asked.

TalonFyre looked at her warmly and whispered the words, "Si itov wux," as he nuzzled her.

This phrase confused Hikari, yet at the same time she was filled with so much joy and warmth that she was near the point of tears that she could only whisper, "What?" in reply.

"I said I love you in ancient draconic," TalonFyre explained with a loving smile.

Hikari put both of her forelegs around him. "I love you too. I don't know what I would have done if I hadn't met you! I love you so much!!!" the dragoness wailed, crying onto his shoulder.

"You crying, Hikari?" TalonFyre asked his beloved, concern showing in his voice.

"I just thought of how I never would have forgiven my father... how a male would have never been in my life... how I might have even killed myself..." she sobbed, causing TalonFyre to embrace her, once again softly as not to endanger the egg.

"Yeah, well all family has rough patches," TalonFyre replied softly, kissing her on the muzzle.

As the tears subsided and the embrace finally ceased, Hikari nuzzled the ex-mercenary once more. "My dad never taught me about Ancient Draconic. I was always too mad at him to learn after... you know..." her voice trailed off.

TalonFyre nuzzled her again, "Like I said, rough patches. Not your fault Rayburn's an ass. I've got the book on it at home too. Now stand back."

The gravid dragoness backed away as TalonFyre spoke, "Siksta Lirkim, Ileisgar." A 350-foot high golden golem rose from out of the dunes. Its horns were like that of a sheep, its eyes made of emerald. The creature's hands and feet were like that of a humanoid dragon with ruby-clawed hands and sapphire-talons on its feet. The entire body was armored with a series of chitin-like plates as well.

"Don't worry, he's my house pet," TalonFyre said in a comedic tone as the golem looked at them intently. The creature blinked for a moment, as if realizing it had seen something that it never assumed it would.

"Vorqic hefoc wer drot confna spical! saeuth ekess ocuir wux tenamalo ghent shio jacida tairais, wux juanth malai!" the golem spoke in what Hikari could only fathom as a friendly manner.

TalonFyre put his paw on his head. "For crying out loud, speak normal!" he ordered, albeit in a somewhat non-threatening tone. The golem cracked its back.

"Holy crap, it's about time!" The golem exclaimed, proceeding to give TalonFyre a fist-bump.

TalonFyre winked, "Heh, too long."

A glare was given to Hikari by the mammoth creature, his eyes narrowing. "Nice to meet you," the dragoness said in a polite, yet somewhat nervous tone, as the golem examined her more closely.

"Yeah, don't touch them," TalonFyre ordered the golem as he pointed a claw at him.

The golem was confused at this. "Why not, and I only see one," the golem responded.

This caused TalonFyre to retort, "Well, there's two there!" his voice becoming angry as he lost his patience.

It was obvious that this golem had no idea why this dragoness was here, or what his master meant by saying there were two.

At this point Hikari looked at the golem with a bit of anger, which quickly became joy when she thought about the words about to flow from her mouth. "I'm gravid. I'm also his mate," she sighed happily.

The golem's mouth dropped. After five seconds of awkward silence, the golem's surprise dissipated. "Well, I'll be a son of a boulder – I thought you were cleaned out Talon!" he said with a smirk.

TalonFyre shrugged in response, "Nope, got it back."

"So, if you don't mind I'd like to get in," TalonFyre said as he pointed to the sand beneath the large beast.

"Heh, sure thing Romeo," the golem said slyly. Hikari giggled at this.

A/N: The golem had said, "Looks like the boy came back! Glad to see you again after all his time, you old moron!" in draconic.

Chapter 49

This is Home

AFTER the short conversation, TalonFyre passed the golem, motioning for Hikari to follow, tossing a rock at the golem. Upon impact, double doors of solid gold opened beneath the rocks.

"Well, this is home," TalonFyre sighed happily as the two walked through the mammoth doors, revealing a large bunker. This "bunker" however, had furnishing beyond luxury. It was stone the color of shining white, almost quartz-like. It also had a room furnished with a large, red and black pillow the size of a small house, big enough for four dragons, possibly even seven.

Hikari was stunned beyond words at this, her mouth dropping as she spouted three words, "This... is... AWESOME!" at which TalonFyre chuckled.

She decided to lie down after this, as not to upset her stomach. She was almost a week gravid, so she needed to make sure she didn't have any problems. It was true, dragons take nearly two months to develop their eggs, however she needed to take care it actually did develop properly.

"And Ultimar..." TalonFyre began smugly, walking over to a large room, "Give me a minute," he continued, walking over to an old portal and proceeding to kick it. The portal opened after this and TalonFyre tapped the doctor's shoulder, "Hiya! Miss me?"

He expected the doctor to be surprised but he merely got a cheerful, "Hey, pal," in response. It didn't really matter however, as Ultimar had done a lot for him. It was almost better that he didn't do anything to make him embittered, although given his nature it would be likely that he never would.

"Yep, it's linked to the whole hospital – Oh, sorry about the sand," TalonFyre gave a sheepish grin as he saw the grainy yellow salt on Ultimar's white tiles.

It was then that Ultimar realized TalonFyre had made a wormhole into his subspace. "How did you..?" the doctor began to ask, baffled at the entire scene.

"Heh, it's ancient draconic technology - Veh, desta loupon douta," TalonFyre said, a proud and smug tone in his voice, "And if you want... Come study it anytime."

"One, I know every language in the multiverse, so I know you just said, 'Yeah, better than yours' in your ancient draconic language, and two, how did you connect to a pocket dimension closed off to the multiverse?" the doctor stated then asked in a somewhat impatient and even possibly angry tone, albeit with a slight bit of worry to it.

"Heh...my secrets are my own," TalonFyre answered in the same smug tone he had before.

Ultimar smiled and replied, "Wux re onelkator, sia thurirl," which caused TalonFyre to sigh in defeat.

Approaching the door once more, TalonFyre smiled, "Want to see the big reveal?" and he passed through without opening them, almost resembling a ghost. "Heh, these are fake," TalonFyre shrugged as the doors disappeared. "It's an open-ended cave with a shield protecting it from sand."

Something concerned the doctor about the portal, however. "Also, I really want to know if those doors allow only us to pass through and not outside evils," he half remarked, half asked the ex-mercenary, a serious look on his face.

TalonFyre shrugged again, "Oh, it's fine. They're set to you guys. Noted you on the door."

Ultimar nodded, "I'm fine with it then."

TalonFyre walked through a large door, placing his paw upon a switch. At this, the room illuminated revealing a vast room made of gold and jewels. "I don't buy much – All in the package." TalonFyre smiled as they walked into the large room. "Hikari, come on!"

Taking her body off the pillow, the gravid dragoness followed suit, walking into the room. "There's a kitchen, nursery, training room, alchemy lab, surgery, even playroom – It's everything we need!" TalonFyre remarked happily.

Ultimar smiled at this, knowing that his friend would have all that he would ever desire.

"Oh Ultimar, can I go somewhere with you alone?" TalonFyre asked intently.

The doctor nodded, "Alright, I'll let you show me whatever you need to."

The two walked into an archival room. "Well, you know how you knew about my past?" the ex-mercenary asked. This caused Ultimar to merely give a small nod.

With the wave of a paw, TalonFyre produced a book the size of the room. "This contains everyone I've met, then it records their lives… Retrieves any memories it needs to," he said smiling and looking at Ultimar.

The doctor gulped, "So… mine too?" looking him in the eyes, a scared expression on his face.

TalonFyre shrugged, "Oh sure." At which Ultimar closed his eyes, clenching his fist.

Chapter 50

Ultimar's Past

    TALONFYRE began to read the book, written here would reveal the reason that Ultimar had become who he was, as well as show who he used to be.
    "I... am Ultimar, the ultimate weapon, the ultimate healer, and formerly, the ultimate slayer of everything I saw as cruel."
    The scientists that created me used genetic technology to develop the ultimate life form - me. The gem they placed in my forehead contains energy that enhances my powers – all energy including magical, spiritual, organic, artificial and chemical. Also, it can't be removed unless I'm dead. They originally intended for me to be stronger, but little did they know, I had already been aware when I was inside my gestation tube. When I was a fully formed baby, I broke the tube and destroyed the lab, leaving only the scientists, who I beat within an inch of their lives, then healed.
    I wandered the galaxies, my power growing as I aged. I became embittered about the way I was created, and obliterated all evil I came across while traveling the galaxy, just to make myself feel better.
    When I was 120, no more than 11 in human years, I finally caught the attention of the IGFSB, or Intergalactic Federation of Sentient Beings. This was after my brutal and merciless attack on an HQ of the IGRSB, or Intergalactic Rogue Science Bureau. They initiated me into their ranks, giving me the position of 5-star Intergalactic Warrior Class as soon as I passed the exam – the highest anyone ever had gotten. I never learned the true names of any of the races, however. I merely knew the 'slang' terms Earth uses.
    I met a very unorthodox Grey after this – Gazar. He had in infatuation with a female Reptilian known as Quartza. I'd never seen such a close pair of friends. They did everything together. She was a bit of a tom-girl, just like Hikari. She always laughed at his overly-dirty jokes and belched loud enough for everyone in the mess hall to hear. The term they used for intercepting information or disrupting the plans of our enemies was and I quote, "Metaphorically butt-drill them".
    After 20 years I had realized no matter how much evil I destroyed, more would keep appearing. I eventually didn't care about destroying evil. No, I didn't care about anything anymore. I decided to quit the Federation after this. They had objections, but they knew keeping a warrior by force was against the first law of their code – Never stop someone from leaving of their own free will.
    After my leave I stopped on a planet of snake-like creatures known as Nagasapiens, where I had decided to end my life. Only I can do such a thing, and voluntarily, as I cannot be controlled by any means in the multiverse. Well, except if the people of Heaven, who reign over it all,

would
do something.

When I was about to do such a stupid thing, I saw a young, lost Nagasapien girl, about my own age. I was 140 at the time, about 13 years old for a human. She was all on her own in the middle of nowhere, and completely exhausted from trying to find her way through the wasteland which we were in.

I couldn't just leave her, so I healed her and created a crater to find water for her to drink. "Where did you come from?" I asked her, a strange look on my face that I never really had before.

"I was sold as a slave to this pig of a king. Before I could arrive at the palace, I escaped along with my friends under my own planning. I went into the wasteland, while they ran into the city. I had escaped capture by dooming myself to wander aimlessly in the desert till I died. The rest of them - I think they were recaptured. I figured I'd rather die than go back, and I hate to think what could have happened to them - all because of *me*!" she cried out in misery. I felt things I never felt before when she had said such a thing – pity, empathy, softness.

"Think of your friends and the place they were being taken to," I requested seriously.

"Why would I want to think of them *or* that palace!?" she yelled, tears in her eyes.

"I can read thoughts, and I *swear* I'll get them back to you!" I shouted, not even thinking. She did as she was asked.

"You'll be safe with me, and I'll free every one of your friends. As well as give that king what he deserves," I assured her, clenching my fist. I flew her to the palace to wreak my vengeance upon them.

"Who goes there? Ah, you've brought the runaway slave! I'll see that the King rewards you handsomely," the guard said as the girl's eyes widened in fear.

"Keep your freaking bull crap to yourself!" I yelled, punching the door ajar. The three guards tried to stop me and were knocked unconscious with backhand chops to their necks, which didn't take me more than a second due to me teleporting behind each of them in succession.

"You didn't turn me in?" the girl asked.

"I came to kick ass, not get some reward from a sick king," I told the girl in a vengeful voice.

I went into the palace, blowing away walls, beating guards out cold. I soon came to the king's chambers. "Hey, you sick little **snake**-monkey, I got a *present* for you!" I snapped.

"Ah the runaway-" he started, only to be interrupted by a low-powered shot of my Ki energy, blowing away his throne and knocking him to the ground.

"Look away, girl. I'm about to perform an operation on this jerk," I sneered with my cruelest expression. I then took away his weapons, searing the wound shut afterwards as he screamed in pain. After I did that, I was about to kill him using a charged shot of Ki to his head, but I was stopped by a small, scaly hand.

"Please, *don't*!" the girl pleaded.

"**Why**!? That guy *deserves* it for what he did!" I yelled angrily.

She shook her head, "You've done enough! He's unconscious! Please, no more violence! I just want to see my friends again!" she continued, tears forming in her eyes once more.

"Right – I'm sorry. Let's go rescue your friends," I replied.

We went into the dungeon, where, sure enough, there were three more young Nagasapien girls. I quickly ripped open the cage, freeing them.

"Are you all okay? Have they pulled you out of the cell yet?" I asked, worriedly. They shook their head no. "Okay, let's get you out of here," I sighed in relief.

"Where do we go?" the first girl I rescued asked.

"Somewhere where we can be free," I answered in a kind voice.

This caused the girl to ask a question I never thought of, "Where can we *be* free?"

I wondered where I could go to protect the first friends I ever made. Just then, as I thought about the word "friend", I felt a new power. A power I constantly use to this day. I waved my hand and used all my strength, creating a portal to a dimension with exactly what we needed – *nothing*.

"How did you do that?" the girl asked in wonder.

I shrugged, "I don't know. I just thought about the words, 'protect my friends' and it just happened."

"Don't you get it?" the girl asked in a joyous voice.

"Get what?" I asked in return, utterly oblivious.

"Your powers - they're meant to protect, not destroy. You thought about protecting others, and they became stronger. You're not *really* a killer," the girl replied kindly.

"You mean, I'm meant to-" I started

"You're meant to give life, not take it away. You're a kind person who took the wrong path. That's all," she said, clasping my hands with hers. I turned red, and didn't know why. I thought about what she said, and realized - it was true.

"Can I have your name?" I requested.

The girl gave a sweet reply, "It's Mian."

"That's such a beautiful name," I whispered, not knowing why. She blushed back. "Why am I red?" I inquired to Mian.

The two other girls snickered. One of them blurted out," I think I know why! He's in love!"

"What's love?" I asked.

They were shocked by this question, and I could have sworn I saw a tear in Mian's eye. "It's when you have deep feelings of attachment to someone," the girl now known as Mian answered, turning even redder.

When we got through the portal, I learned what it meant to care for someone more than myself, gaining a new power - Ki creation, in which I promptly worked on my new house. When I finished, I was satisfied to live there for the rest of my life. However, for the two days I had worked on it I had neglected to mention something, which I would be forced to the moment I stopped my work.

As I landed, Mian spoke in her usual kind voice, "You know, I never got *your* name."

I braced myself. I answered, "It's Ultimar. The ultimate life form, created to be the ultimate weapon," sounding angry at my own words, which felt like venom.

Upon hearing my words, Mian immediately suggested something that my heart warm to this day, "How about me and you become the ultimate healers, and we turn this place into a multiversal hospital?"

I thought about her words, and knew if my powers were meant to give life like Mian said, we'd make a great asset to many dimensions.

"What do you say, Ultimar?" she asked, a puppy dog expression on her face.

"How could I say no, with a face like that?" I answered with a chuckle.

In fifty years, I created a hospital for every kind of being imaginable, with every manner of species as doctors and nurses.

Mian and I got married a few years through at the Sistine Chapel in a peaceful alternate version of earth - by the Pope himself no less. How you ask? I did a bunch of things – charity, building churches, helping the needy, curing diseases, solving the world's problems, all of those things. I always had two rules – never be seen and always make sure you can't be talked about. I planned to leave but I was caught in the act of rebuilding a homeless shelter. They thought I was some kind of warlock or demon at first, but they put the pieces together as to who was doing all these deeds quite quickly.

After this I kind of gained a following of people, but I reiterated I wasn't some kind of deity or angel. I kept saying if I claimed to be divine it would be heresy. That was, as the Pope said it, "The last plain straw before the one with a golden tip" meaning that was all he needed to know. I gave him my entire history after that. He told me he'd never seen such turnover of character.

I was 14 in human years, but in truth I was much older. So was Mian. He asked if we were married and I told him no. I also told him we hadn't even seen each other naked – let alone had sex yet. He made it official – he would marry us and give us the most elaborate ring and wedding. I told him a plain silver ring and normal wedding would be fine since it wasn't expense that mattered but instead the love that it symbolized. It melted his heart. He didn't even have a problem with her being an alien after I took the illusion off. He even gave me the power and authority to bless people for happy lives, as well as other things. I was literally ordained a saint after this in only five years.

We've hardly ever lost a patient, with the devices I created and giving the doctors and nurses a portion of my own power, although they get it stripped away if they use it for evil or too much personal gain.

After all those years healing, I began to hate even thinking of harming another being. That's why when I intervene, my heart aches for the people I hurt, no matter what they've done.

Now for the part I hate most of all. As soon as I was done creating the hospital, I used my telepathic visions to check on the scientists which created me. They didn't learn their lesson. They created a new being, this time much weaker, but one that lusted to be the ultimate weapon. They figured if he wanted to be the ultimate weapon, they wouldn't have problems. They couldn't have been more wrong.

Like me, he broke out of the container. He then proceeded to kill every last scientist. His name – was Sbarre. He lusted for destruction, and like me he made a pocket dimension in subspace, but not a hospital. Instead, he made a war fortress. He came to my hospital from a world he destroyed. He made a deal with me – He wouldn't destroy anything outside his pocket dimension anymore nor would he bring any living thing in against their will, nor trick them into coming. In exchange, I couldn't destroy him. We shook on it. However, he used pact magic to seal the deal without my knowledge. I found out too late.

Once I used my visions to check on him, he was building an army. Due to the deal, he can't interfere directly, but that didn't stop him from sending those abominations he created to other worlds that I hadn't linked to my hospital.

I would never kill them, and he knows this. That's why I have to seal the gates to his world whenever I set up a link to my hospital. I haven't ever forgotten yet, or found a world I couldn't do that to, but he's just waiting for that chance - and he'll take it as soon as he gets it.

I found a friend in TalonFyre. I saved him from being alone, and I know he thanks me for it. He's a bit rough around the edges, but his tomboyish love, Hikari, more than accepts him. I will link this world to my hospital, I just hope Sbarre doesn't realize one thing - I can't seal this world off for some reason…

TalonFyre now gave me the power to have a child, and Mian is now pregnant with my first born daughter. We're going to name her after my wife. Mian means "Pure Soul" in Nagasapien terms. Mina will mean "Pure Wisdom" as I sense she's going to have a sound and wise mind, even more so than me.

Hrothgar, that monster…. he tried to kill my wife! I'm going to kill him. I don't care what I promised Mian, I have to make sure he never kills another dragoness. He even EATS EGGS! My best profession, the thing I excel in the most, is delivering life into this world. This is the most volatile and horrific thing I've seen in a long time. It violates all I stand for, and is something I have to stop!

TalonFyre saved me. He stopped me from making a huge mistake. It would have broken Mian's heart if I would have killed again. I was a fool. I let rage take control of me again, but this is the last time I do. At least, I hope it is.

Hikari is pregnant, or gravid. TalonFyre feels guilty about it, but she lets him know it was only natural for her to be sick. She was worried about the delivery, which passed on to Talon. I promised them I would take care of them and make sure that their son will be born without any complications. Angel is going to be expecting as well.

I don't know why, but I feel TalonFyre is going to be my best friend. I just sense it somehow. I already know I owe him for allowing Mina to be born into this world in two years.

TalonFyre stopped reading after this.

Chapter 51

Grateful to be Second Best

"ANYWAY..." TalonFyre went on, flipping to the page belonging to Mian, "Yup, I saw it and hey, love is blind. Didn't scare me," he then closed the book. "It has her and your lives from birth up until the present. I opted out of the future telling crap – what would life be without surprises?" with this, he put it away. "Feel free to look anytime. Also, there's a lab here and surgery wing here."

The doctor couldn't hold it in any more. He *had* to say it. "You're... I don't know how to say this without sounding cheesy, but you're the best friend I've ever had. I don't even mind you seeing my past – even everyone I killed," he sighed, his eyes becoming full of tears as he uttered the last words.

TalonFyre shook his head, "Nah, it's fine and I need a minute in the training room... It's... I'll show you."

He then pointed to the kitchen, "Hikari, go eat the fridge. It's ready as we speak," smiling as he turned to the doctor.

The gravid dragoness rushed to the kitchen, ready to both fill her stomach and nurture her newly-forming egg. She was excited to be a mother, and her unease about the laying was completely negated now thanks to Ultimar.

"Let's go, I need to get this out," TalonFyre said with a semi-grin, walking to the training room.

Ultimar, however, was lost in thought and regret once more. "I was... a horrible monster... killing everyone that I assumed was evil... without a second thought... Mian... she led me to the life I have now," the doctor whispered, tears streaming from his eyes.

"I saw," TalonFyre sighed in a comforting voice.

After seeing Ultimar in such a state, TalonFyre realized something else about the doctor – he really did have a soft heart. It wasn't cold and merciless as he thought at first, nor was it hard. He was loving, kind, and would do anything to help someone. That was the true nature of Ultimar's heart.

"As I said, love is blind and can cross the universe before we even breathe a word," TalonFyre reiterated, seeing his friend had calmed himself at this point. "Anyway, I'm gonna' need that training room – the one here is a bit old."

Out of the blue Ultimar asked a question that was on his mind for the last week, "Wait... Are you going to be okay with the delivery, Talon?" his expression a mixture of questioning and seriousness.

TalonFyre looked at him with a confused expression, "What? Well, you can help if you want. Let's just say stretching is ok in small amounts," he replied with a strange, wide smile, cringing at the thought, leading Ultimar to roll his eyes.

"Most guys have a hard time with that. I know I did at first," Ultimar replied seriously.

In which TalonFyre merely shrugged, "Meh, I'll suck it up. I'll watch but hey..." he cut off as he teleported to the training room.

The doctor warped into the training room to see TalonFyre smirking. At this Ultimar cracked his knuckles. "Let's get started," the doctor said nonchalantly as he snapped his fingers, showing a large hologram of the sun in the sky.

"Well, you won't need that shit gazer," the ex-mercenary said with a grin, putting his claw to his new ally's forehead.

"This may hurt," TalonFyre warned as he burned a scale through to the inner lining of the doctor's skull, causing him to flinch, but nothing less. This surprised the ex-mercenary, but after the knowledge of the doctor's somber and violent past, he shrugged it off.

"Hey, watch my gem!" the doctor yelled, folding his arms.

TalonFyre was confused and continued, "Now.... Any dragon you encounter - You read its power instantly."

Ultimar pointed to his forehead just above the place that TalonFyre had pressed the scale into his skull, "That gem isn't like your heart, and it can't be damaged or taken out till I die... but I like the look. Don't mess with it. Call me vain, but I like to look good. And that prismatic gem is the top of the list." With this a prismatic gem emerged from the top of his forehead and sunk back in.

"Well, whatever, you may *not* want to shield up," TalonFyre shrugged, glowing jet-black with neon white eyes. "Remember that dark side of me? That was the evil part," he went on, "This.....is for protecting the ones I care for – By the way, look up."

At this the doctor looked to the top of the training room, now covered by an eye. "Peekaboo!" the ex-mercenary chuckled.

Ultimar was astounded and could only muster a few words, "Okay, that's pretty awesome."

"Yeah, well, you know how space is dark? Every mile of that darkness adds up," the ex-mercenary continued.

Ultimar gasped, "So... That eye is..." he took a step back, as an infinity symbol had appeared on TalonFyre's chest upon these words.

"I only run one universe. Hey I have limits... and it's totally in control – The evil side was mixing it up and making it unstable," TalonFyre smirked. "You fixed that, so I'd say you're beaten," his smile turned sarcastic, "But I never said I wasn't gonna' try."

Ultimar smiled, "This is a grand day, my friend, but my combat power, unmasked in my Sigma form, is 500 Sextillion. It's enough to destroy a 500 kilometer ball of solid steel if I used all my power."

TalonFyre's own physical power was only a small fraction of his own, but his spiritual power was at least twice the level of his highest form. The doctor was proud, albeit a bit jealous. Although not the same as envy, the doctor knew it wasn't a good emotion to have. Even so, he was too kind to tell him that the power he held wasn't truly infinite.

"Well you read the symbol, right?" TalonFyre asked with a smug tone in his voice.

"Infinity..." Ultimar sighed, a sad smile on his face knowing he couldn't hide his knowledge very well.

"Yeah, but... any pure dark magic, and I'm talking to bison-shit, throws it off kilter," he turned to the doctor, approaching him and taking his hand, "Which is why... I can if I want and you want... make a bond that bars him from anyone I've met."

The doctor was lost in thought, 'I'm so glad that I met him. Sbarre is no longer a threat to me or my family, let alone the world that I just came to. So what if I'm not the strongest? It's a small price to pay. Besides, Talon won't use his power for evil. I know he's too kind for that. His softness mirrors my own almost. I guess he knows it now too. I'm actually glad I don't have to put up a farce with them anymore. When I told him I didn't mind him seeing my past, I wasn't lying, or at least directly. No, I'm actually glad... so glad that I could share it with someone other than my own workers.'

He was brought out of his trance when Talon spoke again, "So, do you want to do it or not?"

Snapping out of his thoughts, Ultimar smiled brightly, "Yes, and I'm glad I met you."

TalonFyre smiled in turn, "Well, hand me your hand then."

Without hesitation, the doctor put out his hand and TalonFyre cut the symbol, bleeding pure clear energy. He then proceeded to put the doctor's hand upon it. "And.....he's banned," TalonFyre smiled.

Ultimar smirked, "Seems a fitting punishment, for now at least."

TalonFyre shrugged, "It's that easy - just don't smell it. It smells like well....the worst you've smelled times ten." The cut disappeared at this.

"Oh, and remember when he was by you and I targeted him? That was me getting his signature. That, combined with that energy, bars him," the ex-mercenary informed the doctor.

He then chuckled, "Oh and Hikari is watching this. I've sent her the video right now. She'll be happy as ever now. Hey, she knows it's to protect us all. I want the best for her – and you guys," he was going off on a tangent, but Ultimar didn't care. He was just glad that his enemy was out of his life for good.

Chapter 52

Some Powers are Best Left Uncopied

THE gravid dragoness was watching the entire display all the while through the wormhole, her eyes wide. She was taken aback by her mate's power, which surpassed the strongest being on the planet, or possibly ever this entire dimension.

"(Hikari, I take it you're gawking,)" TalonFyre said with a smile, which turned to a frown as he thought of his terrifying power. "Great I've scared her." He smacked himself in the face at the thought.

The dragoness walked in, mouth filled with meat and foodstuffs, "Mh… What do you mean scared?" she gulped the food down upon saying this, licking her muzzle.

"Yeah, I figured," TalonFyre chuckled.

"Well Ultimar, drop in when you feel like it," the ex-mercenary smiled.

The doctor gave a nod, speaking in a comforting tone, "I'll be there for the delivery. Don't worry, Hikari will be fine." TalonFyre nodded in return and teleported home.

Upon returning, TalonFyre found the room covered in meat from Hikari's eating habits, at which he merely grinned, "Well….gold room with meat trim I guess."

"(Ultimar, once Angel and Flare are done being busy, send them the footage as well,)" the ex-mercenary requested kindly.

Ultimar agreed, "(Okay, I'll do that. Also, I hope you don't mind that I copied your banishing power.)"

TalonFyre smiled sarcastically, "(Ah fine. But one thing - that one you copied was a decoy – can't be copied,)" he rolled his eyes in a sly manner. "(And it gives you….let's see here…the skids. Right about *now*,)" he grinned, lying down on the pillow which Hikari had been on earlier.

"(It's only temporary. By that I mean whenever you try to copy my powers it kicks in… There's one I *can* give you,)" with this the ex-mercenary teleported his new friend an endless roll of toilet paper.

"(Ultimate Power ultimately corrupts. Remember that phrase,)" the doctor warned, a somber and serious tone in his voice.

TalonFyre merely shrugged, "(Yeah, you're about to get ultimate blowback.)"

This worried the doctor. What if his new friend became like himself? What if he started to become corrupt with power and began killing the people his saw as the least bit evil, or worse, below him?

"(And hey... The sun purifies the darkness making a balance of the two, meaning the universe stays balanced making my powers balanced. I can fix yours to be the same – Oh, well not now anyway. You're bursting a wormhole open,)" TalonFyre finished his speech with a laugh.

"(I have no dark powers,)" Ultimar replied seriously, knowing that if he did have such powers, it would have been a disaster for the entire universe he was made in.

TalonFyre shrugged again, "(Like I said, balanced,)" he grinned again. "(Now I believe that noise is you… and I wonder if Mian… no she won't want to see it. Give it a day and it'll stop working. Until then have fun painting the bowl. Anyway have fun doctor doo,)" he finished his rambling and cut off his telepathy.

'Talon, I really hope you don't end up going off the deep end like I did… I'd hate to have to do something about it. It's true that you're stronger, but I copied other powers that, if I have to, I'll use. You're not the strongest one in the multiverse, let alone the movie I'll watch if I have to,' Ultimar thought to himself, near tears at the thought of harming his new friend.

Chapter 53

Regrets and True Love

"HIKARI, you finished yet?" TalonFyre called out as he walked into the kitchen where his beloved had begun her meal. He knew she would be eating a lot more as the egg developed, so he assumed that she would have finished most of the food in the refrigerator by this time.

A loud belch was heard as he approached, causing him to smile warmly, "Yup, sounds like it!" he entered the kitchen after this to find Hikari covered in meat, among other things.

"Well Hikari, you full?" the ex-mercenary asked lovingly, putting his paw on her neck.

She nodded, putting her head on his, "Yeah..."

"And feel free to be sick on me whenever. Doesn't matter to me," he went on, nuzzling her.

Hikari shrugged, "It usually happens in the morning." At which TalonFyre realized he had no idea what hour it was.

"Ah. What time is it anyway? I have no clue." He looked outside at this. "Well it's dark. Maybe that's just Ultimar's.....nah." He looked at his beloved, wiping her mouth off gently, "Shall we go to bed for the night, miss piggy?"

The dragoness looked at him intently, "Talon... What did you do.....?"

The ex-mercenary smirked, "Oh nothing... Someone tried to reuse my powers, they got something else." With this he kissed her on the muzzle.

They were interrupted by Ultimar's annoyed response, "(I have diarrhea, thanks to him.)"

This caused TalonFyre to grin. His grin was short-lived, however, due to Hikari's angry expression. "That was cruel... even by my standards," she growled angrily, knowing full-well that the doctor wanted to help with such a thing. Not only this, he had promised to help her get through the laying!

"Fine, hang on...." TalonFyre deactivated it upon seeing his love so upset, he couldn't bear to see her angry at him. "(There, sorry Ultimar,)" he sighed, ashamed of his actions upon his new friend.

"(I think I'll go watch a few movies I haven't seen yet, and it's fine,)" the doctor replied warily.

TalonFyre snickered, "(Yeah, by the way, you have toilet paper still stuck.)"

At this the doctor gave a nonchalant response, "(Okay, I'll get rid of it.)"

"(Don't. Just don't,)" TalonFyre said hastily.

Ultimar could merely give a confused, "(Why?)" at such a response.

"(You were going to send it back at me!)" the ex-mercenary retorted defensively.

The idea of this actually hurt the doctor. Did his new friend really think that low of him? That he would do such a cruel thing after what he said?

"(What?)" Ultimar asked, his pain showing through his telepathy, causing TalonFyre to feel guilty.

"(Yeah, I'm not thinking well.... That power up always knocks me silly,)" he sighed, ashamed of his words.

After the conversation, the two mates walked into a dark room. "Well, here we are," TalonFyre said proudly, lighting a gem, "It's entirely crystal. Even engraved our names over the door."

The door frame read a phrase that caused Hikari's eyes to tear with joy, something that she wanted to see for a long time. It read, 'To eternal love, Talon and Hikari'.

"It's... beautiful..." Hikari whispered, tears rolling down her face.

"And it's the same bed Ultimar gave us, upgraded." He touched the surface of the mattress. "No clue what it is, just got me a better bed... Uh, us I mean." He thought she'd be angry at his mistake but she just laughed.

Above the bed, the plaque read, 'To my dearest Hikari, who made me become the happiest one in the universe...may our love be eternal', at which the dragoness cried harder.

"You okay, Hikari?" the ex-mercenary asked.

The dragoness shook her head, "I love it... so much, Talon. I just... I'm so happy I can't help but shed tears. We'll be together, always." At this she put her neck around his and kissed him. He put his paw around her in turn.

After the embrace, TalonFyre sighed contently, "Anyway, I'm tired," lying on the bed, "Oh man, way better... Dive on, who cares."

It was true, Hikari would have liked to dive on, but she would endanger the egg, which was forming for at least a week. She climbed in bed happily, putting her front leg around TalonFyre as he hugged her close to him.

"Well, night my light of my life..." he yawned, a loving tone in his voice.

Hikari nuzzled him, "That quote from Ultimar's wife... Goodnight Talon..." she yawned as well as her beloved wrapped his wing around her, falling asleep.

To make up for his misdeed, TalonFyre decided to pause the doctor's movie mid-story. "(Oh sorry, that was me,)" he teleported popcorn and a drink to the doctor at this as a kindness. He really did feel guilty about making him so miserable.

"(It's fine, and thanks. Still, remember... absolute power corrupts absolutely. Rule your power, don't let it rule you. Don't become the monster I was,)" the doctor said, both gratefully and warningly.

At this, TalonFyre feel asleep, dreaming of happiness.

And so eight more weeks passed, the two's love growing stronger by the day. Occasionally Ultimar would visit to check on Hikari and TalonFyre, letting them know time and again that she would survive the laying. Still, TalonFyre was concerned. It was Hikari's first time, and it was always the hardest. TalonFyre's mother didn't survive, so the reason behind his worry was justified. Still, Hikari was glad and ready to become a mother, and Ultimar would be right there when it happened.

Chapter 54

It's Time

"HIKARI, you up... chucking..." TalonFyre sighed as he looked at Hikari's sickened expression.

"Yeah. Oh man..." the egg-heavy dragoness groaned, getting up.

"Again, sorry I got you into this mess..." TalonFyre said, a regretful tone in his voice as his love headed into the bathroom, her large stomach showing the egg inside of her.

A splattering was heard as Hikari let go of the bile for a minute on end before she got to where she needed to be, coughing all the while. "Ah, it's fine," TalonFyre shrugged, looking at his beloved as he heated the crystal floor vaporizing the mess, "Self-cleaning."

A sickened expression came upon Hikari's face again. "Hang on," TalonFyre raised his paw, teleporting her to the bathroom, "There."

More vomiting was heard from the bathroom lasting two minutes this time. 'I can't believe what I did to her. She's so miserable and I can't do anything about it,' TalonFyre thought to himself.

"Tha- Ugh!" Hikari grunted in pain as she began to say the words, vomiting more.

"What...Oh," TalonFyre realized that she must have been trying to thank him but she had to relieve herself from her morning sickness. Still, why did she just throw up that much? She hadn't eaten enough to make her this sick.

It was then that TalonFyre realized the pain was for a different reason. "...oh great..." TalonFyre voice was full of worry – the egg was coming. Hikari's body was getting ready to lay.

"(I'm coming, both Mian and myself,)" Ultimar spoke assertively, stepping through the wormhole. He didn't have a surgical outfit on, though. It was a pure blue tank and a white robe underneath. Mian had blue bandages around her midsection and upper body and a white cloth tied around where her belt was before, which he could now only assume covered a more 'personal' section of her body.

"Great timing... Well, anyway, this is happening......" TalonFyre's voice showed great worry. He couldn't bear the thought of Hikari dying! All the scenarios played out in his mind, each worse than the last.

"Let's go, Mian." The doctor walked to the bathroom, ready to help the dragoness onto the pillow in the main room, which could only be assumed to be for delivery.

TalonFyre followed them, "I'll come with. I want to be there. Not the worst I've seen," his voice was as serious as his expression.

Ultimar shrugged, "Alright..."

Inside the bathroom, Hikari's legs were near the point of collapse, and there was a clear substance on the floor, meaning her water had broken. There was no doubt in her mind about what was happening to her at this point. "Talon... please... someone..." Her fears were put at ease when the two doctors entered the room. Ultimar lifted her front legs and helped her into the main room, gently placing her on her back and setting her head on a pillow, a cushion where the egg would emerge and her body on the floor. Hikari gasped in pain – the contractions were starting.

Ultimar placed his hand on Hikari's stomach. "Hikari, I want you to listen to me. Put you mind at ease and take quick-paced, deep breaths. Don't force it, push when your body tells you to, do you understand?"

The dragoness nodded, grunting as another wave of pain shot through her. "Talon… don't leave… please…" the dragoness gasped as she spread her hind legs upon the cushion.

"Mian, massage her stomach to make the laying easier. I'll catch it when it emerges from her birth canal," Ultimar ordered. The snake like lady nodded, as she began to rub the dragoness's stomach to ease the laying.

The sternum of the dragoness began to move as she took the steps that Ultimar had told her to, gasping for breath each time she pushed. The doctor spread her back legs further, creating gloves to mask his scent from the egg and let its mother's scent soak in.

Five painful hours passed, Hikari doing all that Ultimar and Mian instructed. A scream of pain was heard from the dragoness. After that, a somewhat bloody golden egg was in Ultimar's hands.

"Is… is it out yet…? Am I done?" Hikari panted, both out of breath and sweating exhaustively.

Ultimar nodded, "Yes, you did very well."

Hikari smiled at this and set her head down, sleep overtaking her. After this, Ultimar took the egg to the incubation chamber, looking back proudly at the exhausted dragoness.

Chapter 55

The Egg

"THE hell, am I...." TalonFyre groaned as he stood up, dazed, "Must've dozed off again. Anyway, I hope she's ok." He rubbed his head, not realizing he was in his own home.

"Not the worst you've seen, eh?" Ultimar asked rhetorically while crossing his arms, a smug expression on his face. TalonFyre rolled his eyes embarrassedly, realizing he must have passed out after gazing at the least bit of stretching.

"How was everything? I didn't see much," the ex-mercenary asked, a bit of a sheepish look on his face. He closed his eyes and thought to himself, 'Now I feel guilty for not staying up. *Please* tell me she's okay... please... I couldn't bear the thought of losing...'

He was snapped out of his sober train of thought by Ultimar's kind words, "Congratulations... It's a boy. And she's fine. I've never seen such a tough dragoness, not in a while at least."

This caused TalonFyre to sigh in relief. She was fine. The egg was fine. Everything was fine. He began to shed tears of joy at this. He was happy beyond words – he had a mate, a new place to live, a new best friend, and most of all, a new son.

The ex-mercenary looked around, realizing he was in the main room, but Hikari was nowhere to be found. "So where is she, Ultimar? I don't see her anywhere."

Before the doctor could answer, Mian gave a faceless response, "She's resting... in a coma..." causing TalonFyre to panic.

"No... Ultimar said she was fine! She can't be... Please tell me it isn't true!" He clenched his paw tight enough for it to bleed.

"I know you wanted to get back at him Mian, but that was **UNCALLED FOR**!!" the doctor yelled, once again causing the ex-mercenary to snap back into reality.

The snake-like woman sighed. She knew it was wrong and could only give a sad, "Sorry..." in return.

It was obvious to TalonFyre what Mian was angry about. He couldn't really blame her, she was Ultimar's wife. What's more, she was also pregnant. It was only natural that she would be upset with him.

"Yeah.....I knew that... it's ok," the ex-mercenary sighed, knowing it was partially his fault for being so cruel in the first place.

Ultimar put his hand on TalonFyre's front foreleg and gave a sad smile, "I apologize. Nagasapiens can be a lot more... *wrathful* when they're pregnant."

The reptilian woman put her arms around TalonFyre, "Again, I'm sorry..." her voice sounding heartbroken. It was obvious she felt very guilty about causing TalonFyre's worry, even if it was for a few seconds. She was so kind. It was no wonder the doctor fell in love with her, no matter what species they were.

The ex-mercenary put his paw on her hand and gave an understanding smile, "It's fine, Mian."

Noises were heard from the kitchen, leading TalonFyre to smirk, "I hear scarfing…. Yup, that's her." With this, he followed the sounds to find his beloved with a piece of meat in her mouth, swallowing it in a single gulp.

"Well, you seem fine hon," TalonFyre said warmly, looking at his love.

She smiled contently with a bit of pride showing in her face, "I'm a little sore, but at the same time I feel pretty damn good. Not to mention like a total badass." The words caused TalonFyre to smirk. She wasn't going to stop being tomboyish anytime soon, and that response was a big guarantee.

The dragoness looked at her love with a kind, warm and loving expression and said the words she had longed to say since she had become gravid, "Do you want to see the egg?"

"…I guess… I…" TalonFyre became nervous as he received flashbacks of his abandonment. "Yeah, not having that happen," his voice was serious.

Knowing what he was thinking of, Hikari took his paw in hers, "It's fine. You'd never do that, I know it," her voice changed from proud to the most gentle and soothing thing he had ever heard.

His worry vanished and was replaced by relief. He nodded, "Yeah – Well, where is it? I'm not scared too much."

The dragoness led him to their nursery, where a gold egg lay upon a blue cushion with shining silver trim. "Here…" Hikari sighed happily, looking at the result of her hard work and two full months of sickness.

The sight of the egg caused TalonFyre to shed tears once more. He had a son to call his very own. It was too much to keep in. "Damn, no more crying…" his tear-filled eyes showed such happiness that Ultimar began to feel it to his very core.

Due to his psychic power allowing him to sense the emotions of others, Ultimar felt proud, happy, and even a bit somber that he had to leave when it hatched. Still, he knew that this wouldn't be the last time he had to help. He also had to assist Angel in laying soon, as she was due any day now.

"Taiyou…" Hikari whispered, a loving smile on her face. TalonFyre was silent until Hikari spoke again, "His name will mean 'thick sunlight'. It shows both our love and our bond." She turned to TalonFyre with a smile.

Completely taken aback by his mate's knowledge, TalonFyre looked at her, both astonished and full of happiness, "Both of our names?" he whispered joyously. Hikari nodded.

Ultimar gave an approving response, "Okay… Taiyou it is then."

Chapter 56

Hell Hath No Fury

"UH.... Ultimar, I think that....thing I gave you just started up... and you're dripping. Should've taken it out.....ah well happy snail trails," TalonFyre finished his tangent and shrugged.

The doctor put his hand on his face, "I didn't try to even – Ugh..." he ran to the bathroom, leaving his sentence unfinished.

"Well, ok, yeah it's kind of a bad thing to do, but hey – he tried copying my powers. No one does that..." TalonFyre went on once more, a small grin on his face, once again disappearing when he saw another angry expression, this time from doctor's snake-like wife. It wasn't just angry, though. It was pure, unadulterated rage. He looked at her with a shy expression, "Should've made him just puke. Sorry about it Mian, must smell bad."

This did nothing to calm the reptilian woman, however. It was clearly visible that she was still angry beyond words, "That was a dick move TalonFyre!" she screamed. She then realized what had come out of her mouth and gasped, "I can't believe I said that!"

The dragon merely shrugged, "Aw I know and hey, don't worry. It - goes off every now and then – once every several weeks," which in turn caused Mian's rage to increase again.

Knowing that her anger wasn't good for the child, Mian made an attempt to calm herself. She took a breath and asked, "Is there any way to remove it?" her tone now a bit somber and somewhat depressed. The snake-like woman's face, although still a bit spiteful, had a look of desperation in it. She was genuinely concerned.

TalonFyre adopted a regretful look after the display, "Yeah, he's still gonna' have to go another round, but it'll stop."

"I meant to stop that... curse you put on him! Permanently!" Mian continued, now near the point of tears.

TalonFyre put his paws in the air innocently, "It's not - I was only joking!" which caused the woman to continue crying with a hateful expression.

She then looked at him, the spite showing in her eyes. "He didn't try to copy your powers that time!" she screamed at the top of her lungs, her fists clenched to the point where they seemed they might snap in two.

By this point, TalonFyre was filled with regret. He had just realized he had driven a pregnant woman to the point of tears. "Yeah, I know..." he sighed sadly, walking up to the wife of his new best friend, "Here, hit me with your best shot. I deserve it."

"I'm pregnant... no," Mian declined somberly as she turned her head away to avoid the ex-mercenary's gaze.

This in turn caused him to put his paw on Mian's head, albeit gently. He gave a kind smile, "It's fine."

Mian wasn't about to do anything that would endanger her baby, and with her power she would cause a sonic boom when she hit TalonFyre at the level she was emotionally.

"I SAID NO!!!" Mian screeched, her voice echoing throughout the room, reaching the halls. TalonFyre knew he wouldn't get her to hurt him, even though he didn't know why.

"Ok, ok…" TalonFyre turned away, his expression that of shock, discouragement, and most of all, depression. He knew what he did was wrong, but he didn't realize how far-reaching the consequences would be. He walked off towards the bathroom, head held low.

TalonFyre knocked against the bathroom door, receiving an annoyed, "Yes?" from Ultimar.

"Hey, it's removed but it's still gonna' be another round yet… and Mian is mad. She bit my head off, so to speak," TalonFyre said with a tone as guilty as the expression his face held.

This didn't surprise Ultimar at all. He knew full-well how angry Mian would get and how irritable she'd be. Her species was known for how volatile they are when carrying a child, and no matter how kind she was normally, it was still nature that she'd be this way.

"Figures… I warned you…" the doctor sighed in an angry and somewhat sad tone.

TalonFyre shrugged at this, "Ah well, Hikari wasn't that bad but hey…" he then realized what would happen if Mian knew what he was saying. He looked around and whispered, "Uh, she can't hear me can she?" in a worried tone.

"No, I don't think," Ultimar answered, his voice showing the same emotion. TalonFyre sighed in relief, glad he didn't upset the snake-like woman more that he already had. He walked out to the main room after this where his beloved Hikari waited.

Chapter 57

The New Spring

ARRIVING in the main room, TalonFyre looked at his body, once again dirt-covered. "Anyway.....I need a bath," he remarked in a nonchalant tone, shaking off dirt and soot, which landed oh Hikari, and worse – Mian. This caused the snake-like lady to shoot him a glare.

"Woops should've warned you – sorry guys," the ex-mercenary said, embarrassed.

Mian rolled her eyes while Hikari giggled, "Well, now I need a bath too."

At which the snake-like woman growled, "And me."

The problem with this was the fact that no water could be found in a desert – at least not without digging. However, this wasn't a problem for them.

"Hang on....Goldem – mind opening a hot spring?" Talon requested politely.

"Sure thing, boss," the golem replied in the same tone, bringing its mammoth fist down upon the ground, causing water to rise from underneath the sands. "There. Now, back to sleep," the golem sighed, lying down.

Emerging from the cavern, the four saw a large spring before them, bigger than the one they had been in previously.

"Hang on," TalonFyre began, walking up to the hot spring. He transformed into his dark state, a hole-shaped cut appearing on the surface next to the newly-made water-hole. After this a second spring was created. TalonFyre ceased his altered form after this. "There. And if you want I can close it in – walls and door anyone?" he snickered, constructing the architecture out of sand, hardening it afterwards. "Anyway – banzai!" TalonFyre yelled, diving into his newly-made pool. This in turn caused the water to be tainted once more with the ash and soot from his body.

The golem smirked, "Hey Talon, you're dirty!" his tone a mixture of false surprise and sarcasm.

"Aw shut it, Goldem. I WAS dirty!" TalonFyre replied in the same tone, climbing back out of the spring. "Ahh... Now I'm clean."

Ultimar put his hand out in front of his face and spread his fingers. "I got it," he shrugged as he demonstrated another of his abilities – water and earth manipulation. The water condensed into a small spherical shape and a small amount of sand entered. After this the water pushed the ash into the sand, turning it black. The doctor then proceeded to use his telekinetic powers to pull the small piece of dirt out and place it on the ground. Finally the water left its ball-like shape and re-entered the hot spring.

"Well Hikari you're next," TalonFyre said with a small grin. The dragoness dove into the spring without a second thought, laying on her back as she floated on the surface.

TalonFyre pointed to the second spring, "So, you two going in or what? I won't watch – why would I when I have that?" he looked at Hikari and grinned, a giggle coming from her as she looked at him with a smile. "Yeah – she lights me up." he laughed. This caused the dragoness to look at him with a loving gaze, giggling once more.

The two doctors entered the door, a towel forming around each of them as they dropped their clothes on the floor, while TalonFyre headed into his new dwelling place to prepare dinner for his mate and himself.

Chapter 58

She's Still a Pistol

AS he arrived at the refrigerator, TalonFyre took a piece meat from the rack, eating it within less than twenty seconds. He then let out a belch, knowing he'd better get used to doing such things with Hikari's attitude.

"I was going to ask this, but I know the answer," TalonFyre sighed. "Hika – Yeah, all I need to say…" he knew what was coming after this, "I just heated the food up!"

TalonFyre smiled sarcastically, "Give it a few seconds…" at this, his beloved rushed in, knocking him over to the side. "Hey, hey!" the ex-mercenary yelled, getting up from the floor.

"Sorry!" the dragoness yelped, looking away sheepishly.

"It's fine, just eat," TalonFyre shrugged. At this Hikari began to eat in her usual sloppy fashion.

"I married her for happiness not traits," TalonFyre thought out loud, smirking at his next words, "Besides who wouldn't marry such a body. ….Uh…." he then realized he had said everything aloud and gave his mate an embarrassed look.

He once again thought she would be angry, and once again was relieved when his beloved let out a laugh. Unfortunately, her mouth was filled with food at the time, causing TalonFyre to get the brunt of the meat that was inside of her mouth.

"Ew… gross!" Talon gagged, spitting food away from his mouth, "Yuck – It's not mine, I'm not touching it."

After she had finished the meal, Hikari realized she had gotten her mate covered in the food she had eaten. "Sorry!" she apologized again, this time regretfully.

"Again, fine," TalonFyre sighed, wiping the food off and heating the ground to destroy the mess.

Grinning, TalonFyre scraped some of the leftover food off of his body, throwing it at Hikari's face. "Sorry," TalonFyre said sarcastically, laughing. This in turn caused the dragoness to laugh as well.

A wing was placed over TalonFyre by his mate, "How long will it be till he hatches?" she sighed happily.

TalonFyre shrugged, "Ultimar can tell – Wait he's occupied."

Puzzled, Hikari gave a confused, "Why?" thinking TalonFyre had done something again.

"Enjoying a bath – but not alone," Talon said with sly grin.

"Anyway, you guys have fun – I have to take Hikari to my old armory!" TalonFyre called out to them, running out the door and moving through the sands to a large nearby dune, Hikari following.

As he raised his paw, TalonFyre gave a smile, "Come on, I'll show you my swords – And I do mean weapons." At this a large gust of wind blew, revealing another door buried beneath the sands. This in turn had caused the hot tubs to become covered in sand.

"Uh oops – Sorry," TalonFyre apologized. The sand raised out of the tub as soon as the words were spoken and formed into a series of small piles.

"I got it," Ultimar shrugged, using his earth manipulation again.

A latch was unhinged upon the thick, steel door by TalonFyre. Inside lay a hoard of weapons and armor, pure gold and covered in Draconian language.

"Well, here we are. Pre-lit too. Oh, and hold still babe," TalonFyre raised a paw once more, giving her the ability to read ancient Draconian. "There, now go have fun."

The dragoness took in the vast amount of weapons available and eyed a large cannon with rims of white, silver wings and a small tail upon its end. "What is this….? Riliwir Torke, or Crushing Angel… Oh hell yes!" she grabbed the cannon from the wall, smiling broadly. "Wow – this will be fun."

Seeing what his mate had selected, TalonFyre teleported both the cannon and the dragoness to the firing range at the outskirts of the armory. "There, now go nuts. Target's re-spawn as long as you like," TalonFyre said with a sly grin.

Beams of light fired from the cannon at the speed of Mach 2, shattering the targets on impact. "Oh, this is great!" the dragoness yelped happily. "Die-die-die-die-die!"

"All that recoil makes her bounce... Ugh god, I'm better than that," Talon moaned.

Hikari took the cannon on her shoulder and ceased her attack upon the targets. "Could you show me?" the dragoness requested, looking at him with a puppy-dog expression.

TalonFyre gulped, "Well….I can't use it," he smiled after this, "It's for light dragons – it all is. I made it while you weren't looking," he shrugged, "Besides I'm my own weapon since I got that new form."

The dragoness smiled warmly, "You know what lights my fire! Forgive the pun."

At which the ex-mercenary gave the same face, "Yeah, we make a bonfire….oh crap."

"I'm starting to be like you," Hikari chuckled.

"Well, I don't know if that's good or bad," Talon replied uncertainly.

At this Hikari nuzzled him and sighed, "Mates tend to do that," in a warm and loving tone.

TalonFyre shrugged, "No changing me – Can't change the universe."

Upon hearing her mate's response, the dragoness gave a disheartened, "Yeah…" her head dropping.

It was then TalonFyre realized something important. "You changed mine, so maybe so," he sighed happily. This in turn caused Hikari to smile once more, hugging him.

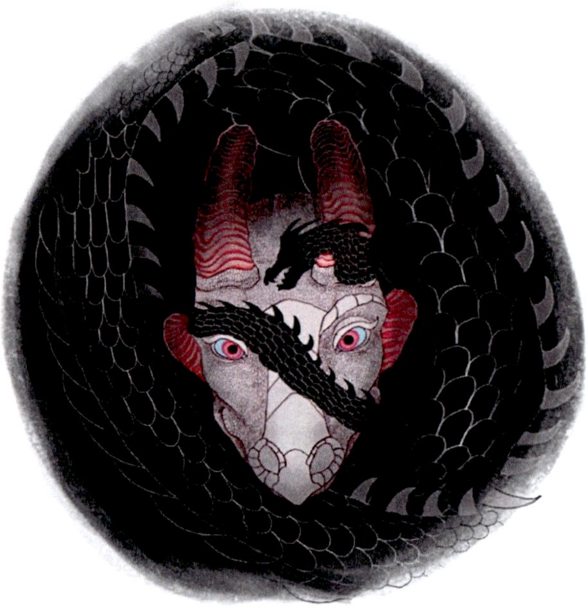

Chapter 59

The Joke Ends Here

"HOW'S it going? You guys enjoying it?" Talon asked his new friend, grinning as he exited the building.

"(Yes, and... oh for crying out...!)" the doctor growled, his stomach lurching again.

TalonFyre smirked, "Must be the last round of what you had earlier. Yeah, it seems like it's purging right......now. Hope you aren't in the hot tub!"

Outside, Ultimar scowled, "I'm not," creating a portable bathroom for himself, causing TalonFyre to laugh hysterically once again.

"(Are the targets re-spawned?)" the doctor asked through his telepathy.

TalonFyre kept his grin, "Yeah and you should be busy right now making horrifying music... And scaring Mian." With this, he materialized a speaker on the outside of the room. "Now let 'er rip!"

By this time Ultimar had lost all patience once more, this time with his new friend. He wanted to show TalonFyre just how outclassed he was. "When I get out of here, I'll show you what the Ultimate Copy can do..." the doctor growled.

TalonFyre shrugged, "I think you just copied something..."

To lighten his mood, Ultimar sighed, "I didn't copy anything. Just diarrhea."

These words caused TalonFyre to fall upon the sands in a fit of laughter, "Oh man, oh man... I'm dying here!"

An idea formed it TalonFyre's head. 'She'll love this.' Without a second thought, he used his telepathy to send the speaker's sounds to his beloved and tomboyish Hikari. "(His Ultimate Copy – He's painting the walls brown!)" TalonFyre joked, Hikari laughing as if she were insane once more.

It once again struck TalonFyre that he had made an error. "Oh – Mian is gonna' be pissed... at...me.... Aw great," he gave a regretful sigh, knowing that he had once again caused Ultimar's pregnant wife to become angry with him.

"Uh, Ultimar – Why is the Jon tipping over? Isn't me - I'm not like that." It was too late to warn the doctor to use his psychokinetic power to keep imminent disaster from occurring at this point, however. TalonFyre put his paw to his face. "Oh, dear lord," he cried.

"Ffffffffffffffff--!" the doctor nearly cursed again, causing TalonFyre to laugh until he vomited on the ground. "Oh, Hikari is gonna' do the same!" he put his paw to his face again, "Oh man, Mian must be hearing this..."

He couldn't help it. TalonFyre had to do it. He raised his hand, his new powers tearing the walls off the bathroom. "And now presenting doctor poo! BWHAHAHAH!" His laugh became loud enough for Mian to hear, who had been sleeping in the sun after her bath.

"Ugh... this is... Ugh! My patience wears thin Talon! There's someone whose power I just copied that could take us both on easily!" the doctor screamed as the entirety of his covering vanished. "De-Materialization..." the doctor growled, his face filled with annoyance.

TalonFyre shrugged, "You still stink... and Mian just walked in."

At which Ultimar's forehead glowed. "I just de-materialized the bacteria. No more smell," the doctor said with a smug look.

'I hope I don't have to use this to threaten you in order to stop you from becoming corrupt. The problem is that there is a limit to how much of such an ability I'm able to copy. Even my Ultimate Copy power has some limits,' Ultimar thought.

"Ultimar, are you okay!?" the snake-like woman screeched as she embraced the doctor, squeezing his mid-section, as she only came up to his shoulders at the height at which her underbelly could move. Not all of a Nagasapien's lower scales were used for momentum. In truth, Ultimar dwarfed her at his height.

He put his arms around her, "I'm fine, Mian. You don't have to worry; it was just a bad joke."

These words caused TalonFyre to look at them apologetically. "Yeah, I went too far..." he sighed regretfully as he approached them, lowering his head to their level.

"Well, Mian... Give me all you got. I deserve it plus I can take whatever you give me," Talon smiled sadly, the infinity symbol glowing. They shook their heads. "I can withstand anything," he insisted, looking hurt.

This caused Ultimar to put his hand up, "Talon, I know that you think we want to get revenge, but it's not our way." Hearing the words, TalonFyre transformed back to his normal state.

It baffled TalonFyre how Ultimar and his wife could be so calm after what he did. Even when his wife was kidnapped, Ultimar nearly refused to fight. He had a feeling that the only reason this doctor tried to kill Hrothgar wasn't because of the fact that he tried to eat his wife, or at least not directly. It was because he devoured new life, which Ultimar cherished bringing into the world more than any other job. He was either crazy, had the patience of a saint, or possibly just hated violence. Maybe it was a combination of all three, or at least two of them.

The oddest thing about him, however, was the fact that he felt like he was almost connected to him in a strange way. It was like something was telling him he was meant to be his best friend until the day came that one of them were to cease living. No, he already was his best friend. TalonFyre presumed the reason he was so comfortable around this doctor was because he knew that no matter what he did to him he would always have his back. He was almost like family to him, and good families never hurt each other. Maybe Ultimar felt the same way since he never had any real family besides Mian. Only time would tell.

Chapter 60

A Visit to the Parents

"WHERE is Hikari – Oh wait...? Stupid question. Well, either the armory or the fridge. I need to build one in the armory – Nah," TalonFyre went off on a rant.

Ultimar shrugged, "You watch over your universe, I'll watch over mine."

At which TalonFyre gave a nod and an understanding response, "Fair enough."

As TalonFyre looked to the doctors, they seemed to be unsure of something. He smiled kindly, "Mian, you can stay if you like – I've set up a room for you to match your tastes... Er, well, you get the idea. Mian, sorry," he didn't truly know what he was saying at this point, however.

"I'm going with Ultimar," the snake-like lady stated in a serious tone.

This in turn caused TalonFyre to shrug, "Oh, ok. Yeah, shouldn't have asked," he looked around, realizing his beloved was no longer in his new home.

TalonFyre grinned, "Well, Hikari is busy firing loads off – Uh, ammo I mean," his expression turned embarrassed. "I'm gonna' go take a map – er, nap," he put his paw to his face, "Yeah, I get tongue-tied when I get tired... or with Hikari – GAH!" he finished his tangent and walked towards his bedroom, utterly mortified. He sighed and turned towards the two, "Bye guys, and sorry again."

Upon reaching the bedroom, TalonFyre lay upon the mattress only to rise when a thought entered his head. He had forgotten about his new parents! Angel was gravid, and she had gotten into that state near the time Hikari had!

"Just remembered something," Talon said quickly, teleporting to Flare's new domicile. "Guys, you ok? Just checking in," he looked around and found no one inside the main room. He became worried, only to hear footsteps from the room of his new parents. He prepared to ready an attack, only to see a familiar figure in the door – Ultimar.

The doctor smiled, "Not yet... two days though," his tone happy and loving.

TalonFyre gave a surprised look, "Oh, Mian, so you're due in two days? Congrats!" At this he proceeded to look for his parents, entering their room. "Guys, you in here?" he looked around, still searching for his adoptive parents.

"They're the ones due in two days, Talon. It's obvious," the doctor said in an annoyed and comedic tone.

"Ohh... Well – Ok, this is awkward. They don't even know I'm here," TalonFyre rambled again.

Ultimar smiled, "Mian and I are staying here until then."

TalonFyre sighed disappointedly, "I'd better leave," leaving a photo of the egg as he teleported back to his home. Unbeknownst to him Flare and Angel were just arriving from their meal, Angel filled completely due to the forming egg nearly ready to be laid.

"It's... it's..." Flare stuttered only for Angel to give a contented and amazed sigh, "Beautiful..." finishing his sentence. At this TalonFyre re-appeared, causing Angel to gasp.

"What? Oh yeah, and I passed out," TalonFyre grinned embarrassedly.

Ultimar shrugged, "Yeah, I expected that," his tone mostly casual.

"Me too," Flare nodded, his own tone serious and comedic at the same time.

"Mmmm-hmmmm," Angel hummed, proceeding to chuckle.

TalonFyre raised his paw, slapping both Ultimar and Flare. Angel he refrained from touching due to the fact she was gravid. Besides that fact, TalonFyre would never hit an innocent female – No honorable man would. Ultimar got the brunt of TalonFyre's blow since the ex-mercenary couldn't hurt him when he wasn't using his "dark form".

"I'd expect you guys to do the same," TalonFyre retorted, rubbing his paw, which became sore after hitting the doctor. He had to hand it to him, his skin really was tough.

It was at this point that Flare decided to speak up, "I got the village nurse to do it. I did too," his face as embarrassed as TalonFyre was when he had told them about the event.

"Do what? Ohh..." TalonFyre gave an understanding nod.

"That's normal," Flare said with a small grin, his voice almost a laugh.

"Well, I've made Hikari happy! She ate the fridge in ten seconds and is chewing through ammo. Feel like seeing some Draconian armor?" TalonFyre went on a tangent again until he said the word, "Litrix," meaning "Armor" in Draconian.

Flare shook his head, "I'm staying with Angel," his voice becoming serious again.

TalonFyre shrugged, "Ok, that's obvious, why did I ask..."

TalonFyre smirked, "And you might want to know... I taught her to speak it too," his voice both smug and happy.

"That's great!" Angel piped in, excited for her daughter's new ability.

"You guys want in? Oh, and Ultimar got showered in crap!" TalonFyre laughed, losing his train of thought.

"After Ultimar delivers the – ...what?" Flare asked, puzzled at the idea.

TalonFyre continued after this, "After the Jon tipped over on him while he was in it!" his voice somewhat a howl.

This caused the doctor to roll his eyes. "That was as crazy as eight nights of idiocy," he grunted, trying to hide a smile.

TalonFyre put his paws up in the air, "Hang on, hang on, let me show you..." he concentrated, sending them a vision of it. He laughed mischievously.

"Oh, sweet merciful...!" Flare gagged. Angel on the other hand went as far as to vomit what she had eaten onto the floor.

TalonFyre put his paw on his head, "Oh man, sorry... Yeah.....my bad, didn't think again," his voice was both regretful and apologetic.

TalonFyre felt horrible. He didn't mean to make Angel sick! He had been away from them too long. Their personalities were vastly different from Hikari's. Angel was the most different, however. Hikari was violent, tomboyish, and was into his earthly sense of humor. Her mother, on the other hand, was very feminine – the complete opposite of what she was. How Hikari came from her baffled TalonFyre, but he didn't care what it was. He loved her attitude. Knowing this, he sent the mental video to his beloved, titling it "Doctor Poo".

"You made a gravid dragoness barf... congrats," Ultimar said sarcastically, his voice showing hidden anger.

"Yeah. Sorry Angel," TalonFyre apologized shamefully.

He was going to leave, but TalonFyre wanted to make up for what he did. He felt horrible. His infinity symbol flashed and a white, spherical gem appeared in his hand. "Anti-sickness. It's real this time," TalonFyre said with a small smile, handing it to Angel.

She swallowed it immediately. "Ugh... thank you..." Angel sighed in relief.

It was true. The gem did help with sickness. However, that wasn't the only reason TalonFyre gave it to his new mother. "Hikari had one – fake though. This one's real – oh and it also makes you burp like your daughter. Side effect," he smirked, covering his ears.

Flare put his paw to his face, "Oh, she will not enjoy that."

A burp was heard from Angel, her face turning red from embarrassment. Being who he was, TalonFyre sent the vision of her mother's belch to Hikari. She would find it funny, and he knew this. "(Hey look, mom did it too!)" Talon said through telepathy, making certain Angel and Flare couldn't hear.

"Again Angel, sorry," TalonFyre said once more, fearing his mother would be angry about her exhalation.

"It's... it's okay. You did it to help me," the gravid dragoness sighed.

"Oh, and after the egg is laid we can go dig through my archives and my armory – all in Draconic," TalonFyre gave a proud smile, as his infinity symbol flashed once more giving the two the ability to read as well as speak in Draconic. "Anyway I'll go check on my queen. Make sure they're safe during the delivery, Doctor Ultimar." With this, he teleported back.

As soon as TalonFyre had landed, he found himself next to a laughing Hikari. "Well, something funny?" he asked, snickering afterwards.

"You... are hilarious!" the dragoness laughed, barely able to contain herself.

"Yup – see? Even your mom burps in the end. ...Maybe I made it that way – just wanted her to burp like you for once!" he finished his tangent and laughed.

"It's only fair," Hikari snickered.

"Anyway, enough weapons today. It's getting dark and I'm tired as hell," TalonFyre kissed her after saying this, "Come on, queen of the universe."

As the two walked to their bed, TalonFyre let out a belch reminiscent to Hikari's burps. "Well – I'm learning," TalonFyre gave a sly grin as Hikari gave a short chuckle.

"You're a pig," Hikari scoffed, causing TalonFyre to cringe. She then added, "...And I love it!" in an excited tone, smirking as TalonFyre laughed at her misdirection.

"I didn't even eat!" TalonFyre screamed at her, his smile letting her know that he was joking.

Though they arrived at the bedroom, TalonFyre stopped and turned to Hikari. "I'm...gonna' stay by the egg," he stated, his voice somewhat low.

Hikari nodded, "Good idea." At this, the two mates entered the nursery, lying down next to their son-to-be.

"Night," TalonFyre whispered, nuzzling Hikari.

"Night love…" Hikari whispered happily.

A voice spoke before the two fell to sleep in a comforting voice – It was Ultimar. "(I've hardly ever lost a patient in 50 years. Over 67 quintillion cases, 124 deaths. Angel is going to be fine.)"

At which TalonFyre gave a snide response, "(Good job….doctor poo,)" falling into slumber afterwards.

Chapter 61

Amane and Taiyou

IT was near 2:00 AM in human time, and Angel was near asleep when she woke up with a pain in her stomach. "Ultimar, get up! The egg is coming!" Flare called out, and once again, Ultimar arrived in his outfit used for bringing new life into the world. Mian slithered into the room as well.

On the floor, her legs already giving out, Angel was grunting in pain and unable to speak. In light of this, she used telepathy, "(Ultimar, please get me something to put my body on so that the egg comes easier.)"

Hearing this, Ultimar created a large pillow for angel to her head on, laying her underbelly-up and spreading her back legs. She looked confused, but trusted his judgement. "Mian, you know what to do. Also, Flare – take Angel's paw and for the life of you do NOT LET GO!"

Ultimar once again instructed in the techniques used for breathing, which Angel didn't know the first time. He also told her it would be easier on her since it was her second laying – she knew this already.

Three and a half hours passed. After a scream from Angel, Ultimar held a wet, semi-bloody egg in his gloved hands. Its color was white, but it had a few gold and blue markings.

"Have… have I finished?" Angel asked, panting and covered in sweat just as her daughter was.

Mian nodded. Flare nuzzled his mate happily as he let go of her paw. "Good… I think I may need a bit of rest now. The laying…" the dragoness fell to sleep without finishing her sentence.

After the ordeal, Ultimar and Mian took the egg to the nursery for incubation. Flare, on the other hand, stayed by his mate's side and lay next to her. "(Amane… Her name will be Amane,)" Angel softly spoke in Flare's mind.

"(What does it mean?)" the light dragon asked his mate curiously.

Her telepathy took a loving tone when she said the next words, "(It can mean many things, but the meaning I desire is 'sound of the heavens'.)" At which Flare moved closer to her, putting his foreleg around the dragoness.

"(It's perfect.)" With this, Flare began to slumber next to his mate.

Back at the nursery, TalonFyre and Hikari were asleep next to their soon-to-be-son's egg. Upon the arrival of morning, the sound of a soft, squeak-like snoring was audible. Due to his own snoring, TalonFyre was unable to hear it. He was awoken by a paw shaking him, finding himself covered in a golden shell.

"Talon!" Hikari screamed happily.

TalonFyre snapped awake at this, "AHHHHH! The hell!?" he screamed, shaking his head.

"I hear snoring… and it's not yours…" the dragoness whispered. This caused TalonFyre to panic once again.

"Huh…" TalonFyre shook himself, the flakes dropping off of him. "The hell was that? You try using me as a stove?" Talon asked, annoyed. He was oblivious to the fact that the shell was in truth the shell of his own son's egg.

The source of the snoring came from under the ottoman in the room meant for dining. "What the heck is that under the table?" TalonFyre asked, ponderingly. The two looked underneath to find a small gold figure.

"GAH!" Talon jumped back, "Ok, weirdest Vespatite ever! Thing must have been asleep on me. Go look." TalonFyre shook off his surprise while his mate looked under the table.

"See it? Must've gotten into the gold stash," TalonFyre scoffed, oblivious until Hikari muttered one word, "Taiyou?" her face both confused and joyful.

"Wow, fast hatching," TalonFyre said in bewildered tone.

Hikari gave a small nod, "I don't care why he hatched so fast, but it doesn't matter to me as long as he's okay."

The words caused TalonFyre to worry a bit. He needed to see if anything was wrong with his son! He placed his head under the table, hitting his head once more. "OW! Gah, why do I even have tables!? Need to get rid of them; tables are just a hazard – for me anyway." He rubbed his head, removing it from under the ottoman.

After the display, Hikari decided to suspend the table in the air with her telekinesis. After this, she picked up the hatchling in her front paws. TalonFyre was silent. There, in her gentle grip, was a small gold dragon. His wing membranes were snow white. His horns were bright pink like his mother's and shaped like his grandfather's. His claws had a yellow tint like his grandparents' but were slightly thicker and larger due to his father. His eyes were a dark green, resembling Flare's. He also, if carefully examined, had a slight blue tint to his sclera. The last part was from the light of TalonFyre's life, Hikari.

"He's… beautiful…" the dragoness whispered, eyes and voice both full of joy. Upon seeing his new son, TalonFyre's eyes began to tear over again. He couldn't contain his emotions.

"And….this isn't because I ended up hurting my head either…" TalonFyre whimpered happily.

"I know, Talon. You don't have to act tough anymore," Hikari whispered once again, her eyes becoming filled with tears as well, as she nuzzled her love.

After the emotional display, TalonFyre attempted to put his nose up to his new son in order to get his scent. As soon as his snout reached the hatchling he received a bite from the small hatchling's mouth.

"Doesn't hurt…" TalonFyre shrugged. After a few seconds, however, the pain became more intense. "…..OW!" Talon yelped.

Hikari was taken aback by this. "That's a no-no, Taiyou," she scolded her new son who cringed.

"Hey, Talon! By the way, he hatched!" the golem spoke, taking them by surprise.

TalonFyre grunted, "The hell did you find out?" causing the golem to fold his arms upon his chest and head as he sunk to the ground looking into the cave.

"Hey, someone has to watch it while you snore away!"

The words caused TalonFyre to scoff, "Oh, shut up and go back to guarding!" At which the golem gave a small roll of the eyes.

Before the golem could do anything Hikari gave it a concerned look. "Did he go out?" she asked, afraid her child could have gotten lost.

"Nah, he just ran from the snoring," the golem answered smugly.

TalonFyre sighed, "Aw jeez..." knowing that even if his beloved Hikari didn't mind, Taiyou may have been upset at the fact that he did such a thing.

"Like I said, BACK TO GUARDING!" TalonFyre growled angrily.

The golem gave a startled flinch, "Sheesh, fine, calm down princess..." as he rose up from the sands. TalonFyre grumbled in a disgruntled fashion.

Before any more words could be said, Hikari put her precious new hatchling upon the ground and he promptly fell asleep. The hatching must have made him exhausted. That, combined with Talon's snoring, would be disastrous for his energy.

A wormhole opened at this time, Ultimar and Mian appearing. The latter had a small, almost invisible, bulge in her pink-scaled, human-like stomach. If it weren't for her thin physique and petite height it would never even be visible to them. It was also apparent that her breasts were larger due to this fact.

"We came to see the hatchling," Ultimar said in a happy voice.

TalonFyre gave another sigh at this, "Yeah, I already got hit on the head and bit – I mean the table hit me – I mean I hit it! GAH!" his voice became frustrated again.

"What, princess mad?" the golem asked teasingly.

TalonFyre could only think of two words to say at this point, "...SHUT UP!!"

"Guess who's a sister to a new baby girl?" Ultimar asked rhetorically in an attempt to lighten the mood.

TalonFyre scratched his head, "Wow, everyone's busy... Not me is it?" which earned him a puzzled stare from Hikari, Mian, and Ultimar.

"Yeah, smooth move Talon!" the golem remarked in a smart tone. This caused TalonFyre to walk out of the cave and begin to argue with his golem companion.

In an attempt to quell the two, Ultimar decide to take the brunt of the anger upon himself. He cupped his hands and called out, "Oh, and Goldem – I think you mean, 'Well, excuuuuusse me, princess' instead!"

The ruse worked, causing TalonFyre to once again enter the cave. "Yeah, feel like another Jon ride!? I can arrange that!" Talon screamed at him.

Ultimar looked down and gave a disheartened, "No..." trying to mask the fact that he was actually hurt by the fact that TalonFyre would suggest such a thing out of anger.

"Yeah, figured as much," Talon grunted.

"You want me to make some toys for your kid?" Ultimar asked, once again trying to lighten the mood.

TalonFyre looked at him, his anger subsiding in a partial amount, "I suppose armor and swords aren't a good idea... or cannons," his face a bit saddened.

"Or me, I'm not a toy!" the golem remarked, cutting into the conversation.

This earned him a shot of dark energy to the mouth and an angry, "Butt out!" from TalonFyre.

Once again, Ultimar started to speak, "I meant actual toys. My Ki-creation ability can give me a Santa-Claus kind of vibe at times, especially around children." A smile appeared as he mentioned the mythical figure, knowing TalonFyre would miss the reference.

"Yeah that'll be fine – I can't make anything but weapons," TalonFyre sighed, missing the entirety of Ultimar's joke due to being discouraged that he was unable to make such things for his new child.

A question irked Ultimar for a long time, however. He decided to voice his concern about the child's future before anything further was said, "Will he have any outside interaction at all?"

TalonFyre smirked, "Yeah, come with me..." walking out of the cave, leaving Hikari and Mian to gaze at the hatchling. Ultimar nodded, but wondered what his new friend would do to help by merely taking him into the desert.

The infinity symbol flashed and TalonFyre turned into his dark form. A wave of his hand turned the desolate wasteland into a semi-dense forest. "There, sand was annoying – besides this place is gonna' have deer now!" TalonFyre said in a happy, yet proud, tone.

Ultimar smiled kindly, "That is what ultimate power is supposed to be used for; to give life, not take it."

"Hey, I was liking that!" the golem growled.

TalonFyre put a paw up and took an uncaring tone, "Oh hush now, change already." At the words the golem changed to a deep green color, his gems becoming plant-colored to blend with the surroundings.

Since he desired to get even with the golem, TalonFyre took a sly grin, "Yeah, well, I'll call you Mossy now. Heh!" he laughed at the golem's misfortune.

"Fine, whatever!" the golem agreed begrudgingly.

"Anyway.....let's go in – I don't want to be away for long." At these words, TalonFyre re-entered the cave, forgetting to de-activate his power.

Even though TalonFyre had done very well at assuring they'd never be hungry, the question on Ultimar's mind still remained. "Do you think he'll have any friends?" the doctor asked in a tone both worried and serious.

At this TalonFyre de-activated his newfound abilities and turned to the doctor. "Well, I was hoping for a bit of an arrangement. The kids we both saved should be pretty close," he put his hand to his face as he prepared himself for the words he was about to say, "Maybe a, UGHH, play date... dammit that word is so nice....bleh... You know, if he gets lonely." At which Ultimar nodded.

The question entered TalonFyre's mind at this. "How are they, by the way?" Talon asked, wondering how the doctor had dealt with the dragoness's abuse and psychological trauma. Ultimar gave a kind smile, "The children are doing well. The dragonesses are also recovering nicely."

After the conversation, TalonFyre approached his new son, who had awakened at this point. He got up his courage and nuzzled him softly. Taiyou, although a bit scared, nuzzled him back. "Hey, didn't get bit for once," TalonFyre chuckled softly.

Taiyou began to emit a soft thrumming noise, Hikari approaching the two.

"Talon... do you think he'll be happy? Do you think we'll be happy? Do you think our family is going to be okay?" the dragoness asked, concerned.

TalonFyre nuzzled his mate, "It'll be fine, Hikari. Everything is gonna' be fine. And if it's not and someone tries to mess with us? I'll kick their ass!" he smirked.

TalonFyre was happy now. He had a family, a best friend who would do anything to help him with a child on the way, a new sister who he had yet to learn the name of, power beyond anything ever seen by the world, and a new life. He was the happiest dragon alive, at least by his standpoint. The power he held, as Ultimar said, could end up corrupting him. However, he knew that as long as Hikari was by his side, he would never fall into such a trap of misguided morals.

Love, a family, a friend, power... this was all he needed to be happy, the last one being the least necessary. He could care less about what happened to his power as long as his family and friend were all kept safe. He'd give up his life for them, no matter what. He also knew the doctor would keep them from dying from any sickness or wounds. This would never have been possible without Flare, without Ultimar, without Hikari... He would have been miserable for his entire life if he had shunned the affections of Hikari, refused Ultimar's help, or worst of all, killed himself. He saw his first friend in Flare, found his love in Hikari, and found a best friend who would never abandon him in Ultimar. This was, hopefully, his happily ever after.

Final Note:

If you would like to see previews for my books (War of the Third Demon part 1 and eventually The TalonFyre Chronicles: A New Life), my DeviantArt Account is FatherOfMusho.

Current ages for the characters:

TalonFyre: 19
Hikari: 17
Angel: 21/39 (18 passed since becoming ageless)
Flare: 22/? (Age Unknown)
Ultimar: 210 (19-20 Human years)
Mian: 208 (19-20 Human years)

Made in the USA
Middletown, DE
26 May 2016